# Who Killed Callaway?

Other novels by John Rhodes

Nutcracker (2004)

Hank's Idea (2005)

Desert Wind (2006)

# Who Killed Callaway?

A Murder Mystery

John Rhodes

iUniverse, Inc.
New York  Lincoln  Shanghai

# Who Killed Callaway?
## A Murder Mystery

iUniverse books may be ordered through booksellers or by contacting:

iUniverse
2021 Pine Lake Road, Suite 100
Lincoln, NE 68512
www.iuniverse.com
1-800-Authors (1-800-288-4677)

Because of the dynamic nature of the Internet, any Web addresses or links contained in this book may have changed since publication and may no longer be valid.

This is a work of fiction. All of the characters, names, incidents, organizations, and dialogue in this novel are either the products of the author's imagination or are used fictitiously.

ISBN: 978-0-595-43777-1 (pbk)
ISBN: 978-0-595-68299-7 (cloth)
ISBN: 978-0-595-88105-5 (ebk)

Printed in the United States of America

In memory of my father, who loved a good detective story, and who introduced me to the works of Dorothy L. Sayers, Agatha Christie, Ngaio Marsh, and many other great writers.

Governors and Staff of The Kings School, Lower Tuckscomb, Glos

| | |
|---|---|
| Lord James Canderblank, KCSI | Chairman of the Board of Governors |
| Doctor Roger Thornby, MA, PhD | Master of Kings |
| Mr. McIntire, MA | Housemaster of Trafalgar House |
| Mr. Robinson, MA | Duty master |
| Mr. Jaspers, MA | Housemaster of Victoria House |
| Doctor Howard, MA, PhD | Senior science master |
| Mr. Feeley, MA | Senior history master |
| Mr. Chadwicke, MA | Housemaster of Kings House |
| Mme Larue | French language instructor |
| Mr. Bottomly, BA | Gymnastics instructor |
| Miss Grantly | The Master's secretary |
| Lady Deborah Canderblank | Lord Canderblank's wife |
| The Hon Victoria Canderblank | Lord and Lady Canderblank's daughter |
| Sir Neville Pondsford, FRCS | Harley Street consultant, Lady Canderblank's doctor |
| H K W Shipman | Lord and Lady Canderblank's secretary |

Boys of Kings

| | |
|---|---|
| Connelly | Trafalgar House, Callaway's calo |
| Jenkins Minor | Trafalgar House |
| Jenkins Major | Trafalgar House |

| | |
|---|---|
| Trumpington | Captain of the School |
| White | Queens House, Callaway's friend |
| Callaway | Trafalgar House |
| Mr. Markham | Callaway's uncle |
| Mrs. Markham | Callaway's aunt |
| General Sir John Trumpington, KCB | Trumpington's father |

## Villagers of Lower Tuckscomb

| | |
|---|---|
| Doctor Henry Thickett, MD | General Practitioner |
| George Green | Publican, The Kings Arms |
| Margie Green | His wife |
| Lucy Green | Their daughter |

## The Police

| | |
|---|---|
| Colonel Percival Dagenham, CB | Chief Constable, Gloucestershire County Constabulary |
| Detective Superintendent George Brownlee | Criminal Investigation Department, New Scotland Yard |
| Detective Chief Inspector Thomas Ford, DSO, MC | Criminal Investigation Department, New Scotland Yard |
| Sergeant Robert Croft, MM | Gloucestershire County Constabulary |
| Sergeant Dorothy Jackson | Gloucestershire County Women's Constabulary |
| Mrs. Betty Croft | Sgt Croft's wife |

*O, what a tangled web we weave / When first we practise to deceive!*
—Sir Walter Scott

# Sunday

J enkins Minor discovered the body on Sunday morning. He was racing down the front steps of Trafalgar House, hastily dressed and late for Chapel, when he tripped over his untied shoelaces. His *Book of Common Prayer* and *English Hymnal* went flying into the thicket of rhododendron bushes in front of Trafalgar, and he scampered to recover his belongings.

Being late for Chapel carried the penalty of "early detention," under which minor miscreants were obliged to get up at dawn and walk the School grounds picking up litter. The essence of the punishment lay neither in the menial task nor the derogatory catcalls of passers-by, but in having to get up so early.

Desperate to avoid being even later, Jenkins groped through the bushes in search of his books, the branches scratching his cheek and all but dislodging his spectacles.

He found the *English Hymnal* lying against a shoe. Beyond the shoe was a leg, and beyond that was the supine trunk of a body with the hilt of a knife sticking out of its chest. Beyond the chest was the hideously distorted face of Callaway, Captain of the Second Eleven cricket team.

Jenkins jerked his spectacles back into their correct position, but what he saw did not improve with focus. Callaway's head lay at an unnatural angle against the lower branches of a rhododendron. It took Jenkins some moments to realize that Callaway was dead, and not simply lying there, for he had never seen a dead body. Yet the staring eyes were sightless, and there were no signs of breathing in Callaway's chest beneath the knife. A line of tiny ants was climbing Callaway's cheek toward his dreadful ruined lips, marching with determination on some ghastly errand upon whose purpose Jenkins feared to speculate.

Jenkins vomited and flailed back out of the bushes. He ran wildly to the Chapel, his arms windmilling and his heart in his throat, and crashed through the doors just as the first hymn was beginning. A part of his mind told him it was "*Onward Christian Soldiers,*" one of his favorites. He raced wildly down the aisle and tugged urgently at his brother's arm.

Jenkins Major was much put out by his little brother's interruption. Like any normal senior at school, and older brothers in general, he almost always ignored his younger sibling's existence. On this occasion, however, he saw his brother's face was white with shock, he saw the fear and horror in his eyes, and the vomit on his coat and tie, and allowed himself to be drawn, with a complete lack of dignity, down the aisle.

"What is it, you little worm? Are you ill?" he hissed angrily as he went, assuming that Jenkins Minor had come down with a violent stomach ailment. Doubtless the elder Jenkins' friends were snickering at them and would never let him live down this indignity.

The younger boy could not bring himself to speak, and went racing back to Trafalgar with his brother at his heels. He pointed a trembling finger at the rhododendron bushes, and Jenkins Major peered in among the big olive-green leaves. Then it was his turn to go racing back to Chapel, his brother in tow, and send the doors crashing for a second time.

On this occasion, the interruption brought the service to a halt and the Master of Kings School angrily to his feet.

"What the *devil* is all this commotion?" Doctor Thornby demanded. "Jenkins Minor, you'll get twelve of the best for this ungodly interruption!"

The threat of twelve strokes of the Master's cane did not deter the trembling boy.

"Sorry, sir—please, sir—it's Callaway, sir!"

"*What* is Callaway, boy?"

"He's dead, sir!"

"Don't be *ridiculous,* Jenkins Minor."

The Master looked round the Chapel for Callaway, but could not see him.

"What do you mean? Where is he?"

"He's in the bushes in front of Trafalgar with a knife sticking out of his heart, sir. He's been murdered!"

◆     ◆     ◆

Kings School stands on a hill above Lower Tuckscomb, not far from Stroud in the Cotswold Hills in Gloucestershire, eighty miles west of London. It was founded by King Henry VIII, as a sop to the monarch's conscience after the English Reformation, during which the crown ruthlessly expropriated from the church, under the pretext of moral renovation, one third of all the land in England.

At first, the School had occupied the former dormitories of a ransacked abbey, and used the old Lady Chapel for its schoolhouse and religious services. Kings School eked out an obscure existence for the next one hundred and fifty years, slumbering through the reign of Elizabeth I, the Armada, the entire Stuart dynasty, the English Civil War, the founding of the American colonies, innumerable wars with France and Spain, and the lives of Shakespeare, Galileo, and Newton.

Finally, in the year 1701, an endowment from Queen Anne and the energies of a vigorous new schoolmaster abruptly breathed fresh life into the moribund School.

The wisteria-covered remnants of the crumbling abbey were torn down, save for the ancient Lady Chapel, and the stones were used to build new quarters: School House for the poor scholars of the neighborhood, Kings House in honor of the founder, and Queens House in honor of the School's new benefactress. The contemporary records of these events, still preserved in the Master's Library, use the plural form of "Kings" and "Queens," rather than the possessive, and this grammatical oversight became a School tradition.

Then, as if exhausted by this spasm of energy, the School again fell back into a deep sleep. Another one hundred and fifty years passed by—the foundation of the British Empire, the American War of Independence, the industrial revolution and the invention of the steam engine, the French Revolution, the American Civil War, the lives of Washington, Jefferson, Lincoln, Wellington, and Napoleon—until the mid-nineteenth century, when fashions changed, and it was considered desirable to send the sons of gentry away to school to learn their Latin, Greek, and mathematics.

Another energetic young schoolmaster emerged from the wisteria and rhododendrons, and expanded the School, adding Trafalgar House and Wellington House and, of course, Victoria House in honor of the young Empress. Why the Duke of Wellington should be honored with his own house, while Horatio Nelson was honored only indirectly through his greatest victory, has never been made entirely clear. Perhaps Nelson's widely publicized indiscretions with Lady Hamilton robbed him of the honor.

Kings became a place to send the sons of soldiers and sailors and the offspring of English families serving in India. It was never as fashionable as Eton College or Harrow School, and it lacked the scholastic innovations of Rugby and the cachet of Marlborough and Charterhouse; but the sons of Generals and Colonels could mingle with boys of their own class before going on to Oxford or to their regiments or into the Imperial Civil Service.

Doctor Roger Thornby, MA, PhD, became Master of Kings in 1904. He had served in South Africa during the Boer War and therefore had the credentials necessary to ingratiate himself with the military establishment; he had also served as tutor to the Viceroy's younger children in India, which gave him access to colonial families. He had little interest in education per se, leaving such mundane matters to his staff, but he was a tireless and effective groveller, and, as a consequence, Kings' enrollment grew, and its endowments and fortunes flourished.

Lord James Canderblank, KCSI, whom Thornby had known in India, was persuaded to become chairman of the Board of Governors; and Thornby further embellished the board with the Bishop of Gloucester and Sir Richard Wimbleton, KCB. Sir Richard had attended Kings and distinguished himself in the Sudan while serving under Lord Kitchener.

When the Great War broke out in 1914, the School's former pupils threw themselves into the battle in the service of King and Country, and Doctor Thornby was immensely proud that almost one in every four alumni suffered injury or death in the mud and carnage.

Now, in 1920, things were finally returning to normal after the war, and the Master planned a grand Open Day, at which a memorial to the Glorious Fallen would be unveiled. There would be the traditional cricket match between the School and the Old Boys; the Governors would all be present; and the parents would flock to see prizes awarded and to enjoy a splendid high tea with strawberries and clotted cream, served in marquees on the Great Lawn.

On Saturday evening the Drama Society and the School Orchestra would perform *"The Pirates of Penzance"* by Gilbert and Sullivan. Among the visitors would be an agent of an anglophile Balkan prince, and the Master was hopeful that the Prince's oldest son and heir might attend Kings in preference to Eton. He was not actually British, the Master explained to the Board, but he was a grandchild of Queen Victoria through one of the old Empress's innumerable daughters.

The Open Day was a triumph; the weather was perfect, and the entire program went off without a hitch. The Governors and distinguished guests were delighted, and the Balkan prince's representative was much impressed. The Master rose the following day in excellent spirits to attend the final event of Open Day, the Chapel service at which the Bishop would dedicate the war memorial.

Everything was proceeding splendidly and according to plan—until Jenkins Minor burst through the Chapel doors.

◆          ◆          ◆

The congregation trailed out of Chapel and milled about in front of Trafalgar. The Master ordered Mr. McIntire, the housemaster of Trafalgar, to enter the shrubbery. He reported back that Jenkins' account was true. The Master sent one of the prefects running to fetch Doctor Thickett from the village, and, as an afterthought, to fetch Sergeant Croft of the Gloucestershire Constabulary as well.

Trumpington, the Captain of the School, made everybody stand back. Mr. McIntire suggested that roll be called to see if anyone else was missing; this sensible suggestion earned him a withering stare from the Master.

Following a moment of indecision, the Master shepherded the Governors and the more prominent parents and guests to his Lodge, where Mrs. Thornby hurriedly served them tea and toast. The remaining parents and staff were ordered back into the Chapel to await developments. The boys were sent to the Gymnasium under the watchful eyes of the prefects.

Lady Deborah Canderblank, the wife of the Chairman of the Board, was much put out.

"We must avoid a scandal, Master, at all costs," she told him crossly, as if this were all his fault. "Perhaps it's all a misunderstanding—in fact, I'm certain of it. Was it really necessary to summon a police constable?"

"What's that?" Sir Richard Wimbleton asked her.

"The mast-er does not need to sum-mon the pol-ice," she yelled at him crossly—the old fool's deafness never failed to irritate her.

"If it's a murder, the Master has no choice," Sir Richard told her.

"Let's not use that ugly word, Richard, if you please," she responded firmly. "We don't know if it's anything more than an accident. We certainly don't want this getting into the newspapers. The less said the better."

The Master was beside himself with anger, and did not try to hide it. The day, he said, indeed, the entire weekend, was ruined. He had invited a newspaper reporter to attend the ceremony and had been looking forward to favorable descriptions of Kings in the press. Now, God alone knew what he would write.

If only that little brat Jenkins Minor had stayed out of the rhododendrons ... What had he been doing there, anyway? Thank God the Prince's representative had left the night before—that particular royal family's opaque allegiances during the recent war had precluded him from attending this morning's ceremony.

And thank God, Callaway's parents were on post in India, and not present to create a public spectacle. He supposed he would have to send them a telegram in the morning.

The doctor arrived in a pony trap and was escorted to Trafalgar. Doctor Henry Thickett, MD, was the local general practitioner. His normal practice at the School ran to outbreaks of measles and occasional broken bones, but murder was very much out of his league. Still, he pushed his way through the bushes and knelt in the mud to examine the body.

The dead boy was wearing a rakish military uniform, and his face and hands were daubed in florid makeup. A false moustache was partially attached to the remains of his upper lip. Heavy black eyeliner accentuated his staring eyes. A copy of a program for the *Pirates of Penzance* lay in the mud beside one hand.

The wooden handle of a knife protruded from his chest. Doctor Thickett touched it cautiously to see if it were firmly in place; it was. He crawled out of the bushes and asked Mr. McIntire to get the body covered with a sheet from the dormitories.

Doctor Thickett and Mr. McIntire proceeded to the Master's study.

"I'm afraid he's dead, Master," reported the doctor. "I was wondering, did you have theatricals last night? He's wearing makeup."

"It's grease paint. Yes, there was a performance of *The Pirates of Penzance* … He was the Major General."

"Ah, that would explain it," said the doctor.

There must have been more than a dozen people staring at him in the Master's study, in various stages of shock, curiosity, and distaste. He noticed several wicker hampers piled high with theatrical costumes in one corner of the book-lined room.

"The cause of death, Doctor?" asked Lord Canderblank.

"He's been stabbed, my lord, but I can't say for sure whether that's what killed him until there's an autopsy."

"An autopsy?" Lady Canderblank boomed incredulously. "Is that *really* necessary?"

"I regret it is necessary, my lady, and there'll doubtless be an inquest, too."

"Such a lot of fuss and fiddle-faddle, and such poor publicity," she said dismissively. "Perhaps the Chief Constable can overrule it."

She turned to her husband.

"James, you'll have to telephone to Percy Dagenham and stop this nonsense."

Lord Canderblank seemed accustomed to receiving imperious orders from his wife and did not demur. She turned back to the doctor.

"With due respect to your experience, Doctor, perhaps a second opinion would be appropriate—a more qualified eye, if I may say so without offense. Sir Neville Pondsford of Harley Street, our own doctor, would doubtless perform the duty. James, you must telephone to him as well. Are the boy's parents *anybody*, Master?"

"His father's a Major in Nepal," the Master replied.

"Of little account? Well, that's all right then."

There was a knock, and the study door opened to reveal a country police sergeant, red in the face from bicycling up the steep hill from the village. He was still wearing his bicycle clips about his trouser legs.

"There's been a report of a murder, Doctor Thornby, sir?" he puffed. "One of your boys came to fetch me."

He pulled a tattered notebook from his pocket and searched for a pencil.

"One of the Upper Six Formers was found dead," began the Master, but Lady Canderblank interrupted him.

"The matter is in the hands of the Chief Constable. Let's not be melodramatic. It hasn't been established that the boy was murdered, as you put it, and his exact medical condition is up to Sir Neville Pondsford to determine."

She stood up, drawing the whole room with her.

"Master, let us get the body removed to Doctor Thickett's establishment immediately, and have the area cleaned up before it becomes a public spectacle for idle eyes. Those rhododendrons were becoming an eyesore anyway, in my opinion—completely overgrown and out of hand. Get them rooted out and burned forthwith. I want the work to begin immediately. Perhaps the grounds staff has some privet hedges to put in their place?"

She paused for breath but had not finished.

"In the meantime, Master, we should all return to the Chapel and complete the service. Bishop, are you ready? James, you will join us once you have completed your telephone conversations."

"I'm not sure that's right, madam, I'm not sure at all," said Sergeant Croft uncertainly, scratching his head and shuffling from foot to foot. "I'll have to keep the body where it is until the Inspector is notified ..."

"Nonsense, and in future you will address me as 'my lady.'"

Mr. McIntire opened his mouth to support the policeman, but the Master cut him off.

"That will do, McIntire."

Lady Canderblank was unstoppable.

"Come, Master, you have work to do! Follow me, everyone!"

She advanced toward the door like a man-o-war under full sail, with the rest of the party trailing in her wake, and Sergeant Croft was obliged to step aside or be bowled over by the rush.

Lord Canderblank made his telephone calls as his wife had instructed. Colonel Percy Dagenham, the Chief Constable of Gloucestershire, promised Lord Canderblank to look into the matter immediately, and Sir Neville Pondsford agreed to travel down by the next available train.

The memorial service, when it resumed, included a reading of the Roll of Honor of the Glorious Fallen, recited in dolorous tones by the Master. A prayer by the Bishop made it perfectly clear that all the slain English soldiers had gone straight to heaven, while the German fallen had received a far less comfortable fate. The service concluded with the playing of "*The Last Post.*"

The newspaper reporter took a photograph of the memorial. He was a lazy and unintelligent man who accepted without question the Master's explanation that Callaway must have died of a heart attack. He did not bother to look at the body.

The Master's weekend was rescued. That evening, Colonel Dagenham telephoned Canderblank Hall to inform the Canderblanks that he had referred the matter to Scotland Yard, and had been assured of the utmost discretion.

"They'll be nothing in the press, I assure you," the Colonel informed his lordship. "Common decency dictates that nothing will be reported until the School has had a chance to inform the parents, and that may take some time. Kings will suffer no adverse publicity."

# Monday

**D**etective Chief Inspector Thomas Ford awakened early next morning. As often, he had had a difficult night. His wounded leg ached in damp weather, and this discomfort triggered ugly nightmares of the battle in which he had been injured.

His reflection in the shaving mirror seemed older than his twenty-nine years suggested. He gazed at the face staring back at him without affection. He considered his features to be nondescript at best—and in that they matched his nondescript life.

He went about his morning routine in a foul mood and limped to the Underground Station through a persistent drizzle that searched the folds of his raincoat collar until it found a way to penetrate and trickle down inside his shirt. There were no seats on the train, and he was already tired when he sat down at his desk in Scotland Yard. His damp clothing clung to him heavily, and he wondered if he might catch cold.

He leafed through a few battered files on the case in Durham without enthusiasm. There were no real clues and no real suspects. The local police were not so much uncooperative as unconcerned, for who really cares about a prostitute beaten to death in an alley?

A constable appeared in his doorway.

"The Super wants to see you, sir."

As Ford entered his office, Superintendent Brownlee looked up from his mass of paperwork. Brownlee was a heavyset and cheerful man who always reminded Ford of a large, golden Labrador retriever.

"Take a pew, Ford. Leg bothering you?"

"It's fine, sir, thank you; it just plays up a bit when it rains."

Ford eased himself into the visitor's chair and found a comfortable position for his leg.

"You wanted to see me, sir?"

Brownlee regarded him over the rim of his uplifted teacup.

"Yes, indeed, I did. You went to school at Kings in Gloucestershire, didn't you?"

"Yes, sir?" Ford replied cautiously, wondering why on earth Brownlee would ask such a question. The very name of "Kings" depressed him.

"Well, it seems one of the boys died mysteriously," Brownlee continued, returning his teacup to its saucer as if he feared he might break it. "Possible foul play. The Chief Constable telephoned me last night to ask for the Yard's help. I remembered from your dossier that you went to school there. Mind running down and giving it a look-see, old chap? Your neck of the woods, and all that?"

Ford minded very much, although continuing the Durham case was equally unappealing.

"What about Durham, sir?"

"Where does it stand?"

"I'm getting nowhere, to be honest, sir," Ford replied, shaking his head. "No witnesses, no physical evidence, no suspects, no motive … Just a poor girl who went down the wrong alley with the wrong man."

His imagination conjured up the squalid scene.

"We've reviewed similar cases in other towns, in case we could find a pattern, but nothing's come up."

"Well, the Yard should never have taken it up in the first place, in my opinion," Brownlee said flatly. "Complete waste of time. Not every murder is the work of a satanic serial killer, for goodness sake!"

He squared his ample shoulders.

"Write up a report and draw a line under it. Say we'll re-open it if another comparable case occurs. Let me have it by end of the day, and I'll send it off to Durham. Ever been there?"

"Durham, sir? No, sir. I haven't."

"Miserable city, cold as hell. The wife's got an elderly uncle there … Damned fine cathedral, though … Magnificent Norman nave … Excellent local beer, I must admit … Go down to Kings tomorrow, if you would."

"Very well, sir," Ford agreed reluctantly.

"The Chief Constable, name of Dagenham, *Colonel* Dagenham, wants to avoid publicity, if possible … Good name of the School, and all that … My school never had a good name in the first place …"

He referred to his notes. He had recently been obliged to start using reading glasses, and he perched them on his nose reluctantly.

"The local officer is a chap named Croft, village copper. Dagenham said he is sound enough, but a bit out of his league in a murder case … Hope this doesn't turn into another Durham for you, old chap. Let me know how you're getting on, will you?"

# Tuesday

**F**ord found Sergeant Croft in his parlor. The village of Lower Tuckscomb was far too small for a police station of its own, and Croft's cheerfully chintzy parlor served as a substitute. It was not unknown for a miscreant to be offered a cup of tea while being booked for driving an unregistered farm tractor on a public thoroughfare, or some similar misdemeanor of the kind that constituted the great bulk of Lower Tuckscomb's crime rate.

A little stone outhouse with a stout padlocked door and a barred window stood in Croft's garden to accommodate the occasional Saturday night case of drunk and disorderly conduct. It had a window box filled with bright red geraniums to sooth its inmates' troubled souls, and morning glories gaily entwined themselves around the window bars.

Croft invited Ford to sit in his own armchair, and Mrs. Croft bustled in with tea and biscuits. The sergeant stood to attention. He appeared to have been chiseled from a single block of granite, placid and enduring.

His iron-gray hair was cropped closely to his skull and had a tendency to stick up rebelliously at the back. A pink crease ran across his forehead, born of years of wearing his police helmet.

"At ease, Sergeant, please! I can't sit here in your own chair while you stand." The soft Gloucester burr of Ford's childhood accent had returned to his voice unbidden.

Croft permitted himself to relax, and accepted one of Ford's cigarettes.

"Thank you, sir. I don't mind if I do."

He sat down gingerly in a ladder-back chair, as if he might break it. His forehead wrinkled with concern.

"Now, about this poor boy—it's just not right, sir, all this hurrying up," he said earnestly. "It isn't right at all."

"What do you mean?"

"The boy dies on Saturday night or Sunday morning. The London doctor comes on Monday, yesterday. He's buried on Tuesday. It's a bit rushed, if you know what I mean?"

"Buried?" Ford asked, startled. "They buried the boy already?"

"Yes, sir. This morning; they buried him at nine o'clock sharp in St. Agnes churchyard. Some of the staff attended, but not the Master and none of the boys. Mr. McIntire, one of the teachers, represented the School."

"You'd better tell me the whole story from the start, Sergeant. Take your time."

"Well, sir, on Sunday morning I was having breakfast when one of the boys from the School came running in," Croft began, settling to the task. "He's a prefect, name of Harold Young, seventeen or eighteen years old, very toffee-nosed, if you know the type, sir."

"I know it all too well, I'm afraid, Croft. Please continue."

"I arrived at the School about nine thirty and went straight to the Master's study. I didn't see the body first, because I didn't know where it was. The Master and a lot of the governors were there with Doctor Thickett—he's the local doctor."

"Yes, I know Thickett—I went to Kings myself a few years back."

"Ah, I thought you looked a bit familiar, sir, if I may say so," Croft responded, scratching his head to assist his memory. "Slow left-handed bowler, if I recall?"

Cricket was the last thing Ford wished to discuss.

"Quite so. What happened in the study?"

"Lady Canderblank was ordering everybody about like a Sergeant Major, sir. She wanted the body moved and the area cleared up. I told her that shouldn't be done, but she said she'd already spoken to the Chief Constable, so the matter was out of my hands. Besides ... I must admit she's a bit hard to resist."

He shook his head at the memory.

"It was the same with Doctor Thickett. He mentioned an autopsy, and she said she already had a fancy doctor coming down from London to take over. There wasn't no saying no to her in that mood. I should have stood my ground, but if the Chief Constable had already approved it …"

"That's all right, Sergeant," Ford replied sympathetically. "Carry on, if you please."

"We went to where the body was, the doctor and me, and one of the teachers, Mr. McIntire, his name is. A sensible man, in spite of being a teacher. The body was under a sheet amongst the rhododendrons."

"Can you describe it as fully as possible, please?" Ford asked, leaning forward.

"Yes, sir. On Sunday night, I made some notes while my mind was still fresh."

He removed his notebook from his tunic, licked his thumb, and riffled through the pages until he found his place.

"The rhododendrons were very big, very old; ten feet high and ten feet thick, all along the front of the building. When you looked inside, there were a lot of dead and broken branches. It was hard to push through. The body was right in the middle, invisible if you were standing outside."

He referred to his notes.

"The body itself was stretched out on its back, with straight legs and its arms at its sides, except for the head, which was twisted up against a rhododendron trunk. Sticking out of its chest …"

"One moment, if I may, Sergeant," Ford interrupted him. "Let's see if I am following you."

Ford pushed himself up from his chair, laboriously got down to his knees, and then, rolling to his back, stretched out on the floor.

"Legs straight, you say? Together or apart, like this?"

"Your legs should be a little apart, sir; that's it, sir … And your arms should be next to your body, sir. Exactly. Now for your head—turn it to your right, sir, and twist it down at the same time. No—twist it down more, sir."

"This is devilishly uncomfortable," Ford grunted. "Here, move that chair so that the leg is against my neck, to represent the trunk of the bush. Like this?"

"Just a bit more, sir. Here, let me …"

"Ouch!"

"I beg your pardon, sir!" Croft apologized.

"Not your fault, Sergeant," Ford grinned. "Is this right?"

"Yes, sir, exactly."

At that moment, Mrs. Croft bustled into the parlor to freshen the teapot, only to discover the Scotland Yard detective prone on her best carpet.

"My goodness, sir! Have you taken a turn?" she exclaimed. "Help him up, Bob—whatever are you thinking of, you great lump?"

"No, no, it's quite all right, thank you, Mrs. Croft," Ford grinned again. "We are just reconstructing the scene of the crime."

Ford struggled to his feet and permitted his teacup to be refilled.

"I'm just toasting some crumpets," she said, and Ford discovered he was starving.

"Just the thing to get you through until lunchtime, sir," she added, as if she could read his mind. "I'll be back in a jiffy."

Had she been less energetic, she might have been plump; as it was she was only well-rounded.

As she bustled from the room, Croft sat down again and glanced at his notes.

"The body was dressed in an Army officer's uniform, with an old-fashioned red uniform coat," he continued. "They'd had theatricals the night before. The face and hands were covering in makeup, and he had false mutton-chop whiskers and a big false moustache. White shirt, white trousers, tall black riding boots. No hat. He was the Major General in the *Pirates of Penzance*, sir, as I understand it."

"How did his face look?"

"Eyes open and staring—bulging like—mouth open and lips dawn back, and the tongue and lips were cut and bloody. Teeth also covered in blood. A bit weird, sir, those cuts—I'm not sure how he got them."

"Other injuries?"

"A kitchen knife with a wooden handle was sticking out of the center of the chest, sir. There were three other stab wounds through his shirt, into his lower chest and stomach."

"Blood?" Ford asked.

"Very little, sir—I was surprised, to tell you the truth. I've seen a bit in the trenches, sir, if you take my meaning?"

"Yes, indeed I do," Ford replied with a shudder. Anyone who had served on the Western Front had had a comprehensive education in lacerated flesh.

He took a sip of tea to obliterate the memory.

"What did you do with the knife, Sergeant?"

"Well, I wasn't sure what to do, sir, to tell you the truth. Mr. McIntire recognized it as coming from the Trafalgar kitchen, and the housekeeper confirmed there's a knife gone missing. As to your question, sir, I've never been involved with fingerprints. So, anyway, I left it in place and wrapped up the handle in a page from my notebook and tied it with string to prevent it from being touched. I hope I did the right thing."

"That was extremely sensible, Sergeant," Ford told him, impressed by his ingenuity. "Whatever prints are on it will be preserved. Was there anything else remarkable about the body?"

"He had vomit on him, but the young lad who discovered him, Jenkins Minor, had sicked up, so he said, and who's to blame him?"

"Pockets?"

"A little bottle of yellowish, pinkish goo, sir; makeup for the show, I assume. It was all over his face and hands. A ten-shilling note and quite a bit of silver—about thirty bob in all. A lot for a boy of that age to be carrying, I thought. Packet of Players Navy Cut cigarettes and a silver lighter—expensive looking, I'd say."

Ford absorbed this information.

"Then it probably wasn't a robbery, one assumes. Was there anything on the ground?"

With a freshly licked thumb, Croft turned a notebook page.

"It was all churned up, sir. By the time I got there all kinds of people had been tramping around. No distinctive footmarks or anything of that sort. There was a muddy copy of the program for the theatricals, which I've got, but nothing else."

He shook his head.

"I looked around as carefully as I could, naturally. There were a lot of cigarette stubs, sir—some old, some new; my guess is that the boys used to sneak in there for a smoke. I picked up the new ones, make of Players Navy Cut, same as the lad's. Apart from that, there were bits of old newspapers and rags—that sort of rubbish; a couple of lost cricket balls, and the books that Jenkins Minor was looking for when he found the body."

Croft consulted his notes to make sure he had omitted no detail.

"That's all I could see, sir, from just looking around."

Mrs. Croft returned with hot buttered crumpets.

"I brought marmalade and raspberry preserves—whichever you prefer, sir," she said, setting the food tray by Ford's chair. "Oh, there're a few scones fresh out of the oven, and some clotted cream and strawberry jam to go with them."

"That's wonderful, Mrs. Croft," Ford thanked her, his mouth watering.

"I hope it's enough," she said doubtfully as she left. "I'll brew a fresh pot of tea."

"Your report was very thorough, Sergeant, if I may say so," Ford said, his mouth full of delicious scone. "Now, what do we know about the victim?"

"Michael Callaway, aged seventeen. His parents are in the Army in India. He stays with his aunt and uncle in London. I've written down the details on a separate piece of paper for you, sir. From what little I've been able to gather, he wasn't well-liked, but that's no motive for murder."

Ford eyed Croft's uniform, which held two rows of medal ribbons: the Military Medal, the two South Africa medals, known as *Mutt and Jeff*, and the three Great War medals.

"I see you did your bit, Sergeant."

"I volunteered to fight the Boers when I was a lad, sir. Full of piss and vinegar, I was, if you'll excuse the expression, sir—off on an adventure. Some adventure that turned out to be!"

The sergeant shook his head at his youthful folly.

"After I got back, I met Mrs. Croft and joined the force. I settled down, like. When the last lot started, I could've been deferred, but it didn't seem right."

"The Gloucestershire Regiment?"

"Yes, sir. Second Battalion, C Company."

Croft glanced at Ford and continued shyly.

"We had a chaplain named Ford up at battalion HQ, very decent bloke, sir—died at Passendale, I'm sorry to say. Would he be a relation, sir?"

"My father."

"Ah." Croft was far too sensible a man to express his condolences. Nevertheless, curiosity drove him on.

"There's a Ser'nt Major Jackson, sir, mate of mine. He mentioned another Ford in the First Battalion, an officer he served under …"

He voice trailed away into uncertainty. Ford's obligation to be polite overcame his reluctance to respond.

"Yes, I know Jackson, a very good chap."

He had no desire to reminisce—he should never have commented on Croft's medals.

"Those days are over, Sergeant, and thank God they are."

He hauled himself upright, conscious of Croft's kindly eyes upon his injured leg.

"Please thank Mrs. Croft for the tea. I suppose I'd better see Doctor Thickett and get up to the School."

◆     ◆     ◆

Ford left Sergeant Croft and walked across the village green to the Kings Arms, where he was given a small room overlooking the young River Coln as it bickered down the valley, just as Ford had been taught in poetry class in school.

Staring out of the window, he tried to recall his Alfred, Lord Tennyson.

*"I come from haunts of coot and hern/I make a sudden sally/And something something something fern/To bicker down a valley,"* he muttered. Or something like that, he thought.

When he returned downstairs, Mrs. Green, the publican's wife, was prepared to provide him with a detailed analysis of the case up at the

School, together with extensive biographies of most of the staff and all of the villagers, and her list of suspects and conclusions to date.

Ford politely excused himself before she was fully launched upon her exposition and walked down to Doctor Thickett's surgery. A scrawny woman with a wailing infant was leaving just as he arrived.

Doctor Thickett did not look up as Ford entered.

"Morning surgery hours are over," the doctor said. "You'll have to come back this evening at five o'clock, unless it's a real emergency."

He continued to write in a notebook, presumably recording the ailments of the sickly child.

"Good morning, Doctor. I am a police officer."

Thickett looked up, adjusted his glasses and regarded Ford with some annoyance.

His angular face was framed with wispy white curls. The lines about his mouth suggested his expression of exasperation was habitual. His white physician's coat was worn, but clean, and its pockets were stuffed with a variety of medical equipment. An elderly stethoscope hung around his neck.

"Is it about the matter at the School? It's all out of my hands."

He stared at Ford more closely.

"Do I know you?"

"My name is Ford. I was at the School before the war. You treated me for the chicken pox."

"Ah, that would explain it," the doctor replied indifferently. "However, as I said, this matter is out of my hands."

"Quite so, Doctor, but I would appreciate your account. You examined the body in situ and here in your establishment?"

"Well, that's true, but I'm sure Sergeant Croft can supply you with the details. He was present, of course. I have nothing to add."

He took up his pen to suggest the interview was over.

"I understand the boy had been stabbed?" Ford asked him, ignoring the gesture. "Can you confirm that as the cause of death?"

"Can't this wait?" Thickett responded, almost rudely. "I have only a brief time for lunch, and then I have my rounds this afternoon."

He made a show of consulting his fob watch.

"I apologize, Doctor," Ford said. "This will only take a few minutes—a formality, I'm sure—and then I need bother you no more."

"Well, all right," said Thickett ungraciously. His professional eye observed Ford's lameness. "You'd better sit down. Let's get it over with; yes, he'd been stabbed."

"How many times, and where, Doctor?" Ford asked as he eased himself into an uncomfortable chair.

"Twice in the chest and twice in the abdomen."

"And this was the cause of death?"

"One doesn't suffer four stab wounds and simply walk away," said Doctor Thickett with asperity.

"That's very true, Doctor," Ford smiled. "I assume that means the knife penetrated the chest cavity and reached the vital organs?"

"You may assume that," Thickett agreed obliquely.

"Can I see the knife?"

"I haven't got it. Sir Neville Pondsford removed it during his examination."

"What happened to it?"

"He cleaned it and ..."

"He *cleaned* the knife?" Ford asked him incredulously.

"Yes, why should he not?" Thickett demanded. "It had paper wrapped around the handle. It was ... messy. So he simply removed the paper and cleaned the whole thing."

"Doctor, are you familiar with the science of fingerprinting?"

"I may have read something about it," Thickett replied vaguely, as if Ford had asked him about the German physicist Albert Einstein's theory of relativity.

He assumed a tone that amounted to a defensive whine.

"I am a general practitioner. I cannot be expected to be familiar with every new-fangled branch of pathology."

"I see."

Vital evidence had been casually destroyed, it seemed, for no apparent reason. Every schoolboy in the land knew all about fingerprints, but evidently this doctor did not.

Ford brought his anger under control.

"Can you summarize your own examinations, please?"

"I examined him at the School. Obviously he was dead. We loaded him into my pony trap and brought him here—a real inconvenience, I may add, for I have no facilities for such situations."

"For how long had he been dead when you first saw him, would you estimate?"

The doctor seemed on surer ground.

"He was cold; there was some rigor; the blood from his wounds was dry—he'd been dead at least a few hours. He was still wearing theatrical makeup, so I assume he had died after the play on Saturday night."

"Where did you put him when you brought him down here?"

"On that examination bed."

He nodded toward a narrow bed that stood against the wall.

"The next day, yesterday, Sir Neville arrived from London and looked at the body," Thickett continued, speaking quickly as if anxious to conclude the interview. "Tobias Jones, the undertaker, arrived shortly after Sir Neville and put the boy in a coffin, and he and his men moved him up to the church."

"What did your examination reveal, Doctor?" Ford asked.

"Reveal? Why, nothing beyond the wounds. In any case, Sir Neville undertook the examination."

"How deep were the wounds? Enough to cause death immediately, by penetrating his heart, or did he bleed to death?"

"I can't really say. The knife was several inches long and well stuck in, so it might well have punctured his heart."

"Was there much blood when you removed his clothing?"

"We didn't remove his clothing; Sir Neville just opened his shirt. We left the details up to Jones, the undertaker."

Ford felt his anger returning.

"Were there any other injuries or marks of a struggle, Doctor?"

"None that I saw …"

"What was the condition of his finger nails?" Ford pressed on.

"I have no idea."

"Did you examine his neck, Doctor? I understand he was lying at a very strange angle when he was found."

Doctor Thickett showed increasing signs of impatience.

"His neck? Why would I examine his neck?"

Ford took a deep breath to calm himself.

"Am I to understand that you and Sir Neville looked at the body without removing its clothing and without conducting any form of post mortem examination? Then Sir Neville removed the knife and cleaned it? Then the body was immediately placed in a casket by Mr. Jones, still in its original clothing and still wearing theatrical greasepaint?"

"Are you implying some form of impropriety?" Doctor Thickett spluttered, turning red in the face. "I resent that, Ford; indeed, I resent that very much. Sir Neville was in charge, and I simply assisted him."

"Doctor Thickett, I'm implying nothing," Ford replied without expression. "I'm simply trying to understand what happened. When you were finished with the body, did you discuss the case with Sir Neville—to agree on your notes, perhaps?"

"Not really; he was in a hurry to catch the next train back to London. Sir Neville just wrote out a death certificate and left."

"What cause of death did he record?"

"Er … it was death from natural causes, I believe."

Ford stared at him silently.

"Well, Lady Canderblank had made it clear she didn't want a fuss," the doctor added, somewhat sheepishly. "She had suggested that phraseology to Sir Neville. Any other cause of death would have required a coroner and an inquest and an autopsy. She didn't want any fuss."

Now the doctor was looking *very* sheepish.

"There was nothing to be gained. After all, the boy was dead, his parents are in India, I believe, and there was the good name of the School to consider …"

His voice trailed away.

"Quite so, Doctor, Ford replied heavily. "One final question, if you would be so kind, and I'll leave you in peace: how long was Sir Neville here?"

"Oh, perhaps five minutes—ten at the most. He had hired a motorcar in Stroud, and the man was waiting."

Ford permitted himself to absorb this information.

"Thank you, Doctor," he said, rising carefully to his feet. "I apologize for taking all this time. I'll try not to bother you again."

He turned toward the door and paused.

"Oh, what happened to the knife, Doctor?"

"The knife? I really don't recall. I assume Jones took it with the body."

◆    ◆    ◆

Ford's heart sank as he drove up the hill to Kings. He had loathed the School, likening himself to a prisoner and counting every day of his term of sentence. He remembered creating an imaginary scientific equation in which his spirits sank in inverse proportion to the elevation of the hill, multiplied by the inverse of his distance from the School. The closer he got, then as now, the more miserable he felt.

He had been here for five years, a period of one thousand, seven hundred, and six days, of which four hundred and fifty-four had been holidays, leaving him a balance of twelve hundred and fifty-two days of misery.

The Chief Constable had supplied him with a car and with a young constable to drive it, and now Ford and Croft sat perched on the back seat as it snorted up the hill. The constable's evident lack of expertise was offset by his enthusiasm, Ford noticed with foreboding.

They drove through the absurdly oversized Gatehouse—a remnant of the west front of the old abbey—and entered the School grounds. Ahead of them stretched the verdant length of the Great Lawn with the School buildings ranged on either side of it.

There were the Houses in which the boys lived, the ancient Chapel, the new Gymnasium, the Infirmary, the Science Labs, the Master's Lodge, and all the rest. At the far end stood the ornate mass of the Old School, which housed the Great Hall, the classrooms, the Common Rooms, and the offices occupied by the senior members of the staff.

School lessons were in session, and the scene was devoid of humanity.

They drove to Old School and drew up beside a resplendent Rolls Royce. Ford noticed the driver eying it defensively, as if it might set their more modest police Humber car to shame.

"Thank you for an excellent ride," Ford felt compelled to say to the driver. "Now, Croft, let's see what we can see."

Ford found his way down the too-familiar passages and halls to the Master's Office. The droning of schoolmasters' voices reached him through some of the doors he passed, while from others escaped the roar of temporarily unsupervised adolescents.

The formidable Miss Grantly, the Master's secretary and gatekeeper, sat at her desk in the outer office, attacking the worn keys of a complex, elderly typewriter with her bony fingers In school legend, she was the fruit of a union between a dragon and a witch.

Ford approached her, feeling as if he had been transported back to a time when he had invariably entered this room with trepidation.

"Good morning, Miss Grantly. My name is Ford. I don't know if you remember me?"

"I remember everyone," responded Miss Grantly tartly, scarcely glancing up at him through her severe steel-rimmed spectacles. "You are no exception, I assure you."

She completed her typing with a few more abrupt pokes at the keys.

"The Master has visitors. You'll have to wait."

A murmur of voices could be heard through the closed doors of the Master's inner sanctum. Ford stood humbly before her, and she relented.

"I'll tell him you're here."

She tapped on the doors and disappeared inside. Some minutes passed as Ford surveyed an endless line of old school photographs that adorned the walls. Miss Grantly returned.

"You'll have to wait, as I thought."

◆    ◆    ◆

Beyond the doors, Lady Canderblank was taking morning coffee with the Master. She had insisted that her daughter Victoria accompany her, and the young lady sat draped on one arm of her mother's chair looking distinctly bored.

"Ford ... Ford ..." said Doctor Thornby thoughtfully. "There was a Ford here in the old King's day, if I'm not mistaken. Let me see."

Doctor Thornby maintained an elaborate filing system of his own design, in which he recorded the School history and subsequent career of every boy who had attended Kings. To this end he required Miss Grantly to scan the newspapers for reports in which the alumni were mentioned, and to maintain an extensive network of busybodies who liked to keep track of their own former colleagues.

"Yes, here he is," he said triumphantly, pulling a vanilla folder from a filing drawer. "Now, let me see ... Ford, Thomas Albert, The Rectory, Little Pagscombe, Gloucestershire. His parents are Doctor Albert Ford, DD, and Mrs. Ford. He was born in 1890 and attended Kings from 1903 to 1908."

"What was he like?"

"I have no idea, Lady Canderblank ... He was in Kings House, so perhaps Chadwicke can recall him. I see from the records that he was a cricketer ..."

"Here, give that to me," demanded Lady Canderblank, and snatched the file from him. She adjusted her pinz nez spectacles to read the first page.

Ford, Thomas Albert
Doctor Albert Ford, DD, and Mrs. Ford
The Rectory, Little Pagscombe, Glos.
Born 1890
Attended Kings 1903 to 1908
Victoria House; House Colors 1904, House Prefect 1906, House Cricket Captain 1907, 1908

Cricket: Colts XI, 1904, First XI, 1905, 1906, 1907, 1908; Rugby: Second XV, 1906-07, 1907-08; Compton Prize 1907, 1908
*Regius* Magazine 1906-1908; Editor 1908
Falmouth Prize 1908
History Upper VI; Hampton Exhibition, Kings College, Cantab., 1908

"Bit of a cricketer, slow left hand bowler and a steady bat, as I recall," said the Master.

"He wasn't a school prefect, I see," Lady Canderblank observed, interrupting him.

"He wasn't really the right type, if my memory serves me; his father is a country parson of no account."

"The Compton Prize?" Victoria Canderblank asked vaguely, peering over her mother's shoulder. "The Falmouth Prize? There are so many prizes, I can't keep track of them."

The Master assumed a tone of instruction. He might not be able to remember clearly every undistinguished ex-pupil, but he was an expert in the minutiae of Kings tradition.

"The Compton Prize is given to the pupil who, in the opinion of the sports master, is the most distinguished sportsman of his year. The Falmouth Prize is awarded by election; all the masters vote to select the boy who has shown the best academic promise and accomplishments. I seem to remember that Ford's election caused a bit of a controversy. Several of us thought young Percy Brighton was a more appropriate choice."

"Well, as I recall, Master," said Lady Canderwick acidly, "Harry Brighton was on the verge of donating all that money to the new science laboratory, and selecting his son for the Falmouth Prize was the least we could have done. In fact, as I predicted, no prize for the son, no donation from the father."

She tossed the folder onto the master's desk. Several newspaper clippings spilled from it.

"However, whether or not this police person won some prizes, in conditions of controversy or not, is scarcely the point. The point is, what are we to say to him?"

"Shouldn't we just let him in and let him ask questions?" Victoria asked innocently.

"Certainly not—I have no intention of being questioned," her mother snapped. "Master, you must be very firm that the medical conclusions are indecisive. There is no reason to suspect foul play—after all, who could possibly benefit from a boy's death?—and the appropriate course of action is to let sleeping dogs lie."

She permitted herself to become irritated.

"Colonel Dagenham assured me that any investigation would be a mere formality. I expect you, Master, to keep this person in his place."

She stood and prepared to leave.

"Furthermore, I have to say that it concerns me very much that a former pupil should have ended up in the police force. We can scarcely attract the better sort of families to Kings if their boys must mix with future riff-raff."

With that she stalked from the room, followed by her daughter. Ford stood waiting in the outer office, but Lady Canderblank ignored his riff-raffish presence. Her daughter spared him a glance and an almost imperceptible nod.

Ford let them pass and then, with Croft following behind, entered the Master's study. Ford continued to feel the intervening years had fallen away, and he was back in school, under the arbitrary justice of an absolute dictatorship.

The Master had two offices, as befitted his illustrious station. Just as the Prime Minister maintains an office in 10 Downing Street and a second in the Houses of Parliament, the Master had this public office in Old School—guarded by Miss Grantly—and a second private office guarded by his wife, in the Master's Lodge.

This office was lined with bookcases interspersed with filing cabinets and display cases filled with silver trophies, and in it he conducted the official business of the School. The upper walls were covered by portraits of more than four hundred years of former Masters, so that one could trace the history of men's fashions from the doublets and long stockings of

Tudor England, to the dark suits and starched white shirts of modern dignitaries.

Ford stood before the Master's desk, humbly waiting to be noticed, while Croft assumed a pose of sphinx-like immobility beside the door.

Doctor Thornby decided to grant Ford the lowest level of courtesy possible in the circumstances, without outright rudeness, and to treat him as if he were a tradesman with some task to perform about the School. He shuffled the clippings back into the file, closed it, and looked up at the policeman.

"Yes, Ford, what is it?"

Ford was glad that the Master had dispensed with formalities. It enabled him to concentrate solely on the job at hand.

"Good morning, Master. I wish to establish everybody's movements when Callaway died last Saturday evening, from approximately ten o'clock when the show ended until midnight."

"That's a Herculean task," Dr Thornby objected. "You can't be thinking logically. All the boys, all the masters, all the visitors ... It could take weeks!"

He shook his head decisively.

"Really, Ford, I would hope you could keep things in a better perspective. Surely one doesn't need—what's the word?—*alibis*, I believe, in a simple case of suicide, or whatever this was. I recognize you have a job to do, but I will not tolerate any further disruption to the smooth operation of the School. Do I make myself clear?"

He had a commanding presence gained from years of authority over those who could not fight back. His face, with its straight nose and full lips, reminded Ford of an elegant Greek statue. When he stood, as he did now to emphasize his point, he was tall and well proportioned.

"I appreciate your concerns, sir, but I believe we can do it with efficiency," Ford responded respectfully but unabashed. "I shall need a complete list of all the boys, the staff, and the visitors. The masters can question the boys. Sergeant Croft and I can collect their statements and interview the staff. That will leave the visitors, and we can deal with them outside the School."

The Master appeared exasperated. "Why is all this necessary, Ford? Surely you can't be implying that anyone associated with Kings can have anything to do with this tragic event?"

"The sooner we can establish their whereabouts, sir, the sooner we will be able to prove that. It's as much for the protection of the School as anything else."

Doctor Thornby snorted but could see no flaw in Ford's argument. He sat down again.

"Oh, very well," he conceded ungraciously. "If you must, you must. Miss Grantly can supply you with the lists. Is there anything else?"

"Yes, sir, if I may. I can address the masters at this morning's break and get the process rolling. The sooner we've completed it, the sooner we can leave the School undisturbed."

"I really don't see why any of this is necessary, but I suppose we had better get it over with."

"Indeed, sir," Ford agreed. "I regret it's a necessary formality. And, in that regard, I must ask you to make a note of the visitors you were entertaining that night; and, of course, an account of your own actions, and Mrs. Thornby's, for the sake of completeness."

"What *I* was doing?" the Master expostulated, as if Ford had taken leave of his senses. "What possible bearing could that have on your investigation? Really, Ford, I hope you're not letting yourself get carried away."

"I hope not too, sir."

Ford waited. The silence grew longer while Doctor Thornby struggled with his dignity.

"Oh, very well!" he snapped.

Ford continued as though the Master were being completely cooperative.

"What is your impression of what happened, sir?"

"My *impression*, Ford?" Thornby repeated incredulously.

"Yes, sir. One of the boys has been killed, and although the Harley Street surgeon made out a certificate specifying 'natural causes,' scarcely a specific description, he died in violent circumstances. Unless you can suggest reasons to the contrary, I must proceed on the basis that he was murdered."

"*Murdered?*" the Master replied, as if the idea were completely absurd. "Really, Ford, why would anyone wish to murder a Kings boy?"

"That is what I wish to determine, sir. What were the contents of the telegram you sent his parents? May I see the copy?"

"That's a personal matter, Ford."

Ford did not reply, and Doctor Thornby recalled that as a child, Ford had had a streak of obstinacy about him. He had never broken any rules; in that regard his record had been spotless. He had been quiet to the point of silence. He had given the impression that he was enduring Kings, rather than reveling in its many benefits.

His obstinate manner had displayed itself on the cricket pitch, where he had seemed to refuse to submit to a batsman, as if he were saying to himself, "I will *not* let this chap beat me," and in the classroom, where he had seemed to refuse to let his textbooks withhold their secrets, as if his silent monologue ran along the lines of, "I *will* learn to conjugate this verb," or "I *will* find the correct value for x, even if I have to sit here all day."

He had been a silent warrior determined to overcome sporting and academic obstacles, determined to maintain his privacy, and determined to leave Kings untouched. Most adolescents are extravagantly anxious to impose their opinions and particularly their needs upon the world, but Ford had offered nothing and asked for even less.

"Oh, very *well*, Ford. I also telephoned his relatives in London where he stayed during the holidays."

Doctor Thornby took up the copy and passed it over.

WE REGRET TO INFORM YOU THAT MICHAEL DIED OF NATURAL CAUSES ON SATURDAY NIGHT STOP HE WILL BE BURIED ON TUESDAY STOP LETTER FOLLOWS SHORTLY STOP

"Did you write as well, sir?"

Silently, Doctor Thornby passed over a copy written in what Ford recalled to be Miss Grantly's hand. It consisted mostly of fulsome descriptions of Callaway and ornate condolences. One paragraph read:

> Michael was found dead outside his House. In consultation with our medical advisors, we have sadly concluded that he suffered a heart attack, perhaps brought on by his exertions in the operetta.

When Ford still offered no comment, the Master said defensively, "There was absolutely no need to mention any further details, Ford. No need, if I may say so, for unnecessary drama. His parents will conclude that he died in the glow of his triumph upon the stage, and that is how all of us at Kings will also remember him."

"If I may ask you again, sir, what is your impression of what happened, sir?"

"The School is rife with rumor, and I fear you may stir the pot. The boy is dead, obviously by taking his own life."

Ford did not question this bizarre conclusion, and the Master became more emphatic.

"Suicide is ugly, and there is no benefit to be derived from causing pain to his parents or dragging the details through the scandal sheets of the popular press to gratify the lurid curiosities of the lower classes. The sooner we can forget the entire matter, the sooner Kings can pursue its purposes."

Doctor Thornby stood up and continued in tones of absolute finality.

"I have agreed to tolerate your presence, Ford, only because the Chief Constable has given his personal assurances of discretion and dispatch. I understand that, as a legal matter, you must consider the possibility of murder, but I assume that is no more than an investigative formality."

He stepped around his desk and stood close to Ford. The difference in their heights caused him to look downwards.

"I expect you to concur with the obvious, Ford, and in a very few days. No one *wished* to murder him, *ergo* he was not murdered."

He paused before continuing.

"In the spirit of cooperation, we will now see the masters as you requested. But if you step outside the boundaries of decency, discretion, or prudence, I promise you that you will regret it very much."

Ford had to remind himself that he was almost thirty and no longer a schoolboy under the Master's absolute authority. He had a vision of sitting in the detention room, writing out five hundred times, "I will not step outside the bounds of prudence."

◆     ◆     ◆

Dr. Thornby led Ford and Croft to the Senior Common Room, where the teaching staff was gathered for tea and a brief respite from the constant presence of mutinous adolescents. The air was redolent with tobacco smoke, and the clatter of teacups on saucers rose above the hubbub.

Ford glanced round the room, remembering the battered armchairs and threadbare carpeting, the elderly shelves piled with papers, and the over-stuffed notice boards. When he was in school, the shabby room had always seemed luxurious because it had at least a threadbare carpet, whereas the floors trodden by the boys invariably consisted of hard materials impervious to the assaults of children's feet.

He recognized many of the older masters, but the younger members of the staff were all new. The war had cut down a complete generation like a scythe, leaving a gap to be filled by those young enough to have escaped the harvest, or even, Ford noted with surprise, a smattering of women.

Decades of school-mastering had given the staff a common appearance. They tended toward baggy tweed suits with pockets bulging with lists and marking records and sundry forbidden objects confiscated from their charges. They were all capable of speaking very loudly to subdue the roaring of teenagers. They were skilled in sarcasm, honed by evaluating the faltering answers of boys who had not done their homework. They exuded a communal pessimism born of fruitless years spent attempting to fire the imaginations and enthusiasms of sullen youths unwilling to be taught.

On Ford's appearance, the din of conversation and chinking teacups and saucers died. One or two of the older masters made as if to welcome him, but Doctor Thornby cut them off and introduced him briefly and gracelessly.

"Very well, Ford," he finished. "Be as brief as possible."

"Ladies and gentlemen," Ford began, speaking into the sudden silence, "as we all know, the circumstances surrounding Callaway's untimely death are unclear. My purpose is to clarify them. To do so, I need to establish the precise cause of death and to rule out the possibility of foul play."

The room gave him rapt attention.

"It is in this latter regard that I need your help. We need to establish where everyone was from the time the play ended on Saturday night until one o'clock on Sunday morning. That's the time interval in which we assume he died."

No one stirred.

"I would ask you to ask all the boys to account for their movements. I'm sure that most simply went back to their Houses and to bed. Please ask them if they saw anything, or if they have any other information that might shed light on this unfortunate incident. Sergeant Croft will assist you in this matter. I suggest you hold House meetings, and then see in private any boy who has a contribution to make. In the case of Trafalgar House, I will assist Mr. McIntire personally. Are there any questions so far?"

There were none. The masters were passive, and it struck Ford that he was handing them a piece of homework. Perhaps the analogy could be useful.

"Therefore, please supply Sergeant Croft with a list of all the boys under your supervision. A tick mark will suffice to indicate that a boy returned to his House, stayed there, and was in bed by lights out. If that was not the case, please place a cross against the boy's name and add a note of explanation at the bottom of the list. You may use the same technique for any additional information a boy offers."

Several of the masters nodded. Their assignment had taken shape in their minds.

"That takes care of the School. In the case of the staff, I would be grateful if you would supply a short paragraph summarizing the movements of yourselves and your households."

There was more nodding; Ford had an inspiration.

"There were also a number of visitors and school servants and groundskeepers. Perhaps I could request Doctor Howard to undertake the construction of the list of visitors, and Mr. Feely to address the remainder?"

Doctor Howard, the senior science teacher, had been one of Ford's favorites, and he was a stickler for completeness and accuracy born of countless years of carefully recording the results of scientific experiments, even those in which the outcome had been utterly predictable. Ford remembered Mr. Feely, a history teacher, as a prodigious busybody. The prospect of officially sanctioned prying would delight him.

"Please have your lists completed by no later than tomorrow at five. Are there any questions?"

There was a universal buzz of agreement. Ford fantasized that the masters might even compete for excellence in their submissions, as if they were being given grades. Perhaps he should make a comment about the importance of correct grammar and clear, legible handwriting, as an ingratiating joke, but told himself not to be carried away.

"I appreciate your help," he said. "And, of course, all of this is subject to the Master's concurrence."

The Master was strongly in favor of no investigation at all, although he had to admit a certain admiration for Ford's efficient organization. Looking round the room, Doctor Thornby saw it would take a brave man and a good reason to deny the masters their opportunity.

"Certainly—I was planning something very similar, but we'll do it your way, Ford."

He had obviously decided to enter into the moment.

"Five o'clock sharp tomorrow, gentlemen," he added, ignoring as he always did, the unfortunate addition of females to his staff. "Let there be no laggards!"

♦    ♦    ♦

The meeting broke up in a babble of conversation, and Ford threaded his way through the crowd to Mr. McIntire.

"Good morning, sir," he said, shaking hands.

"Let's take a turn around the lawn," said McIntire. "Give me five minutes to get my next class started."

Ford waited no more than five minutes and McIntire joined him on the steps of Old School.

"I left that criminal White in charge; there'll be a riot before luncheon," he said.

They set off across the grass.

"I take it you're not pleased to be back, Ford. I assume this particular moment of greatness has been thrust upon you?"

McIntire was an English teacher whose conversation was peppered with quotations from Shakespeare. He was a dour and stocky Yorkshireman, ill suited to King's enveloping snobbery, and Ford wondered why he had remained here for so long.

McIntire seemed to be thinking with him in parallel.

"You were as much a fish out of water as I am," he said.

"Well, sir, in my case, time has knit up the raveled sleeve of care," said Ford, falling into McIntire's idiom. "I'm sorry you're having to go through this mess."

Ford had liked McIntire, who had been a rare beacon of normality in his dreary days at Kings.

"Lady Canderblank has let me know it's my entire fault," McIntire responded dryly. "Have you met her ladyship?"

"I have yet to have that honor thrust upon me, sir." He gestured toward Trafalgar. "What happened on Saturday night?

McIntire had seen nothing unusual on Saturday night, except that the boys were exceptionally boisterous from the excitements of the day. He and the assistant housemaster and the prefects had chased them into their dormitories by eleven fifteen.

The seniors, who lived in little rooms on the third floor, had all signed in to the Late Book. It was a Sixth Form privilege to sign a register rather than attending a physical roll call. Callaway's name was there with all the rest and he had written the time, 10.35, beside his name.

McIntire had waited until the prefects reported that everyone was accounted for, and then he'd locked up. There were three exterior doors; the front door, the kitchen door in the rear, and McIntire's own private door on the side of the building. He had noticed nothing amiss, and—belonging to a local Shakespeare society that was putting on a production in the summer vacation—retired to re-reading *Romeo and Juliet*. He had gone to bed at one o'clock, having heard nothing.

"When young Jenkins Minor unleashed the dogs of war on Sunday morning, Lady Canderblank assumed command," McIntire continued. "The doctor and the policeman examined the body and removed it. By lunchtime, she had had the shrubbery chopped down and the entire area dug over. By teatime there were new privet hedges, and she would have expunged the entire incident from our collective memories if she could have."

They had wandered over to Trafalgar and now stood looking down at the freshly turned earth and diminutive bushes.

"Did you get a good look at Callaway before he was removed, sir?"

"Yes. It was I who put a sheet over him."

McIntire's description of the corpse matched Croft's exactly. He reported it without emotion.

"Did you notice anything unusual on the ground or in the bushes?"

"It was a bit messy. Lots of rhododendron branches, some broken … lots of cigarette ends. Now the seniors have to sneak behind the potting shed for a smoke—such an inconvenience for them on a rainy day! The Sergeant—a good man, for a southerner—collected a couple of the fresh butts, and there was a copy of the program for *The Pirates of Penanze* … and young Jenkins' Chapel books, of course …"

His voice trailed away.

"What was your visceral reaction? How did you think he died?"

"I assumed he had died by *a bared bodkin*—there was a bloody great knife sticking out of his chest! Although ..."

"Yes, sir?"

"It's strange. There wasn't any room to move, let alone fight, although several of the branches had been freshly snapped. It occurred to me he'd been killed elsewhere and dragged into the bushes, but that didn't seem possible, either."

They entered Trafalgar and climbed to Callaway's room on the top floor where the senior boys had quarters to themselves. On Saturday night, McIntire told Ford, the other two seniors had had permission to stay with their respective relatives, and Callaway had been the sole occupant of the seniors' floor.

McIntire unlocked the door to Callaway's room.

The room was long and narrow. A bed stood beside one wall, and against another, a wardrobe and a small writing desk. A large window with a wooden chair beneath it occupied the far wall. There were neither pictures nor any other forms of decoration to offer hints of its occupant's personality.

"Have you searched the room, sir?"

"No. I assumed it would be checked for evidence. We took a suit and shirt and tie to bury him in, but nothing else. Lady Canderblank wanted the entire contents removed and burned, but Sergeant Croft was very insistent."

Ford sat down in the narrow bed to rest his aching leg.

"Good. What was Callaway like, sir?"

"Frankly, he was a little prick, but that merely establishes him as a typical Kings scholar," McIntire responded. He noted Ford's infirmity but made no comment, and sat down on the chair to avoid having to do so.

"Callaway had the usual bad habits. He was a mediocre student and mediocre at sports," he continued. "He had a reputation for larceny but was too clever to be caught. In short, he was a rather unpleasant young man.

"However, to be fair, he did show promise in singing and drama, and he worked very hard to improve his natural talents. He did a very good

Lady Macbeth last year, and he was terrific as the Major General on Saturday. He was good-looking in a petulant sort of way. In fact, I assumed that the combination of his good looks, his acting abilities, his general self-absorption, and his meanness of spirit, marked him out for a successful career on the stage."

Ford choked back a chuckle.

"What about friends, or particular relationships with other boys, or his attitudes toward the staff? I understand that he was unpleasant, but I need to find a reason why he was lying in the bushes downstairs with a knife in his chest."

"Indeed you do. His only real friend was White, a young hooligan in Queens—born to be a bookie, I'm sure. Callaway was too selfish to be popular. Doubtless he made his calo's life miserable."

A *calo*—the word was derived from a Latin word meaning servant—was a junior boy assigned to run errands and do menial jobs for a senior. The older boys were known as *doms*, from the word meaning master.

McIntire glanced at Ford. "I appreciate your dilemma, but if everybody at Kings with Callaway's personality got killed, the Great Lawn would resemble the aftermath of the second battle of the Somme."

Ford flinched—he simply could not help it.

"God, I'm sorry. Were you there, Ford? That's very tasteless of me." McIntire seemed genuinely contrite.

For a moment Ford was transported in time and space. He recalled the choking smoke that reduced visibility to the length of his arm, so that he could scarcely make out the bodies of the dead men he was stepping on, and the deafening din of exploding howitzer shells; he and every other hapless soldier a tiny cog in a vast military machine, a multitude of half-blinded, half-deafened men stumbling to their deaths ...

Ford collected himself and pressed on.

"Who was Callaway's calo?"

"A fourth form boy called Connelly."

Ford rose awkwardly.

"I need to find someone who had both access to Callaway and also a reason to kill him, sir. Someone who could have come and gone before you locked up. Can I ask you to question the boys about anyone coming up and down these stairs? I know that's a bit of a task—people would have been running up and down constantly—but we need to find an outsider, or the shadow of suspicion will fall directly on Trafalgar." He reflected. "All that assumes that Callaway really did sign the Late Book, and at the time he recorded."

McIntire also rose. "You're suggesting someone forged the entry?"

"It would have been a wild risk, and we can get an expert to verify his handwriting … But something is amiss, sir; if someone killed Callaway and carried him down the stairs, he would have been seen for sure. It would have to be an adult or one of the senior boys to be strong enough."

Ford glanced out the window to where the rhododendrons had once stood.

"If he was killed down there in the bushes, someone must have forged his name, for no apparent purpose … Or, Callaway came in and went out again …" He laughed. "As you can see, we know nothing!" He looked round the stark bedroom. "Perhaps there's something here. I'll search the room."

"Do you want me to leave, Ford? It occurs to me that I fall within the boundaries of suspicion." McIntire did not look particularly worried.

"Yes, you do, sir, but I have no particular reason to suspect you, and doubtless Mrs. McIntire will provide you with an alibi. Can you take the bedclothes apart to see if there's anything in them, and check the mattress? I'll start on the wardrobe."

In twenty minutes, Callaway's room had been searched from top to bottom. There was nothing remarkable, nothing to suggest anything more than a humdrum school life. Even the evidence of Callaway's vices was banal: a packet of cigarettes hidden in a shoe, a French publication featuring naked women, and a collection of beer bottle tops retained as if they were trophies from forbidden parties.

The desk drawers had revealed a jumble of schoolwork and a collection of correspondence tied in string. On top of the papers was the start of a letter that read: "Dearest Mummy, Why do you deny me—"

The sentence was unfinished.

Ford remembered that Sundays were letter-writing days. Obviously Callaway wanted something that his parents were refusing, and had made an early start in penning his complaint. Ford scooped up the entire mess to read at his leisure.

They went downstairs to Mr. McIntire's room and opened Callaway's box—each student had a small box for personal items and valuables kept in his housemaster's safekeeping. By tradition, the master was honor-bound not to inspect the contents, and the boy was honor-bound not to place in his box anything which "might bring dishonor to Kings."

The box contained a ring with a latch key and a door key, presumably from Callaway's home; a gold-plated wrist watch inscribed, *MC 12/12/ 1919*, which Mr. McIntire deduced was Callaway's sixteenth birthday; a vicious-looking sheath knife, legal in the outside world but strictly forbidden in Kings, and therefore handed over at the beginning of term; and a sealed envelope containing a surprising amount of money.

Mr. McIntire whistled. "That's more than I earn in a month!"

"Is his family well-to-do, sir?"

"I don't think so. His father's an Army officer, and Callaway was here on a scholarship."

"Well, someone was being generous," Ford muttered.

The money bothered him. It was beyond Callaway's means, and it arguably suggested he was up to no good. Whether it's presence here constituted a motive for murder was an entirely different matter.

"I'll take the keys, sir, and give you a receipt. I'll go and see his relatives tomorrow."

Ford took a perfunctory look at the kitchen from which the knife had been removed, made a list of the rooms overlooking the shrubbery, said goodbye to McIntire, and returned slowly to his car, just as Old Clappers began to toll.

Old School was topped by a tall octagonal clock tower that held 'Old Clappers,' a titanic bell cast in 1784, whose sonorous tones marked not only the passing of the hours but also the ending of lessons.

During school hours the Great Lawn was all but deserted until Old Clappers tolled. Within a minute of its tolling, the school buildings disgorged several hundred boys through their various doors; boys who ran, walked, slouched or dawdled, according to their various natures, to their next lessons, at which time the buildings swallowed them up again, and peace and calm were restored.

The constable who had driven Ford and Croft was nowhere to be seen. Suddenly the School seemed oppressive and he was anxious to leave, but the thought of the long walk down the hill to the village left him hesitating, and he was reluctant to beg a favor from Doctor Thornby.

"Are you looking for a ride?" a bright voice burst upon him.

The young lady whom he had seen leaving the Master's study earlier that morning appeared in his vision, as if by magic.

"I ..."

"I'm Victoria Canderblank," she interrupted him. "We would have met this morning if my mother had not been in a foul mood. And you are unquestionably the enigmatic Chief Inspector Ford. Now that we know each other, let me give you a lift."

He found himself in the luxurious interior of the Rolls Royce.

"Have you solved the crime, if crime it be? God, what a depressing place this is. It gives me the creeps!"

She rattled on while they rolled imperiously down the hill. In a remarkably short time—too short a time, it seemed to Ford—they stopped outside the inn.

"Will you come and interview me?" she asked with a dazzling smile. "I'm a witness, after all!"

Her eyes were an extraordinary shade of blue.

"I shall make a point of it, Miss Canderblank," he promised gallantly, and climbed from the car.

"Be sure you do, Mr. Ford," she called gaily through the window, and she was off in a cloud of petroleum fumes.

Ford crossed the green to Croft's cottage, and Croft's wife opened the door.

"Good afternoon, Mrs. Croft. Would you please ask your husband to visit me over at the inn this evening, after he's had his dinner?"

"Of course, sir."

Her kindly features still held remembrances of the beauty that must have beguiled her husband in his youth.

She hesitated before continuing. "You should get some rest, sir, if I may say so without offense. You look pretty much done in."

"I'll go to bed early, I promise, Mrs. Croft. I appreciate your concern."

◆ ◆ ◆

Croft found Ford in the public bar enduring Mrs. Green's analysis of Callaway's death. Ford was learning, to his surprise, that the murder had very likely been the result of a satanic ritual—a possibility, he was forced to confess, that he had not considered. The ritual had been interrupted before its completion, which explained why parts of Callaway's anatomy had not been removed for human consumption.

When Croft arrived, Ford promised Mrs. Green that he would pursue this line of investigation with all the energy it clearly deserved, and drew Croft to the fireplace where they could talk undisturbed.

"It's a rum place, that school, sure enough," said Croft as he accepted a pint of best bitter. "I've never really been inside it, so to speak. It's a world of its own, with all those rules and such like. Reminds me of the Army in some ways, except the Army made more sense."

"I know exactly what you mean, Sergeant," Ford said. "The difference between a gentleman and a common man is that a gentleman is isolated from the world during his formative years and taught all sorts of obscure stuff and nonsense under harsh conditions, while the common man is taught things of practical value, if he will learn them."

Croft raised his eyebrows in surprise. There was more to Ford than met the eye, he decided.

"Leaving aside the finer points of English academic traditions, Croft, how did you get on today?"

"Surprisingly well, sir, to tell you the truth. All the masters are taking their tasks very seriously. The one sure fact we've developed so far is that Mr. Jaspers, the old Greek and Latin teacher, swears he saw Callaway at his window at a quarter to eleven." He took a swallow of beer.

"Does he, by Jove!" Ford exclaimed. "Is he certain?"

"He's very definite, sir, and I believe him. He was walking his dog, which he does every night, and he looked up and saw him. It seems that Mr. Jaspers is writing a book—a monograph, as he called it—on the buildings at Kings, and he studies them as he walks by. He says he was looking up at Trafalgar, considering—wait a minute, sir; let me check my notes—considering 'the proportions of Italianate revival architecture,' sir, and saw young Callaway."

"That gives us a time, and a place, Sergeant. That's the first piece of hard evidence we've had all day."

"Quite so, sir. As for the rest, we're collecting all the statements. Almost everybody is being vouched for by everybody else, and we'll have to see if anyone is left over at the end. It's a bit like musical chairs."

Ford brought Croft up to date on his own activities, and Croft was clearly pleased that Ford was including him as a partner to be informed, rather than as a mere subordinate.

Then Ford proceeded to make plans.

"I'll go to London tomorrow to see the Harley Street specialist and Callaway's relatives. I'll read Callaway's letters on the train. I also have to attend a meeting for my boss. I'll take the last train back tomorrow night; perhaps you'd arrange for the constable to meet me with the Humber."

He took a sip of beer, remembering that the easy taste disguised its potency.

"In the meantime, I'd like you to make sure the gathering of information gets completed up at the School, and I'd like you to get a detailed statement from the undertakers, and get the knife. I know you'll be careful how you handle it; perhaps it will still have some fingerprints ... Let's hope we can avoid an exhumation ... Then, the day after tomorrow, we'll see what we can conclude."

He paused.

"Let's see, am I forgetting anything? Of course, your drink: another for the road?"

Croft let himself be persuaded.

"Very good of you, sir."

With a second pint clasped in his hand, he gesticulated toward the landlord behind the bar.

"Just to let you know, sir," he said in a lower voice, "Green was up at the School on Saturday night. He was attending to the catering. They had a firm over from Stroud for the sandwiches and such, and Green supplied the drinks; cider for the guests at the interval and brandy for the Master's guests after the theatricals. His daughter Lucy helped out at the Lodge. Not that I'm suggesting anything, but they're on the list."

"Thank you; that's helpful to know."

Mrs. Green descended upon them with more news. It seemed that a sheep had been found dead up in Twenty Acre Meadow, close by the School. Its cause of death was still uncertain; however, those with an ounce of common sense between their ears would clearly see it for was it was—yet another straw in the wind pointing toward black magic and devil worship.

"I'll look into it first thing tomorrow, Margie," Croft said without inflexion.

"It sounds to me like a wolf in sheep's clothing," Ford said, and Croft almost choked on his beer.

# Wednesday

F ord left Gloucestershire by the earliest train and traveled up to London, working his way methodically through the contents of Callaway's desk, leaving the stack of correspondence until last. The loose papers were a morass of essays, notes, and indifferent attempts at poetry. An incomplete short story suggested Callaway'd had a streak of sadism in him, but, alas for Mrs. Green's theory, not satanism.

The last paper was the incomplete draft of a letter to his mother, beginning: "Dearest Mummy, Why do you deny me—"

Turning to the packet of correspondence, he read it from top to bottom, and then re-read it, making notes as he went. The correspondence consisted of three parts.

The first was made up of letters from his parents in India, which gave updates on their domestic news and contained comments and responses to the weekly letters he must have written them as required by school rules; the second consisted of letters from his relations in London, to which, judging by their complaints, he must have responded infrequently; and the last contained a few other pieces of odd mail.

There was also a letter to his parents, dated several weeks before, which he must have forgotten to post.

> Dear Mum and Father,
> I hope you are well. I am well. School is as usual. The weather is warm. We are doing Pirats of Penanz this term and I am the Major General. I have a couple of good songs. I hope Annie is well. Things are REALLY expensive, please send me a fiver by return.
> Love
> Michael

Ford riffled through his parents' letters looking for a reference to whatever it was that his mother was denying him, but there was none. Indeed, his parents had invariably responded positively to whatever it was he had asked for.

> We also enclose yet another five pound note, but we really hope, Michael, that in the future you can manage to live within the very reasonable sum we agreed to ... If you really want to go to France this summer instead of coming home to India, we'll be very disappointed, of course, but we wouldn't want to spoil your fun.

The miscellaneous correspondence was not much help either, Ford noted.

> Dear Sir, We regret that this book is banned under English laws governing pornography ...

> Dear Mr. Callaway, When we agreed to open an account, we made it clear that we expect prompt payment ...

Ford closed his eyes as the train made its final dash toward London. The pattern that emerged was that of an indifferent student, a spendthrift always asking for more, a boy with prurient interests; there was nothing here to suggest that Callaway was anything other than the rather unpleasant youth Mr. McIntire had described—and certainly not anything to suggest a motive for murder.

◆     ◆     ◆

Ford left the Home Office in a light drizzle and headed back toward Scotland Yard. He had just attended a meeting on Brownlee's behalf, the principal purpose of which seemed to be the provision of a forum in which junior civil servants, fresh from Oxford and Cambridge, could lecture seasoned senior police officers in what they described as "the objectives of police work."

Ford reflected that if he were successful in his career and climbed the ladder of promotion, he could look forward to an ever-increasing amount of paperwork and an ever-increasing exposure to such civil servants, until a day on which his job would consist solely of completing forms, writing reports, and attending meetings.

After this metamorphosis, he would be indistinguishable from senior officers in the Ministry of Agriculture or the Board of Trade. Indeed, it might be feasible to establish an exchange program in which government servants from different departments could change places by a random lottery and yet still be responsible for the same requisitions and budgetary submissions.

In those circumstances, it might well be that they would receive the same lectures from the same callow civil servants, in which the phrase "the purpose of $x$ is to foster the well-being of the British public" could be completed by substituting "neighborhood police patrols," or "beef and diary products inspections," or "excise tax simplification," for $x$ as appropriate.

"Good morning, Chief Inspector!"

Ford was so startled from his bureaucratic reveries that he jumped. Victoria Canderblank stood before him, her face framed in a floppy yellow rain hat, her smile a ray of sunshine in the gloom.

"Good Lord, Miss Canderblank, please excuse me!" He hurriedly raised his hat to her.

"I'm sorry to surprise you," she said, still smiling. "You must have been miles away."

"I was contemplating the dismal fate of police officers."

"Ouch! That sounds painful."

It began to rain heavily. They were standing directly outside a pub, and it seemed logical to take shelter in the saloon bar until the squall had passed.

"Is the fate of police officers as gloomy as all that?" she asked, as she accepted a glass of sherry.

"No, not really. One retires after twenty-five years and focuses one's attention on stamp collecting or fishing, and slips quietly into old curmudgeonhood."

"Do you collect stamps, or do you fish, Mr. Ford?"

"Neither, I fear."

"Then what *do* you do, when you're not detecting?"

"I play a little golf," Ford admitted.

"Do you really? So do I—perhaps we'll encounter each other on the back nine! In fact, my father's a member of a club near Oxford. Perhaps we could play a round on Saturday morning?"

Before he could either accept or decline the invitation, she had hurried on to working out the details, sipping her sherry as if the round were a foregone conclusion; and then she was gone, hurrying off to take advantage of a break in the storm, leaving him with a sharp memory of her smile and a paper napkin on which she had written out the arrangements in fuzzy ink.

◆　　◆　　◆

Sir Neville Pondsford kept Ford waiting in his elegant outer offices for more than half an hour before admitting him to the consulting room. Since no one was ushered out, Ford assumed he had been kept waiting to create the illusion that there were many urgent matters on the doctor's agenda—as Ford had to admit, perhaps there were.

"Sir, I am the police officer investigating the circumstances of young Callaway's death at Kings School," said Ford without preamble, presenting his card. "I am sure your time is valuable, so I will be as brief as possible. I have interviewed Doctor Thickett. I understand from him that you examined the body and entered a cause of death of 'natural causes' on the death certificate."

"Yes, I did," Sir Neville replied nonchalantly.

He had the sort of patina that only comes from wealth and social position, and stands as an impenetrable armor against the trials and tribulations suffered by lesser mortals.

"I understand from Doctor Thickett that the examination took no more than five minutes and did not extend beyond a visual inspection while the body remained fully clothed?"

Sir Neville shrugged. "Thickett was the boy's physician—I was simply asked to assist as a personal favor."

"Since you signed the certificate, sir, it is, of course, entirely your own responsibility rather than his. Did you make notes, Sir Neville?"

"Notes?" Sir Neville asked, arching one eyebrow quizzically in a manner Ford had never been able to achieve. "Notes? It is not my custom to make *notes* at post mortems, my dear fellow. I'm sure the local doctor completed the necessary formalities."

Ford continued, as unperturbed as Sir Neville.

"I fear he took no notes either, sir, and therefore I must ask you to confirm his verbal report. There was a large kitchen knife protruding from the body. I understand you removed it. What did you do with it?"

"Do with it? I have no idea! I probably laid it down on the table; I certainly did not take it away with me, if that's what you're inferring. Is it missing?"

Sir Neville looked at his wristwatch to emphasize the many calls upon his time.

"I understand you cleaned it?"

"Perhaps I did ..."

"Sir, it had been wrapped in paper to preserve any fingerprints or other clues it might have revealed. I understand you removed the paper and cleaned the knife, thus obliterating the evidence."

"Common decency required that the knife be removed and tidied. It was a question of propriety. I saw no countervailing need to observe forensic niceties."

"I see, sir," Ford said quietly, absorbing this information. "How long was the blade?"

"Oh, three or four inches, perhaps—a paring knife rather than a carving knife, I would say."

"In your opinion, sir, multiple wounds of that depth in the chest cavity would normally cause death—in the absence of *countervailing indications?*"

Sir Neville appeared not to notice the irony in Ford's voice. "Of course."

"Thank you for your time, Sir Neville," said Ford with some finality, as if he had no more questions.

It must have occurred to Sir Neville that this was not a good point on which to end the interview.

"Er," he began as he picked up Ford's card, which he had previously tossed unnoticed on his desk. "Inspector—Chief Inspector, I'm sure you will appreciate that the selection of the cause of death phraseology was entirely to spare the poor boy's parents unnecessary suffering. I did what I could to smooth over an incident that, if unnecessarily extended, could only cause more anguish. It was my duty as a doctor. We are expected to exercise discretion. I'm sure you have a similar responsibility in your profession, Chief Inspector."

"Were you advised by anyone as to the *preferred* cause of death, sir? Did someone suggest that, in the circumstances, it was best to take that approach?"

"Naturally I took the parents' absence into consideration, the need to avoid disruption in the School, and the potential damage that press attention might generate. But I discussed the cause of death only with the local chap, Doctor Whatever-his-name-is."

"Doctor Thickett, sir. Obviously, the Canderblanks would not have suggested you make a long journey simply to look over the shoulder of a country physician with credentials and experience far beneath your own."

A faint chink appeared in the armor of Sir Neville's imperturbability. "Naturally, I discussed these matters with the Canderblanks and the Headmaster, since they were the ones that requested me to attend the examination. They were quite rightly anxious that a molehill not be turned into a mountain."

"Were you also advised or requested to remove and clean the knife, sir?"

Sir Neville permitted himself the merest touch of incredulity. "Of course not! What an absurd idea!"

"Thank you, sir. I have only one final question. I assume you rendered an invoice for your services?"

Sir Neville was clearly not pleased that the commercial aspects of his practice should be mentioned.

"Naturally, since I was there in a professional capacity," he responded, almost keeping his irritation from his voice.

Ford prepared to leave, and Sir Neville stood up with another glance at his watch. He advanced around his desk, and Ford watched as he smoothly rearranged his features into an expression of affability.

"I hope I've been able to assist, you, er, er … Ford. Are you almost finished? Where do your investigations lead you next?"

Ford turned back.

"Oh, I'll ask for an inquest, Sir Neville, as a matter of fact. And I'll seek an order for the body to be exhumed and a full post mortem conducted."

"Surely you jest!"

"I fear not, sir," replied Ford. He kept his tone neutral.

"I shall report to the coroner that a death certificate was written out for natural causes, when the body in question had a four inch blade sticking in its chest, and that no medical notes had been written to describe the state of the corpse. I shall further report that the knife was cleaned, possibly in order to remove any microscopic evidence and prevent any use of fingerprint identification. And that the body had then been handed off to the local undertaker without any consultation with the police or a police surgeon."

"But that would suggest …" Sir Neville gasped for words.

"I'm not sure what the professional disciplinary implications would be, sir. I'm not an expert in that field. I'm not sure if it's gross negligence or malpractice. I'm not familiar with the exact definitions, I'm afraid."

Shock drained the color from Sir Neville's face.

"As far as the law is concerned, sir, where I'm on firmer ground, the signing of a false or deliberately misleading death certificate is perjury, and there's obviously a *prima facie* case to be made for criminal conspiracy, since you were paid to make a perjurous affidavit. And, of course, deliberate destruction of evidence by cleaning the blade is an obstruction of justice, which is also a felony."

Sir Neville collapsed back into his chair. "That would *catastrophic!*"

"Perhaps, perhaps not—obviously it's up to the proper medical authorities and the Courts, sir. One never knows. But none of that is my immediate concern, which is that I can't proceed with the primary investigation until I know how the boy died. That's why I need the inquest, sir. Thank you for your time, Sir Neville."

Ford again turned to leave.

"Wait, for God's sake, man! I—the boy's *neck* was broken! That's how he died—the knife wounds were post mortem!"

Ford stared at him as he absorbed this statement, his mind grasping at a jumble of implications. The doctor appeared to be stricken; his armor of imperturbability had been pierced. Ford did not doubt that he was hearing the truth for the first time.

"How do you know the boy's neck was broken, sir?"

"The angle of his head and its lolling action when the undertaker moved him." Words tumbled from Sir Neville's lips. "Third or fourth cerebral vertebra, most likely, C3 or C4. More than likely his skull was fractured also—he'd obviously fallen from a considerable height. The back of his hair was matted with dried blood."

"Fallen, sir?" Ford asked, still grappling with this completely unexpected explanation of Callaway's demise. "How do you know that?"

"I had the misfortune once to see a man fall from a fourth story window and to attend to him as he died. That man's terminal position was exactly as Thickett described the boy's, with the same neck injury. But the key is that the boy had bitten through his tongue and lip. Only a great force could achieve that, and it's identical to the condition of the dead man I saw."

Ford needed time to think. Callaway must have fallen to his death from his window, which was, Ford realized, directly above the bushes. Both Mr. McIntire and Croft had commented on broken branches.

But *why* had he fallen? Was it an accident or suicide—or could he have been pushed? And why, for God's sake—after he had fallen—had someone *stabbed* him?

"Tell me more about the knife wounds, sir."

"The blade was short and thin, almost like a dagger. It would have penetrated easily. I would hazard a guess—more than a guess, a professional estimate—that the blows were administered by thrusting upwards, rather than stabbing downwards. I made a mental note of it at the time."

Such an act would be most unnatural, thought Ford. He tried to imagine the situation, but the doctor was still talking, his hauteur stripped away.

"Listen, Ford ... Chief Inspector, I'll admit that I've been a complete idiot. I shouldn't have let her talk me into that foolish certificate. Normally I would not have cleaned the knife as she wished, but since it obviously wasn't a murder weapon, I saw no harm in it. The Canderblanks are friends, and Debbie Canderblank can be very insistent, frankly. But I swear I had no ulterior motive."

Now that the dam of confession had been breached, his words became a torrent.

"Well, to be completely, candid, that's not quite accurate. The Canderblanks are considering an investment in a new orthopedic clinic I'm setting up. Needless to say a scandal would be ruinous—literally *ruinous!*"

He stood up.

"I know what you must think of me, but I happen to be a damned good doctor, and I'll wager my reputation—if I survive with a reputation—that my diagnosis is correct."

Ford looked at him steadily.

"I do not ruin lives and careers by choice, Sir Neville. I simply need to know everything that affects my investigation into this boy's death."

He stopped to consider.

"In the event that I conclude an exhumation or other similar action is necessary, I will permit you to request it. You will be able to say that you've had second thoughts, or something along those lines, and there would be no scandal. You would be applauded for your caution and candor rather than criticized for your initial negligence."

A sob of relief escaped Sir Neville's patrician throat.

"If, however, I find any basis for doubting what you have told me, or if you are anything less than unconditionally cooperative in the future, or if I find any indication of further collusion with the Canderblanks, I shall proceed as I intended."

Sir Neville began to thank him, but Ford cut him short and left.

◆   ◆   ◆

Ford found Walnut Crescent in North West London, where Callaway's aunt and uncle lived, in the late afternoon. He supposed it was just close enough to describe itself as part of Hampstead, although Camden would have been more honest. He calculated that he just had time for his interview with Callaway's relatives before catching the last train back to Gloucestershire.

"Mrs. Markham?" he asked the woman who answered the door at Number 37, and he presented his card.

"My name is Ford. I'm the police officer investigating your nephew's tragic death. Please accept my condolences."

The woman ushered him into the front parlor, a room crammed with overstuffed furniture, potted plants, and bric-a-brac. The numerous pictures were exclusively of a devotional nature, except for a photograph of Callaway in school uniform, which had been given a prominent position on the mantelpiece and dressed up in black ribbon. Mrs. Markham carried an air of faded gentility, while her husband, when he appeared, had something of the bulldog about him.

Between Mrs. Markham's tremulous whispers and Mr. Markham's staccato growls, Ford was able to build a picture of Callaway at home—moody and uncooperative, resentful of making contributions to household duties, disappearing for hours on end to trawl the book shops in the Charing Cross Road.

He had no friends and fiercely resisted even the most trivial social contacts. In contrast to his guardians, he preferred to rise late and go to bed late, clearly a point of longstanding controversy. His bedroom was a fortress he defended against all-comers.

Callaway had had, Ford learned, two supreme faults.

The first fault, revealed through Mrs. Markham's resentful eyes, was Callaway's utter refusal to discuss any remotely personal subject, so that she had literally no idea of his hopes and fears, nor of his likes and dislikes, beyond such banal trivia as a fondness for sardines and a hatred of rice pudding. From Mr. Markham's perspective, an even greater fault had been his absolute refusal, in the face of every conceivable threat, to go to church or participate in any church activities whatsoever.

"Mr. Markham's a church warden," explained Mrs. Markham. "It looked bad that Mickey wouldn't go to church."

For a moment Ford was nonplussed; no one had referred to Callaway by his first name, far less by a family diminutive.

"Particularly since we're High Church," she added, as if family solidarity were particularly important to those with a preference for ornate displays of religious devotion.

"Mrs. Markham couldn't do her housework," Mr. Markham complained, "even in term time, because he had the key to his room and always kept it locked."

"I found this key," said Ford, digging it out of his pocket. "Is this the one?"

"Aha!" barked Mr. Markham in triumph, and rose as if to snatch it.

"Unfortunately, sir, I'll have to be the first person in. I'll have to search his room before I can give you a free rein."

Throughout the interview, Ford could detect no particular sadness or regret that their nephew had died so unexpectedly, nor any curiosity as to the causes. It appeared that Callaway, despite his familiar nickname, had not been lovable. In fact, Ford formed the conclusion that caring for their nephew had been a burden to be endured.

"What arrangements did you have with your sister, Mrs. Markham? I assume that you agreed to give him a home while he was here in England, and take care of the financial details, and so forth?"

"He arrived almost five years ago, Chief Inspector," she whispered. "Clara, my sister, asked us to take him in so that he could attend Kings. Mr. Markham and I have not been blessed with children, so we, of course, agreed."

Her voice grew stronger as the story continued.

"We assumed he would go on to the university, or into the Army like his father, but Mickey wouldn't hear of it. He wanted to go to France for the summer, and then I think he had intentions of being a writer—I can't be sure, because he refused to discuss such matters. I wrote to Clara, of course, and she recognized that he couldn't stay here indefinitely, but he wouldn't go back to India either."

"He wouldn't do what he was told," Mr. Markham added. "Never did; the original prodigal son."

"His parents sent you money to support him and pay his school fees?"

"Yes, although he was always trying to cadge more," Mr. Markham growled. "Although we shouldn't speak ill of the dead, of course," he added hastily.

Unexpectedly, he crossed himself, and Mrs. Markham hurried to do so too, as if the display offset their lack of remorse.

"But we didn't pay the fees on Clara's behalf, only his allowance and school expenses," Mrs. Markham said, returning to financial matters. "He had a scholarship."

"I didn't know that," Ford said in mock surprise.

"Yes, it was all arranged by Lady Canderblank; it was very gracious of her," gushed Mrs. Markham, becoming animated. "She even came to visit us before he arrived, and sat in that very chair! She chose Darjeeling tea, and complemented my shortcakes."

"Did she, by Jove!" Ford exclaimed, hoping his enthusiasm would encourage her, but Mr. Markham cleared his throat loudly, and she relapsed into passivity.

"May I enquire as to your occupation, sir?" Ford asked.

"I work for the Westminster Bank."

"Mr. Markham is the Chief Cashier at the branch in the High Street, with men under him," she expanded. "It's a very large and important branch."

His position was clearly a source of pride, for her animation had returned, and Mr. Markham, to the extent that he could, looked smug.

"Mrs. Markham devotes her not inconsiderable talents to St. Johns," he responded. "It's a positive beehive of charitable works."

Markham seemed anxious to return her complement, and to convey the impression that they were substantial and generous people, indeed pillars of the local community, perhaps to counterbalance the evident aridity of their relationship with their nephew.

Ford nodded to acknowledge their obvious moral and social standing, but said nothing further, in the hope that they might fill the silence.

"Doctor Thornby telephoned us personally," Markham rewarded him. "He suggested that we should be spared the inconvenience of traveling to the funeral, and the emotional upset for Mrs. Markham."

Ford nodded again. Mrs. Markham arranged her features into a pattern conveying grief.

"He said it was unnecessary to send flowers," she added.

Mr. Markham became defensive.

"We've asked the vicar to offer a special prayer next Sunday. It's the least we could do!"

Suddenly both the conversation and the claustrophobic room sickened Ford. He decided not to raise Sir Neville's interpretation of Callaway's death. He was certain that the Markhams were not remotely involved, and he had no stomach for the defensive guilt a suggestion of suicide would provoke, or the endless speculation that would arise at the suggestion of murder.

"Perhaps I'll take a glance upstairs," he said, and the Markhams arose to lead the way, clearly relieved that the formal interview was over.

Ford went over Callaway's room slowly and methodically, with the Markhams hovering at his shoulder, but besides several books that caused Mr. and Mrs. Markham to draw in their breath sharply in distaste, there was nothing else of note. The untidy desk drawer contained the same desultory mixture of papers and letters as at school, and like his room at Kings, this room also conveyed no sense of its occupant.

It was as if Callaway had expected his aunt and uncle to search his room in his absence, and had made sure that any private materials had been removed or securely hidden.

"Unfortunately," Ford said, "I have a train to catch. I'll take these papers with me and return them shortly. In the meantime, I regret that I must relock the door until I return."

Mr. Markham opened his mouth to protest, but Ford cut him off.

"You will, of course, be anxious to assist in a police investigation, sir, even though it's inconvenient. I thank you both for your cooperation, and, again, please accept my condolences."

The Markhams looked mulish, and a thought struck Ford.

"It's my duty to advise you that entering this room until further notice is an obstruction of justice."

They both registered shock, and he was certain they would make no such attempt. He locked the door as he was speaking and turned the handle to make sure it was secure.

"I'll return at the first possible moment. In the meantime, you have my card. Thank you, again. Good evening."

Before they could form an objection, he limped down the stairs and let himself out of the house. Hurrying down the road as best his aching leg would permit, he was delighted to find a taxi discharging its passengers near the corner.

"Paddington Station, driver, if you please."

He leaned back wearily on the aging seat cushions. The interview with Sir Neville Pondsford had been draining. Ford was used to dealing with hostile witnesses, but the experience was always exhausting.

But he believed the doctor's final version of the story, and he believed that Callaway had probably fallen to his death. It explained why the body came to be in the rhododendrons without the necessity of an improbable knife fight in the dark, or someone transporting a dead body around Kings without being noticed.

But in what circumstances had he fallen? And, if not by accident but by his own volition or another's, why?

*God, what a sterile existence Callaway seemed to have lived!*

The combination of his obsessive secrecy and the Markhams' moral rectitude had precluded family affection. Alone and unloved at both home and school, he had had only his own thoughts to keep him company, or so it seemed.

Suddenly, Ford stood at the edge of his private cliff. His own existence was delimited by his barren flat in South Kensington and his grimy, impersonal office desk at Scotland Yard, piled with documents itemizing the anguish of others. The void of self-pity opened up beneath his feet, beckoning, just as it might have, perhaps, to Callaway. Some are born lonely, some achieve loneliness, and some have loneliness thrust upon them.

"Paddington, guv," said his driver.

"Right," said Ford.

# Thursday

F ord was awoken by an insistent banging, and took a moment to realize that he was in the village inn. The cause of the loud pounding on the door revealed itself to be Lucy Green, the daughter of the house, looking disheveled and unwell. She was bearing a tray of precariously balanced tea and toast, which she placed on his nightstand with the sketchiest of curtsies and hurried wordlessly away.

There was a note on the tray from "Robt. Croft, Sgt., Glos. Const.," inviting him for breakfast and to hear his report from the School. The tea and toast immediately lost their attraction and Ford dressed rapidly, wondering what delights Mrs. Croft might serve him.

Mrs. Croft's notion of breakfast was based upon the assumption that no other meal might be available for several days—poached eggs served with a large slice of cured ham, followed by toast with butter and marmalade, followed in their turn by the first tiny, pungent, and delicious raspberries of the season, accompanied by fresh cream.

Ford stole an admiring glance at Croft's waistline. Obviously a great deal of bicycling would be necessary to work off the effects of his wife's cookery.

When the dishes had been cleared away, the two men continued to sit at their ease at the kitchen table, and Croft, with evident pride and excitement, produced his reports.

"They all did it, sir, all the masters, every last one of them. Old Mr. Jaspers was fair running across the lawn to get to the Common Room by five o'clock; it was a sight to see! I read over them last night, sir. Do you want me to summarize, or would you prefer to read them cold, like?"

It was a display of modesty that Ford seldom encountered in Scotland Yard, where even the most junior constable was completely convinced he could solve any case, and in a matter of minutes.

"Please give me your analysis, Croft; that would be very helpful."

Ford accepted a fresh cup of tea from Mrs. Croft, and Croft accepted a cigarette from Ford.

"I'll leave you to it," said Mrs. Croft.

"Please don't leave on my account, Mrs. Croft", said Ford. "I'm sure we have no secrets from you."

"Thank you, sir," said Mrs. Croft, beaming. "I'll just go out and feed the chickens."

"Well, sir, there were three hundred and five people at the School that evening," Croft began, referring to a sheaf of papers which contained his notes—clearly his notebook had proven inadequate to the task.

"There were two hundred and ten boys, thirty-five masters and their wives, twelve other school workers—domestics, grounds staff, and such-like—and forty-eight visitors, mostly parents. Almost everyone was at the play, except for the workers, some of the wives, and three boys in the sana-torium with the measles, and the nurse to look after them."

Croft took a sip of tea to fortify himself.

"After the theatricals ended, at about a quarter to ten, everyone milled about for a bit outside the Old School, congratulating the performers and chatting, and then went their separate ways."

He peered at his notes.

"Most of the visitors had been put up in Stroud, and there was a chara-banc to carry them off. Four of them were dropped off at the pub, and the rest went on. They're all accounted for, and unless one of them stole back from Stroud later, they weren't at the scene. The ones staying at the pub sat up drinking until one o'clock, according to Mrs. Green, and weren't capable of going back anyway."

"I can imagine," Ford murmured.

"Exactly, sir. There was a foreign gentleman, the representative of a Prince, who returned directly to London by train from Oxford. I'm mak-ing inquiries to see if he really was on the train."

He licked his thumb and turned a page.

"Most of the junior boys were rounded up by the prefects and went back to their Houses. With certain exceptions, sir, everyone was back where he or she belonged by ten twenty, sir." He paused and gave Ford a questioning glance. "Is this helpful, sir?"

"Very helpful indeed, Sergeant. Please carry on."

"The quality was staying at the Master's Lodge, and they went back for brandy and coffee and refreshments. That was Doctor and Mrs. Thornby, Lord and Lady Canderblank and their daughter, Sir Richard and Lady Wimbleton, and the Bishop, sir. Lucy Green was there serving, and the housemaid."

"Ten people in all."

"Correct, sir. Between ten thirty and ten forty-five, they all went to bed, except for Lord and Lady Canderblank, who went out for a stroll. Doctor and Mrs. Thornby vouched for each other, and so did Sir Richard and Lady Wimbleton, of course, so strictly speaking, that leaves the Bishop and Miss Canderblank without someone else to vouch for them. The housemaid lodges with the gatekeeper, and she was home by eleven. Lucy Green went home at the same time. She walked down the hill to the village, and her mother says she got in at about midnight."

It was clear that Croft had spent considerable time marshalling the facts. Ford knew several Scotland Yard detectives who would not have been so careful.

"Leaving out Trafalgar House for the moment, sir, all the boys in all the other Houses were in their Houses, if you follow. The only boy who doesn't really have a provable alibi is Trumpington, the head boy, because he doesn't have to sign anything or report to anybody and has his own room with his own door. He can come and go as he pleases on account of his privileges."

Ford knew from his days at Kings that the post of School Captain carried godlike rights and powers.

"All the masters who are married are accounted for by their wives, and the unmarried masters all say they'd gone to bed, or sat up reading, or such like, and there's no obvious reason, at least to me, to disbelieve them."

Croft turned another page and drained his teacup.

"Now, sir, for those who weren't indoors. Between ten thirty and eleven thirty, when Trafalgar was locked, Mr. Jaspers was walking his dog, and he met Miss Larue, the French lady teacher, who was out for a smoke. Mr. Bottomly, the gym master, was out for a run round the playing fields. He does that every night; it seems, rain or shine, to keep fit."

He accepted another cigarette from Ford.

"Mr. Robinson, the duty master, left School House at eleven and walked all round the School, checking all the doors except for the Houses. He says everything was as it should be. He saw Mr. Jaspers entering his House after walking his dog. He finished up at the Gatehouse at eleven thirty, and old Peters saw him. They closed the gates together. Mr. Robinson walked back to School House and got there five minutes later. He saw no one on his way home, sir."

Ford sat back, calculating.

"Let me take a couple of notes, if I may, Sergeant. We have Lord and Lady Canderblank, Mr. Jaspers, and Miss Larue out walking. We have Mr. Bottomly out running. We have Lucy Green on her way home. We have Mr. Robinson doing his rounds as the duty master. Am I correct so far?"

"Quite correct, sir."

"Assuming that no one is lying, a risky proposition in a murder case, then everyone else was accounted for except for the unmarried masters, two guests at the Lodge, and Trumpington ... Right, I think I've got it. Please continue."

"The remainders are the School servants and groundskeepers. They all say they were at home. Them with wives have alibis and them that don't, don't. Then there's George Green, who'd been supplying the liquor, sir."

"Why didn't he and his daughter go home together?"

"He says he was finished before her, on account of the late party at the Lodge, so he just drove his trap home without her. It's my impression, sir, that they've had a falling out, but I didn't press too far."

"What about the servants and grounds staff? Anything strike you as suspicious?"

"I've known most of them for years, sir. I'd be surprised if any of them would have anything to do with a Kings boy. Village and School don't mix, if you take my meaning—like oil and water. Still, they can't be ruled out altogether, strictly speaking."

"Very true," Ford said. "Some of the guests left; what about people entering the School?"

"Well, anyone could climb over a hedge or a fence, sir. But as far as vehicles go, the back gate was locked at eight, same as usual, and no one entered or left, according to the gatekeeper. As far as the front gate was concerned, there's a list of who came and left, but no one without proper business, as far as I can see so far. The front gate was open and unguarded for a few minutes about eleven, sir, when the gatekeeper was helping with the foreign gentleman's car—which wouldn't start, sir."

Croft sat back and reorganized his notes.

"That's about it, sir."

"That's excellent work, Sergeant."

Mrs. Croft had returned to the kitchen, and Ford made sure she heard the complement.

"Now, let's stretch our legs for five minutes, and then and I'll bring you up to date with what I did in London."

Ford stood up and gazed out the window. The sparkling morning looked irresistibly inviting. He and Croft made for the back door, but the sergeant was intercepted by his wife and dispatched upstairs to confront a blocked toilet.

Ford wandered out into the garden. Flower borders bursting in color surrounded an immaculate lawn; every single plant seemed to be the largest specimen of its species Ford had ever seen.

"Its all in the manure, sir," Mrs. Croft told him, joining him by the roses. "Tea leaves for the roses, chicken poop for the bulbs, cow manure for the herbaceous borders, and well-rotted compost for the fruits and vegetables."

"Well, it's a splendid garden, Mrs. Croft. It does you proud."

"It's all to Bob's credit, sir, not mine. It takes his mind off the job and gives him some exercise."

She glanced up at him.

"Do you have a garden, sir?"

"No, no, I live in a flat. I had a window box once, but everything died."

It seemed an apt metaphor for his domestic existence.

"Oh, dear. I'll give you some geranium cuttings and some cow manure to take back with you to London, if you like—there's nothing like a cheerful window box to raise the spirits. Now, if you'll excuse me, I've got some baking to finish."

She bustled off, and Ford followed her back to the kitchen where he found that Croft had vanquished the reluctant toilet, and together they returned to Callaway's death.

Five minutes was sufficient for Ford to describe the bones of the interview with Sir Neville.

"I wish I'd been there to see it, sir," Croft said with a chuckle. "He treated me like I was something the cat brought in."

Ford smiled and went on to describe his visit to the Markhams.

"It's really very strange. Obviously Callaway was a very unpleasant youth, and I can understand them not being too upset. But they never asked how he died; they never asked about the funeral; they never asked about his effects …"

He rearranged his aching leg beneath the table.

"His room was like a hotel room—completely impersonal. Some books, but not as many as you'd expect from someone who was constantly in the Charing Cross Road, which, as you know, is lined with bookshops. How did he occupy his time? He spent hours in his room, by all accounts." Ford paused, then asked, "What did you learn about him from the School reports?"

"Pretty much the same thing; no friends, except for the boy White. No real interests or hobbies, as far as I can tell. Kept himself to himself, like. Nothing to indicate that someone had a reason to murder him, sir."

"Well, someone did! I'll interview the people on your list who may have seen something. That may take a day or two. I'll see White and Callaway's calo. In the meantime, Sergeant, I'd like you to go back to Trafalgar. Our villain may well be a member of the House. Speak to all the boys individually."

"Right, sir. What am I looking for?"

"Two things: a motive for murder, and as accurate a picture as we can draw up of everyone who went up and down those stairs, and when."

Mrs. Croft drew a batch of freshly baked scones from the oven and laid them on the table with cream and strawberry preserves.

"Mrs. Croft, I'll never be able to get up!" Ford protested. "You'll be the death of me!"

"There's nothing like a spot of home cooking when you're away from home, sir."

"Well, this tastes delicious," said Ford, with his mouth full of hot scone. "Tell me, is Mrs. Green a friend of yours?"

"Not a bosom pal, like, sir, but I see her out and about, of course."

"Anything to the notion that Mr. Green and Lucy have had a falling out? Some sort of family row?"

"Well, sir, in Bob's position we probably know more about people than we should, and we've learned to keep our mouths shut. There's a rumor—just a rumor, mind you—that Lucy's no better than she should be, sir, as the saying goes, and she's gone and got herself in trouble, and her father, quite naturally, is furious. It's just gossip, but since you asked …"

The memory of Lucy bringing him his morning tea leapt before his eyes.

"By George, Mrs. Croft, she wasn't at all well this morning. Obviously it's speculation, but it would explain why Mr. Green didn't take her home. They'd probably had an argument. So … is there anything else being bandied about in the village, Mrs. Croft, which might shed some light on the events at the School?"

"Well, sir, it's all guesswork. I wouldn't want to put any more faith in what people are saying than in Marge Green's theories about witchcraft!"

"What do you think yourself; any comments?"

She paused and spoke carefully.

"If you're asking my opinion, and of course it's just a guess, I'll bet my life that it wasn't old Mr. Jaspers."

"Why not?"

"Well, sir, if he murdered the boy, what would he have done with the dog? You can't stab someone while you've got a dog on a leash."

"That's an excellent point, Mrs. Croft. It hadn't occurred to me."

Ford was genuinely impressed with her insight.

"What else?"

"That's the only thing I've been able to think of, sir."

"Well, keep thinking, if you would. Do you know Miss Canderblank?"

"Not really, sir. I know the housekeeper over at Canderblank Hall, and she says she's far less stuck up than her mother. She recently moved up to London, and my friend says it was to get away from Lady Canderblank."

"I saw her in London yesterday, quite by chance," Ford told them, recalling her glowing presence on a gloomy day. "She invited me to play golf."

He shook his head in puzzlement.

"I wondered if she was trying to find out about the investigation on behalf of her mother, who seems to have moved heaven and earth to dispose of all the physical evidence. And, of course, as we discovered yesterday, Lady Canderblank arranged for Callaway to go to Kings, so there's some sort of a connection."

"That may be, or perhaps the young lady has a different motive for wanting to see you, sir."

Ford found himself blushing.

"Good heavens, Mrs. Croft, I'm simply not in her league!"

"You never know, sir, if I may make so bold, what will turn a young girl's fancy."

"Surely not, Mrs. Croft!"

"Leave the Chief Inspector alone, Betty, for goodness sake!" Croft chuckled. "Never mind the missus, sir; she means no harm."

"Of course not, and no offense is taken, I assure you."

Indeed, the incident had endeared them both to him. It was very pleasant to be sitting in this comfortable, unpretentious room, being fed copious amounts of excellent food at frequent intervals.

In contrast, his own "home" was empty, cold, and unappealing.

"Mrs. Croft, your hospitality is overwhelming, but I must get going before you tempt me with any more to eat. Sergeant, will you go up to the School with me now or later? I'll try to catch the 'wanderers'—young

Connelly and so forth. Later, I'll take the car on and see the quality. I'll leave the Greens for last."

"I'll come up and make a start on who went up and down the stairs in Trafalgar, sir."

He stood and pulled on his uniform tunic.

"If I may say so, this is a damned sight more interesting than trying to find out who's pilfering Mrs. Mallet's chickens. And I still have to see the undertaker, sir—'Jones the Coffin' as we call him."

◆     ◆     ◆

Ford sat in the Master's Library, a finely appointed room lined with book-cases bearing leather-bound tomes bequeathed by various former masters and students. The more valuable books—a first printing of Marlowe's *Faustus*, for example—were secured in glass cases together with the deeds and letters patent that recorded the School's long and illustrious pedigree.

A portrait of the founder, King Henry VIII, hung above the mantel-piece, and a full-length rendition of Queen Anne stared down the length of the polished library table from the far end of the room. They didn't seem impressed by their surroundings.

The Library was no longer used for anything as humdrum as the mas-ters' academic researches, and now served as a formal meeting room for Doctor Thornby and gatherings of the Board of Governors. The Master had given Ford access with great reluctance, as if he feared that Ford might deface some priceless manuscript.

Ford heard someone tap nervously on the door, and a boy appeared, sliding in between the doorframe and the half open door as if hoping to enter unnoticed.

"Connelly, isn't it? James Connelly?" Ford asked.

Connelly was an unremarkable fourteen-year-old with coal-black eyes set in a white face. He was trembling with nervousness, but Ford disre-garded that, for all fourteen-year-olds tremble before policemen, some with good reason.

"Yes, sir."

"Sit down, Connelly."

Connelly sat down in a hard wooden chair and watched Ford. His nervousness transferred itself to the constant rapid tapping of one heel against the chair leg. His head was thrust forward and his shoulders were hunched, as if he expected an assault. His hands were clasped tightly in his lap. One thumbnail was attacking the other. Ford gave him a moment to compose himself.

"You were Callaway's calo? He was your dom, I understand?"

Kings, like many other schools, perpetuated the tradition generally known as "fagging," under which the junior boys were obligated to act as personal servants to the senior boys. In a normal five-year school career, one would suffer two years of servitude, followed by a year of freedom, followed in turn by two more glorious years in which one had one's own servant.

The custom was not officially recognized or sanctioned by the School, but it was built deeply into its institutional psyche as an immutable tradition. Defenders advanced the argument that it bred respect for one's elders, and then bred a sense of responsibility for others when roles reversed. Abolitionists pointed out the obvious risks of brutality and exploitation. From time immemorial the abolitionists has always lost.

"Yes, sir," Connelly answered.

"What was he like? Was he reasonable?"

"Well, sir, he was my dom," Connelly replied cautiously.

"I understand," Ford told him. "I was a calo myself, Connelly. I hated my dom with a great passion. He was fat, lazy and spotty—an ear-twister and a hair-puller. He made me give him my allowance."

Ford spoke from bitter memory, and Connelly knew he was speaking with an honesty the boy had seldom seen in adults.

"When I became a dom myself, I never once called my calo."

"You didn't, sir?" Connelly asked in surprise.

"No. I hated the whole system, and I refused to take advantage of it when I could."

"There are a couple of seniors like that now, sir, but everyone thinks they're weird." Connelly's foot had ceased its endless tapping.

"I'm sure they do. The calos hate being calos, and live for the day when they become doms and can get their revenge. But, of course, you can't get your revenge on your own dom; all you can do is make another boy's life miserable and perpetuate the system."

"I never thought about it like that, sir. Dad says it's good for my character."

"Well, some people do think that." Ford thought the idea preposterous but refrained from comment.

"Dad says people against it are Bolsheviks, sir," Callaway continued. "Are you are a …"

He managed to cut himself off.

"Am I a Bolshevik, Connelly?" Ford chuckled, completing the unspoken question. "Only when it rains. Now, what was Callaway like as a dom? What did you have to do? Clean his shoes and so on? What else? My dom made me smell his socks. They were disgusting!"

Connelly's white face stared at him for a moment, and then crumbled into wracking tears.

Ford felt a cold, empty hollow in the pit of his stomach. He let the boy continue until his first spasms of misery and loathing subsided, and then provided him with a large handkerchief.

"Did he make you do certain things?" asked Ford gently.

The boy nodded and was overtaken by another storm.

After a little while, Connelly was able to bring himself to speak.

"How long will I have to go to jail for?" he sobbed.

His whole body was shuddering and another storm was threatening.

"Boys of your age don't go to jail. Besides, you absolutely and definitely did *not* commit a crime. Whatever may have happened, you were acting under duress."

"He—he did it, and then he said it was a crime. He said it had to be secret, because if I told anyone, I would go to jail. He said Oscar Wilde went to jail, and I looked it up in the public library during the holidays, and it's true."

Connelly could not stop talking now that the secret was revealed.

"He made me do all kinds of things, and I didn't dare say no, because he had a little whip thing that really, really hurt. I wanted to kill him, but I didn't know how. When he died, it was the best moment of my life. But I didn't kill him, sir—I swear on the Bible, I *didn't* kill him!"

"Did you go to his room on the night of the play?"

A fresh spasm of grief overcame the boy.

"Yes, he told me to. He was in the bushes smoking when I got back from the *Pirates*, and he told me to come upstairs after lights out. But when I got there, he wasn't there. I waited, but he still didn't come, so I went back down to the dorms."

Ford waited for him to recover.

"Did anyone see you? Did you see anyone else in the bushes?"

"Just White, sir. He was having a smoke too. Callaway told me what he was going to do, and White laughed. It was awful."

"Was that usual for White to be there? Was he a friend of Callaway's?"

"He was Callaway's *best* friend, sir."

"Did you see anyone on the stairs when you went up to his room?"

"No, sir, not really, just someone in the play."

"Who was that?"

"It was one of the Major General's daughters, sir, in costume, sir, I didn't recognize who."

Gilbert and Sullivan had included a female chorus of "daughters of the Major General" in the *Pirates of Penanze*, Ford knew. Presumably, these parts had been played by boys whose voices had not yet broken.

"Was it a tall person or a short person?"

"He was coming down as I was going up. I didn't really look. I was worried that Callaway would be angry at me for being late. He was taller than me, I think, sir, but then I saw him going up again as I went back down, and he might have been the same height, or shorter."

Ford tried to digest Connelly's statement.

"You saw this person twice?"

"Yes, sir," Connelly replied earnestly. "The first time, he was coming down from Callaway's room, or at least from the seniors' floor, and then he must have changed his mind and gone up again as I was leaving. Honest to God, sir, cross my heart and hope to die."

"Now, listen carefully to me, Connelly," Ford said, abandoning his attempt to understand this information. "You are *not* going to go to jail. If you've told me the truth, and told me everything, you have absolutely nothing to fear. If you think of anything else, you can reach me through Sergeant Croft. Do you understand?"

A final spell of weeping shook the boy, but this time Ford sensed it was caused by relief, rather than fear or guilt.

◆    ◆    ◆

Trumpington replaced Connelly and presented a very different persona. He had the easy charm that is so often, and so erroneously, associated in works of fiction with the English aristocracy.

He had outgrown the gawkiness of youth and the awkwardness of adolescence. He was full of self-confidence, was clearly familiar with success, and his stint as School Captain had made him comfortable with command and authority.

He was not, however, as wise in the ways of the world as he thought he was, for he took command of the conversation from the very outset, and then discovered that he had to set its direction while Ford followed him. Thus he found that he had to guess what Ford's questions might have been, and what information Ford might have gathered.

Unlike Connelly, he sat at ease. He seemed to find the notion of being interviewed both boring and wryly amusing.

"To be absolutely frank, Callaway was a bit of a bastard," he began before Ford could open the questioning.

"Was he, indeed?" replied Ford.

"Well, yes, as you have doubtless already gathered."

He paused to flick a grain of dirt from his spotless trousers.

"Rules are rules, and I had to punish him a time or two, I can tell you," he added, speaking as if he were forty years old. "If one doesn't enforce the law, it becomes a joke, as I'm sure you would agree. Still, one hopes he wasn't an out-and-out reprobate; doubtless he would have come to his senses after taking a knock or two in the real world. It's just, one supposes, the effect of inferiority engendered by being surrounded by one's betters."

Trumpington was uncertain how to address Ford. He understood that the policeman was a Kings old boy, but with a checkered history. Trumpington had looked him up and seen that he must have been a good cricketer, and bright enough to win a scholarship to Cambridge, but that he had never become a school prefect. Only a character flaw or a less than desirable background could explain that anomaly.

Now he was a policeman—definitely not the profession of a gentleman. Perhaps the simple use of his last name would be appropriate, just as one might address a respected butler or a head gamekeeper.

"Anyway, I'm sure he would, Ford—come to his senses, I mean."

"That's helpful to know," Ford replied neutrally.

"He had no friends among the decent chaps; just White of Queens, and he's an even bigger shit than Callaway was. I know the Master is very keen to enlarge our enrollment, but, really, one has to draw a limit somewhere."

"Indeed one does."

"I knew Callaway, of course; in my position one knows everyone. But I spent no time with him; one doesn't keep company with bastards. Our views and values were far apart."

He shrugged elegantly.

"Beyond that, Ford, I really cannot offer you any insights, I'm afraid. If he was murdered, and I understand that's very open to question, despite your presence, I think one can safely assume it was a passing tramp, hoping to steal the contents of his pockets. Came upon him, did the deed, passed on into the night. I'm sure of it. Perhaps you would serve your cause to better effect by searching the local bridal paths and coppices."

Trumpington sat back and regarded Ford blandly.

"It's an interesting theory—I'll make a note of it," said Ford, scribbling in his notebook.

"Let me see …" Ford continued, returning his gaze to Trumpington. "A tramp passing unnoticed through the School grounds enters the rhododendron bushes outside Trafalgar for some unknown purpose, and sees

Callaway wearing a theatrical uniform. They may or may not have spoken, but the tramp concludes that Callaway is a good candidate for a robbery—indeed, a sufficiently good candidate to be worth murdering. Perhaps the uniform created the impression of wealth, or perhaps the tramp was shortsighted."

Ford scribbled another note, then continued.

"In any event, the tramp leaves the bushes, enters Trafalgar, finds the kitchen, takes a knife, and returns outside, still unnoticed. He re-enters the bushes. Callaway is still there, fortunately for the tramp, and the tramp stabs him to death. He robs him, but fails to find the almost thirty shillings in his pockets. He also ignores an almost full packet of cigarettes, a silver cigarette lighter, and Callaway's wristwatch; perhaps he was overcome by remorse, and left these items as keepsakes for Callaway's family. The tramp leaves the bushes, crosses the School grounds, and leaves the scene of the crime undetected. I must admit, it's not a theory I would have formed."

"You're making it sound ridiculous!" Trumpington said crossly. "Besides ..."

"Yes?"

"It's of no importance," Trumpington muttered.

"I see. Where were you, between ten fifteen and eleven thirty that evening?"

"Where was I?"

"Where were you, between ten fifteen and eleven thirty that evening?"

"Well, I suppose I'd gone back to my room and was reading."

"Did you go out again?"

"Why are you cross-examining *me*? I'll ask you remember I'm Captain of the School."

Ford groaned to himself. Why was everyone connected to this case so affronted by the notion that they had to account for their time? Why must he cudgel every interviewee?

"You will have to make a sworn statement about your movements on that evening. Such a statement is subject to the laws of perjury. It falls within the general rubric, *the truth, the whole truth, and nothing but the truth, so help you God*. If convicted of perjury, you would serve a considerable sentence in jail. At your age it would be an adult institution, and you would be in the company of a population of men very much *not* to your liking, nor you to theirs. Perhaps it might be best if we break off this interview to permit you to consult your father's solicitor?"

"That ... that won't be necessary," said Trumpington hurriedly, his veneer of superiority cracking. "The fact of the matter is that I did go for a stroll, and I did see someone entering those bushes. I couldn't see who it was. That's why I thought of a tramp."

"At what time was this?"

"Probably a little before eleven, because I set my alarm for the morning when I got back and it was eleven when I set it."

"Describe the person you saw."

"I couldn't see, as I said. It was dark."

"Callaway was wearing very distinctive clothes; a bright red coat and white trousers. The trousers would have been visible even in poor light."

"It definitely wasn't him."

"Was it a small person? A junior, perhaps Callaway's calo?"

"No, it was someone bigger than Connelly; an adult."

"Did you see this person when you were entering or leaving Trafalgar?"

"When I was leaving—I mean, when I was walking past—I mean ..." Trumpington's voice trailed away.

"Perhaps, in the long run," said Ford judiciously, "it would be better if you simply gave me a full and accurate account. The only circumstance in which I would advise against it is if you murdered him yourself."

"I went for a walk," said Trumpington, speaking rapidly. "I was passing Trafalgar, and I thought I'd take a walk through. It's something I try to do as Captain of the School. It's good for discipline. My father liked to visit his men in the trenches. Good for morale. Breeds respect amongst the lower classes."

Trumpington reminded himself of Ford's background and felt reassured by his own.

"However, all the boys were already in their dorms, so I left again. As I was leaving, I saw someone disappearing into the bushes. I ... I assumed it was one of the seniors going in for a smoke, but when we found out that Callaway had been killed, I decided it was a tramp."

"You didn't go in after him?"

"No. I went back to my room."

"If the person was entering the bushes, you saw his or her back?"

"Exactly."

"Was it a man or a woman?"

"Er, I'm not sure."

"Come, Trumpington, the person could not have been ten feet from you, and lit by the light of the doorway. One can tell a man from a woman even if you see only the person's back."

"Oh, very well, it might have been a woman."

"*Might* have been?"

"Well ... probably."

"Is there anything you wish to add?"

"That's the entire incident, Ford."

Trumpington's demeanor was returning to its former self-confidence.

"I beg to differ. If you saw a female figure, but you thought it might be a member of Kings disappearing for a smoke, then of course it could not have been a female. Was it a boy or man dressed as a woman? Is that the impression you formed?"

"It's easy to be mistaken ..."

"I see. You were in the direct proximity of a murder, a fact that you have failed to mention previously to Sergeant Croft. You saw someone entering the bushes. If it was a member of Kings, it was to smoke; a serious violation of school rules. If it was not a member of Kings, you could reasonably assume that that person was up to no good. But despite your repeated references to the need to maintain order and discipline, on this occasion you chose to do nothing. You were compelled neither by duty nor by curiosity."

Ford saw Trumpington's self-confidence ebbing once more. He pressed on.

"After Callaway's body was discovered, you felt it unnecessary to report your observations to the police. You also failed to mention that you saw a woman, or a boy, or man disguised as a woman—a bizarre observation, under most circumstances, except immediately following a school play in which boys play female parts."

Trumpington opened and closed his mouth several times, but offered no further explanation.

"You acted as the property master, I believe, with responsibility for all the costumes?"

"Well, naturally I didn't do the work myself."

"What happened to the costumes?"

"They were collected and stacked in Doctor Thornby's study for return to the theatrical company."

"Did you sign off that everything had been collected?"

"Yes, I did, except for Callaway's stuff, of course. That miserable bastard was always late for everything! Really, Ford ..."

Ford regarded Trumpington squarely.

"I have to tell you that I believe you are lying. In my experience, it is extremely hard to maintain a consistent lie over a prolonged period of time, Trumpington. I have no idea what your current motivations are. Perhaps you saw Callaway entering the bushes and followed him to demand his uniform, only to discover he had been stabbed. Perhaps you saw his murderer entering the bushes and took no action. Perhaps you recognized the person entering the bushes."

Trumpington's patrician face drained of color.

"In these circumstances, your failure to act at the time, and your failure to notify Mr. McIntire immediately, have caused considerable cost and confusion. Had you acted appropriately, you might have prevented the murder or enabled the perpetrator to be apprehended in a timely manner. Whatever your motives, they were clearly not those worthy of a School Captain."

Trumpington flinched, and Ford continued.

"Perhaps this other person is a figment of your imagination and you killed Callaway yourself, by accident or design."

Trumpington took in a breath to deny it, but Ford overrode him.

"Did you recognize the person, or not?"

"No."

"The man dressed as a woman?"

"Yes ... I mean, no."

"The person wearing a Major General's daughter's costume, even though you signed off that all the costumes had been returned?"

"No ... I mean, yes. I mean they were returned, I swear it, and it was a costume."

"You recognized the person, didn't you?"

"I ..."

"He was a member of Kings, wasn't he?"

"I ..."

"I wish to see you again in the morning. In the meantime, I suggest you reflect upon your position and decide whether you wish to amend your original statement before committing it to writing and signing it. Rest assured, I shall continue to investigate this incident until I am satisfied, and I am currently very far from satisfied."

◆　　◆　　◆

Ford's last interview was with Callaway's crony, White of Queens House. White was a habitual breaker of school rules and carried himself exactly in the manner of shifty belligerence exhibited by petty felons the world over. He would, of course, deny all wrongdoing. An authority figure such as Ford would be a natural antagonist.

He combined his rebellious nature with a love of money and a cool head for mathematics. The combination made him a natural gambler. He was always prepared to give odds on a cricket or rugby match, and after lights out he was always available for a hand of poker.

Like many a regular offender, he began by seeking a clarification of the ground rules.

"Is everything I tell you confidential, Chief Inspector? You can or can't tell Doctor Thornby?"

His question almost endeared him to Ford, who was by now surfeited with Connelly's emotional traumas and Trumpington's haughty superiority.

"Anything you tell me may eventually turn up in court as evidence. You may be a sworn witness at a trial."

There was a gleam in White's eye; he loved detective stories and was fascinated by criminal law, believing instinctively it might play a significant role in his future.

"However, I am under no obligation to report what I do not consider to be germane to the case. Thus, for example, if you joined Callaway for a smoke in the bushes, it would not be necessary for me to report that fact unless it's necessary to sustain a case against you or someone else."

"In that case, yes, I joined him for a smoke in the bushes, sir," White replied without hesitation. "We usually did. We talked for about fifteen minutes, and then I went back to Queens."

"What sort of a mood was he in?"

"Usual, except he was pleased with his performance in the *Pirates*. I must admit he did pretty well, and he got a lot of applause. He was bathing in it."

"Basking in it?"

"Vocab isn't my strong point. Actually I don't have *any* strong points, to be honest. Anyway, we talked for a while, and then I shoved off."

"Was he nervous?"

"Nervous, sir? No, that wasn't like him. He said he had to meet someone else, but he didn't seem bothered."

"Did he, by Jove! Who was it? Was it his calo?"

"No, it wasn't Connelly; he'd already popped in and popped out. It must have been someone else he was waiting for."

"Then, who was it?"

"I've no idea. Didn't ask, didn't say. Anyway, just as I was leaving, I heard someone else coming in from the other side. I heard Callaway say, *'Oh, it's you.'*"

"Are you certain? Those exact words?"

"Yes, sir," White answered firmly. "I remember very clearly—it's the last thing I ever heard him say before he snuffed it."

"How did he say it?"

"Oh, casually, as if it were normal."

"*'Oh, it's you?'* Like that?"

"Yes."

"Did the other person speak?"

"No—at least, not that I heard."

"Who did you think it was? Weren't you curious? At the time, did you make any assumptions?"

"Not really. To tell you the truth, I wasn't feeling all that well and needed to get to the crapper absolutely as soon as possible, so I buzzed off back to Queens. I only just made it in time, if you know what I mean?"

This frank admission seemed to complete White's contribution to Ford's understanding of what transpired on Saturday evening.

"Is there anything else you can help me with?"

"Well, I expect you know about him and Connelly? I saw Connelly blubbing just before I came in to see you."

"Yes, I know. You don't seem to have done anything to prevent Callaway's treatment of him."

"Well, it's human nature, and it happens all the time," White said defensively. "We're locked in here, and we don't even *see* a girl for weeks at a time. Not that I …"

He must have felt he was on shaky ground, for he hurried on.

"There was bad blood between Callaway and Trumpington."

"Over what? Constant violations of school rules? Smoking and smuggling in beer?"

"No, something else, I think. Callaway had some kind of hold on him. He said that Trumpers was eating out of his hand. He could make Trumpers do anything he wanted. Stuff like that. It may actually have been true; Trumpers let us off for smoking a couple of times, which he'd never done before."

"That's interesting," said Ford. "What are the boys saying about Callaway? What kind of person was he?"

"Oh, the official line was that he died of a heart attack, although everyone knows that he didn't. Then Thorny switched to a theory of suicide, which is obvious bunk, and now he's settling for Trumper's loony theory of a tramp."

"What do *you* think?"

"Well, sir, Callaway was a bit weird. Sort of obsessed with sex and things like that. He was planning to break into Miss Larue's room to see her underwear. He wanted me to help, but I wouldn't; it was too risky ... I only like to take risks when I can calculate the odds."

Again it must have occurred to him that this was not a good subject to discuss with a policeman, and he returned to the point abruptly.

"He liked snooping through other people's things. It wouldn't have been his first spot of breaking and entering ... He was good at making enemies; we were only friends because we spent so much time in detention together."

White was warming to his task, and Ford was careful not to interrupt his flow.

"In my opinion, it was an inside job, not a tramp. Someone he'd crossed. An adult—none of us boys have the balls for a thing like that, regardless of the provocation."

It was an astute observation, Ford reflected.

"Listen, sir, not to change the subject, but what's it like being a tec'? Do you have to be a copper on the beat first, or can you sort of jump straight into it?"

"I got in straight from college. It's mostly boring, but occasionally you catch somebody. Are you interested, White?"

"I'll lay odds it's one side of the law or the other for me, sir," White grinned. "Destiny, or something."

Ford smiled.

"If you'd like to know more, there's a pamphlet I could get you. I'd prefer you on our side."

"Would you really, sir?" His interest seemed genuine.

"I'll post it to you. In the meantime, let me know if you think of anything else."

◆     ◆     ◆

That evening, as Ford nursed a pint in Green's public bar and thought back over the events of the day, his mind was drawn not to Trumpington's tortured dissembling, or White's squalid revelations. It was not even drawn to Connelly's woes with Callaway, but through them to his own experiences.

When Ford was a junior at Kings, his own dom, whose name was Townsend, had not done to Ford what Callaway had done to Connelly, thank God, but he had been viciously cruel. Ford recalled his unbridled joy when Townsend had eventually left Kings.

They had not met again until the war. It had been on a "reconnaissance in force," a probe toward the German trenches in the dead of night. God knows what Division HQ had imagined it was trying to achieve; the whole episode had been an unmitigated disaster.

Just as they were approaching the German wire, enemy flares lit up the whole of no-mans-land as brightly as a summer's day. In that harsh light the German machine guns began systematically cutting down the British infantry. Ford and his men had retreated in chaos through the mud, through the flooded shell holes filled with bloated floating corpses, and through the tangles of barbed wire that snatched at their uniforms and equipment, pursued by the clatter of machine guns from behind and the whining of bullets about their ears.

Then the Germans began firing mortars that burst amongst the fleeing men. The fortunate—those whom the shells killed instantly—were tossed into the air like rag dolls, while the less fortunate were merely maimed or dismembered.

Ford was stumbling toward safety with the rest when the man beside him went down with a scream. The man's leg had been severed. Ford picked him up, threw him across his shoulders, and staggered on; soon he was covered in sticky, warm blood. Ahead of him a man was yelling, hopelessly entangled in coils of barbed wire, brightly lit, a certain victim for the machine gunners behind them.

"Help me, for God's sake, help me!" the trapped man screamed.

Ford was passing close by him, weighed down by his burden.

"My God, it's you, Ford! Get me out! Cut me loose!"

Ford turned at his name. It was Townsend.

"For Christ's sake, Ford, you little shit, get me out of this!"

"I have to take care of this man first," said Ford, and moved on.

"You bastard, Ford, you complete *bastard!*"

Ford found his own trenches and toppled into them. It was always strange that such hellish places could be so desirable after a patrol into the terrors of no-mans-land. The Colonel was there together with two elegant staff officers, assessing the carnage their plans had brought down upon their own troops.

"Not to worry," one was saying, "We can sustain fifty percent casualties; we have those new reserves from England. We'll try again tomorrow night with more troops. You never know when you might catch Jerry napping."

A medical orderly had relieved Ford of his groaning burden.

"Damned good show, Ford, bringing back one of the chaps," said the Colonel. "Good for morale, and all that. Creates the impression we care what happens to the men."

"Yes, sir." Ford said. "There's an officer out there hung up in the wire. Townsend. I don't know what unit he's in."

"Townsend?" asked one of the staff officers. "Did you say Townsend? That must be Spotty Townsend, I saw his name on the list. Damned good chap; I roomed with him at Oxford."

"He was alive when I last saw him. Someone should go back."

"God, look at the time!" said the staff office hastily. "We have to get back to HQ."

"What? Oh, yes indeed," said the Colonel. "Damned good job, Ford, and good luck with Townsend."

Ford had taken three exhausted men and climbed back up the ladders into hell. They'd found Townsend quickly enough, but not his head. They brought him back anyway.

That was the way Ford had won his Military Cross.

# Friday

At the usual loud banging on his door, Ford struggled from his bed and grabbed his robe. It seemed only minutes since he had turned out his light; he felt as if he had had no sleep at all, and now Lucy Green was knocking with his morning tea.

Ford would have to interview her today. He had been avoiding interviewing the Greens for fear he might have to move out, and there was no other inn in Lower Tuckscomb. He pulled on his robe and opened the door with some reluctance, but, instead of Lucy, he found himself staring blearily at Croft. Ford realized that it wasn't morning at all, but the middle of the night.

"Sorry to wake you, sir, but there's been another death up at the School—Trumpington, the Head Boy."

"*What?* Come in! What happened? What time is it?" Ford sleepy fingers fumbled to tie his sash.

"Just past midnight, sir. Trumpington apparently fell from the Gymnasium roof. Mr. Robinson, the duty master, found him and sent the gatekeeper down the hill."

"Give me five minutes to get dressed, and we'll go up together."

"Right, sir. I'll go and wake up Doctor Thickett, sir, if you agree. Apart from anything else, we can ride up in his trap—it's a damned sight better than bicycling, sir, and it's coming on to rain."

"Excellent! I'll see you downstairs."

Croft's banging had awakened the household. The Greens stood at their bedroom door in their nightclothes—he in a belligerent mood while she asked hopefully if another satanic ritual had been discovered. Lucy evidently kept late hours, for she was still dressed and wearing makeup, and Ford glimpsed her unused bed through her open door.

Shortly, Croft was driving the sleepy horse slowly up the hill to Kings while Ford and Thickett, in the back of the trap, sat huddled against the weather.

Trumpington's body lay spread-eagled on the flagstone pathway that ran in front of the gym. Mr. Robinson was standing guard over it, his hissing hurricane lamp shedding a thin white light across the scene, illuminating a fine mist-like rain.

"Good evening, sir," said Ford. "It's an unfortunate business. Has anything been disturbed?"

"No, Ford. I've been on guard," Mr. Robinson replied.

"Excellent. Who have you informed?"

"Just the Master and Mr. Jaspers, his housemaster."

"Has anyone else seen the body?" Ford asked.

"Well, Peters, the gatekeeper, and Mr. Jaspers. Poor man—he's very shaken!"

"I expect Doctor Thornby was shaken also."

"He didn't come," Mr. Robinson told him.

"Sergeant, if you please," Ford said. "Go and see Mr. Jaspers and make sure Trumpington's room is secure. Quick as you can. Nothing is to be touched."

"Right, sir." Croft disappeared into the shadows.

"Please proceed, Doctor Thickett."

Ford watched as, for the second time in less than a week, Thickett was kneeling down beside a body and verifying that a boy was dead. He probed the inert form and moved it cautiously.

"There are multiple broken bones. I suspect his back is broken. His injuries are consistent with a fall from the roof. The body is still warm, and there's no rigor; he's been dead less than two hours, I would say."

Thickett must have realized that this was his chance to distance himself from the examination of Callaway.

"I will need to do a more thorough examination, of course," he said, rising stiffly to his feet, "and I'd prefer to do it with the aid of a police surgeon."

Ford glanced at his wristwatch. It was one o'clock in the morning.

"Thank you, Doctor. When did you discover him, Mr. Robinson?"

"At eleven thirty, Ford, just as I was completing my rounds. If it helps, he wasn't here at ten forty-five, according to Mr. Jaspers, who was walking his dog."

"Thank you, that's very helpful."

Croft reappeared, moving swiftly for so large a man.

"His room is locked, sir. I have Mr. Jasper's keys. The Master was there when I arrived, sir. I told him to leave everything undisturbed."

"He was in Trumpington's room?"

"Yes, sir."

"Very well. Please go into the gym and get up onto the roof, if you would. I'm sure Mr. Robinson will show you the way. See what you can see."

Croft and Mr. Robinson departed.

"Be careful up there, Sergeant," Ford called after him. "One is more than enough."

Croft raised his hand in understanding as he disappeared round the corner. Ford took the hurricane lamp and walked in widening circles around the body, searching the ground for anything untoward. Apart from two shattered slates from the roof, there was nothing to see.

Trumpington's clothes revealed only the detritus to be expected of any schoolboy's pockets. There was also a key ring and a separate key, as if it didn't belong with the others.

His broken body indicated nothing but a fatal fall. His hands were cut and bloody, as if he had scrabbled desperately for a handhold before he fell.

"We may as well get him into the cart, Doctor, if you would be kind enough to assist me."

The dry patch of stone paving where the body had lain revealed a small leather notebook. Croft and Mr. Robinson returned just as Ford and the doctor completed their struggles to place Trumpington as decently as possible in the cart. Croft picked up the notebook and handed it to Ford, who put it away without a glance. The rain became a little heavier.

"Do you recognize this key, sir?" Ford asked Mr. Robinson.

"Let me see … yes, it's a Gymnasium key."

Trumpington had entered the building on his own volition.

"There're a couple of broken slates up there, sir," Croft said, "and the gutter's come adrift. But there's nothing else, sir, at least as far as you can see in this light. There's an attic, and the windows open directly onto the roof. It's exactly above us."

"Was the window open or closed?"

"It was ajar."

"When did it start to rain?"

"I don't know, sir."

"It rained quite sharply from eleven to eleven fifteen," said Mr. Robinson. "Then it stopped quite suddenly. Ah, I see what you mean, Ford; he must have fallen immediately before it started to rain, to account for the dry ground beneath him."

"His fingers are cut," Ford said. "Look—here and here, across the inside of his knuckles. Could he have hung on the gutter for a moment, and it sagged suddenly and knocked him loose?"

Croft examined Trumpington's hands closely.

"It's very likely, sir."

"Would you mind going back with the lamp? See if there's anything on or in the gutter itself. If there's some blood, we need to be quick before the rain washes it away completely."

"Right, sir."

"May I ask why that's important?" Mr. Robinson inquired.

"If he hung on, trying to save himself, then it probably wasn't suicide, sir," responded Croft, before Ford could speak.

"Exactly so," Ford added, impressed by Croft's acumen.

"Doctor, please take the body back down to your surgery. I will arrange for a police surgeon to come in the morning."

◆    ◆    ◆

The night was very dark without the lamp as Ford stumbled across the Great Lawn to Victoria House. As he drew nearer, he saw a dim light in

Mr. Jaspers' windows. He entered the house—Victorian Gothic he noted, remembering Mr. Jasper's architectural studies—and knocked on the housemaster's door.

It was opened not by Mr. Jaspers, however, but by Doctor Thornby.

"Mr. Jaspers is exhausted, and I sent him to bed," the Master said quietly, nodding toward an inner door. "I was afraid the shock might be too much for him."

"I see, sir."

"Another terrible accident!" Doctor Thornby began *sotto voce*, out of consideration for Mr. Jaspers' slumbers and distress, but as he continued his voice grew louder.

"God knows what his father will say—God knows what the *Governors* will say! What in God's name was he doing on the roof of the Gymnasium? What a tragedy! The boy was clearly marked out for a distinguished career, like his father before him! On to Oxford in the autumn, and then, who knows? The sky was the limit—indeed, he had mentioned the Royal Flying Corps as a possible start to his career. Such a gifted young man—such a natural leader!"

Croft slipped quietly into the room and nodded to Ford, indicating that he and Mr. Robinson had found blood upon the guttering.

"It is a tragedy, sir, just like poor Callaway's death," Ford agreed, cutting off the Master's flow. "Did you find anything of significance in his room, sir? Anything which might explain what he was doing up there, or why he might take his own life?"

"No, I couldn't find anything out of the ordinary—nothing at all," said the Master.

"Did you remove anything from the room, sir?"

Doctor Thornby bristled.

"I resent that question, Ford. I resent it very much indeed!"

Ford sighed inwardly.

"I appreciate that, sir, and I will make a note of it and report it to my superiors. However, the question remains; did you remove anything from the room, sir?"

"Certainly not!"

"Thank you, sir. Why was it that, upon receiving news of Trumpington's death, you did not go to see his body, but came directly to his room instead? Was there something that you expected to find—a suicide note, perhaps?"

"This line of questioning far exceeds your boundaries, Ford!" Doctor Thornby did not seek to hide his fury. "I have spoken to you before about discretion and prudence!"

"Then let me change the question, sir. Have you spoken to anyone else since being informed of Trumpington's unfortunate death? Obviously you have spoken to Mr. Jaspers, Mr. Robinson, and your wife, and you spoke to Sergeant Croft when he came here a short while ago. Have you spoken with anyone else?"

"I refuse to answer. I feel as if you have plunged me into the serpentine coils of a novel by Kafka."

"Then I will change the question again, sir. When did you last see Trumpington? Have you had a conversation with Trumpington since five o'clock this afternoon, when I interviewed him?"

"No, I did not. Again, I protest your tone and manner, Ford. I shall leave before I lose my temper completely. Goodnight, Ford!"

"You are free to leave whenever you choose to do so, of course, sir. Before you go, however, I will have to ask you to turn out your pockets and give the contents to Sergeant Croft."

A sound similar to a snarl emanated from the Master's throat, but a voice interrupted him. Mr. Jaspers was standing at his bedroom door, his white hair resembling that of a man struck by lightning. He had thrown an elegant smoking jacket, tailored in crimson velvet; beneath this splendor his rumpled pajamas looked like impoverished relatives.

"Give him the note, Master, please. It's the appropriate thing to do—in the best tradition of Kings! The best course with an unpleasant truth is to face it."

He sounded as if he were speaking to a recalcitrant fifth-former.

The Master snarled again, turning his head from side to side like a trapped animal seeking escape, and then snatched a paper from his pocket and threw it at Ford's feet. Ford noticed that Croft's face was dark with anger, and for a fleeting moment he feared Croft might do harm to Thornby. He shook his head fractionally and saw Croft's fists uncurl.

"Thank you, sir," Ford said carefully, and laboriously bent over to pick up the paper.

The note was scrawled in handwriting Ford recognized as Callaway's. He read it silently.

> *For starters I want five pounds. I want complete silence about you-know-what. And remember, I'm just as good as you are.*

Ford raised his eyes to Thornby's, and the two gazed at each other for a moment. Ford nodded to Croft, who politely opened the door for the Master.

Doctor Thornby gathered himself and strode from the room, but paused in the doorway.

"You will *not* ruin that boy's reputation, Ford," he thundered, with enough force to wake the whole house. "You will *not* bring dishonor to his family or to Kings! I *forbid* it!"

"Can I lend you an umbrella, Master, or some boots?" Mr. Jaspers asked solicitously. "Your slippers will get wet."

The Master snorted disdainfully and stormed out. His feet could be heard shuffling on the marble floor of the hallway, but it is hard to exit in high dudgeon when wearing slippers. The outside door closed with a slam.

"Are you familiar with *The Pirates of Penzance* by Gilbert and Sullivan, Ford?" Mr. Jaspers asked in the silence that followed the Master's departure.

"I am, sir."

"Then you will recall the refrain that seems so apposite in the present circumstances: *'With constabulary duties to be done, a policeman's lot is not a happy one.'*"

"Apposite indeed, sir."

♦     ♦     ♦

Trumpington's room was in some disarray, as if the Master had searched it hastily; his damp footprints could still be seen in the carpet.

Trumpington's box had been in Mr. Jasper's inner room, and therefore had been beyond the Master's reach, but Ford found that it contained only innocent possessions, such as a gold pen, a gift from his father, and, unlike Callaway's box, no money.

Trumpington's room was redolent with duty, rectitude and achievement. The walls were lined with school photographs, and the mantelpiece was filled to overflowing with framed family portraits. The bookshelf was filled with textbooks. Trumpington must have been interested in military history, for he had annotated several works—biographies of Marlborough, Wellington, and Napoleon, and a two volume set on the Crimean War.

The desk drawers contained what seemed to be every letter Trumpington's father had ever written to him, all signed by *Pater*, Latin for *father*—an upper-class affectation Ford loathed—or simply by *P*. A few notes had been written by his father from the Western Front, making the war sound like an adventurous camping expedition interrupted by occasional assaults on the *fiendish Huns*, and stressing the inevitability of British victory.

A letter from Sir Robert Baden-Powell complimented Trumpington on his plan to establish a Boy Scout troop at Kings, and made reference to a new course for scoutmasters which had been inaugurated the previous year at Gilwell. Another was from Lady Canderblank's personal secretary, and was positively regal in tone: *"I am instructed by Her Ladyship to complement you on your recent appointment as Captain of the School ... "* Another letter of congratulation was written, this time in the first person, by his future Oxford tutor on the occasion of his recent scholarship.

There was a series of letters from a certain Leticia Gravenby, all of which seemed well-worn, as if they had been read many times. The first mentioned a recent meeting at a house party, and invited Trumpington to go riding with her. It was signed, *"Yours Sincerely, Leticia Gravenby."*

Evidently, the encounter had been a success, for subsequent letters, which balanced interest in Trumpington's doings with her own preparations for becoming a debutante in the coming season, progressed to *"Best Regards, Leticia"* and on to *"Affectionately Yours, As Always, Lettie."*

Notebooks were crammed with school notes, and books contained underlined passages and marginal notes. Trumpington had been an earnest and painstaking student, even if his report cards were filled with B minuses and C plusses. "Tries hard" was a universal comment. A letter from Mr. Jaspers congratulated him on winning his Oxford scholarship in history. *"Frankly, not your strongest subject, but you have taught me a lesson in the rewards of diligence."*

In all this evidence of a golden and untainted career, there was not one hint of why Callaway should have written to him, *"For starters I want five pounds. I want complete silence about you-know-what. And remember I'm just as good as you are."*

Ford, having kept the notebook that had fallen from Trumpington's pocket until last, now drew it out and opened it. It proved to be a combination of lists of miscreants and their punishments, such as *"June 4^{th}, Harding, Lower 5^{th}, spitting, two hundred lines: 'Spitting is prohibited on School Grounds,'"* and appointments, of which the very last entries from the previous day, read, *"Ch. Insp. Ford, Master's Library, 4 p.m.,"* and *"Master, in Hall after dinner."*

There was no mention of an assignation upon the slippery tiles of the Gymnasium roof.

There was a little pocket in the leather cover. It contained a small grainy photograph of a pretty young lady with smoldering eyes, with *"L"* and *"XXX"* written on the back in Miss Gravenby's handwriting, sealed with an impression of the young lady's lips in faded red lipstick.

There was also a tightly folded five pound note.

Ford recalled his interview with Trumpington the day before. At first he had pretended that he knew nothing, but as the interview progressed he had admitted being on the scene of Callaway's murder. He had been inside Trafalgar—he could have gone up to Callaway's room to argue or plead with Callaway about whatever it was that gave Callaway a hold over him, and he could well have pushed Callaway from the window.

The person that he claimed to have seen entering the bushes could have been Trumpington himself, knife in hand, to finish the job. Ford had judged it best to let the boy stew in his own juices overnight and press him again in the morning, but now he might never know with certainty what Trumpington was hiding.

*"For starters I want five pounds. I want complete silence about you-know-what. And remember I'm just as good as you are."*

Callaway was blackmailing Trumpington, demanding both money and Trumpington's silence about *"you-know-what."* Perhaps *"you-know-what"* was Callaway's relationship with the wretched Connelly, but what could Callaway have possibly discovered about Trumpington?

Perhaps it didn't matter. There was a good possibility that Trumpington had been involved in Callaway's death and then taken his own life in remorse.

"So, how would that have worked?" Ford asked himself.

Trumpington discovers that Callaway is assaulting Connelly. He confronts him, but Callaway counters by saying that he knows something equally damaging about Trumpington. It is a standoff, but Trumpington has far more to lose from exposure. Callaway sends Trumpington a note demanding blackmail payments.

Trumpington decides to confront Callaway—or pay him. He follows Callaway after the performance of the *Pirates*. Perhaps he skulks in the shadows watching the comings and goings as Callaway and White hide for their smoke. Connelly enters and exits, and, *"Oh, it's you,"* visits Callaway. The rhododendrons must have seemed as busy as the main concourse of Waterloo Station during the evening rush hour.

Perhaps Trumpington *is "Oh it's you,"* and pleads with Callaway. At the time of his death, Trumpington had no more than sixpence, apart from the carefully folded five pound note; perhaps he had given thirty shillings to Callaway as a down payment against the fiver. That would explain why Callaway had so large a sum in the pockets of his costume. Finally Callaway enters Trafalgar, signs the book, and goes to his room.

Trumpington faces the dismal prospect of paying for Callaway's silence in perpetuity. Callaway had written that Trumpington was no better than Callaway was—that must have been particularly galling to the arrogant Trumpington.

He has been collecting costumes from the play; he returns to his room and slips one on; he returns to Trafalgar and goes up to Callaway's room.

He enters Callaway's room, where Callaway is seated in his customary position at the window. They begin to argue. Callaway's attention is focused on the argument, and he inadvertently loses his balance and falls to his death—or Trumpington pushes him.

Trumpington rushes downstairs and enters the bushes. He passes Connelly on the stairs, but Connelly is distracted and doesn't recognize him. Trumpington cannot be certain that Callaway is dead. He returns to Trafalgar and steals a knife, again without being recognized. Returning to the body, he stabs it to make sure that Callaway will never reveal his secret. He runs back upstairs again to make sure he left no trace of his presence.

The plan seems to be working until yesterday's interview, in which he accidentally places himself at the scene of the crime—his school reports indicate that Trumpington was not very bright. Faced with the prospect of another harrowing interview, he goes to the Master, perhaps to confess, perhaps for advice. Whatever Doctor Thornby says is not encouraging; he goes up to the Gymnasium roof and ends his life rather than face public humiliation and ruination.

Ford stood and stretched wearily, and Croft entered the room, having completed taking written statements from Mr. Robinson and Mr. Jaspers.

"Anything, sir?" Croft asked.

Ford gazed around the room with its stuffed bookshelves and neatly made-up bed, and its photograph-bedecked mantle, and he shook his head. "There's nothing here, Croft, but I have a possible explanation."

Ford repeated his hypothesis to Croft.

"That's very neat, sir, if I may say so. If I understand you, it would also explain why the Master came here to search the room, instead of doing the obvious thing of going to look at the body. He'd have kept that note from Callaway to preserve young Trumpington's reputation and not upset his parents. It would have been destroying evidence, but perfectly well intentioned."

"An excellent point, Sergeant," said Ford, impressed again. "Perhaps I should call you *Detective* Sergeant"!"

"Oh no, sir. I can't work it all out like you can," Croft chuckled. "Although I must say it's very interesting, like a riddle or one of those puzzles like, 'If Harriet walks east for five miles at nine o'clock, and Arthur walks west for seven miles, starting at ten, when did it start raining?'—you know the kind of thing, sir."

"My explanation is, as you say, very neat," Ford pondered. "But is it correct?"

Ford examined Trumpington's alarm clock.

"It's four-thirty! We have to see the Master first thing, and we still have to conduct those other interviews."

"I took the liberty of waking up the driver, and we have the motorcar, sir. If I may suggest it, you could go back to the pub for a shave and then join me and the missus for a spot of breakfast. We could be back up here by six."

◆    ◆    ◆

Fortified, indeed weighed down, by Mrs. Croft's titanic conception of breakfast—on this occasion, based primarily on a vast supply of pancakes, but certainly far from limited to mere pancakes alone—Ford telephoned to the Chief Constable, reporting the news of Trumpington's death and requesting a meeting later that morning.

He also left a message for Superintendent Brownlee, who was not yet at his office. Ford had carefully placed the five pound note in an envelope, and Croft had telephoned to have it sent up to the Yard as soon as possible. Perhaps, just perhaps, its surface would reveal the fingerprints of whoever had given it to Trumpington.

Then Ford and Croft entered the motorcar, which chuffed its way back up the hill to Kings. The driver, Ford noted, had invested in a pair of dramatic black leather gauntlets, and Ford wondered if he was waiting for an appropriate occasion to take down the canvas top and don a pair of goggles.

"Same drill as before, Sergeant, if you please: get the masters to establish everyone's whereabouts last night."

"Right, sir."

"I hope this won't become a routine."

In Miss Grantly's absence, Ford knocked on the door of the Master's study and entered. Doctor Thornby was on the telephone and broke off the conversation abruptly. He looked so haggard that Ford felt a pang of sympathy.

"Good morning, sir," Ford said, but the Master did not grace him with a reply. Ford hardened his heart and ploughed on, regardless of Thornby's hostility.

"As you are doubtless aware, removing or withholding evidence is a serious offense, covered by both the laws concerning obstruction of justice, and by laws that make one a potential accessory to any crime which may have been committed."

The Master stirred, but Ford held up a hand.

"Please let me finish, sir. It may very well be that Trumpington was instrumental in Callaway's death, and then committed suicide. Certainly the evidence supports that as a possible explanation."

"Doubtless that outcome would please you," the Master said dangerously.

Ford continued as if he had not spoken.

"In that case, I would be able to end the enquiry into Callaway's death without further action, and I would see no benefit in portraying Trumpington's death as anything but a tragic accident. It might well have been, for example, that he saw a kitten trapped on the roof and was attempting to rescue it when he slipped and fell; a sad but noble death. The fact that two boys died within a few days of each other would be, to the outside world, no more than an unfortunate coincidence. The good name of Kings would remain intact."

Doctor Thornby again began to speak, and again Ford held up his hand.

"However, that outcome is dependent upon reaching the conclusion that Trumpington *did* cause Callaway's death, and, for the time being, I am not prepared to reach such a conclusion. In these circumstances I would suggest you reconsider your answer to my question earlier this morning. Did you see Trumpington after dinner last night, and what transpired in that conversation, sir?"

The Master appeared chastened. Strain and lack of sleep was drawing little wrinkles beneath his eyes, and he seemed much older than he had two days ago.

At last, Thornby spoke. "He was very upset by an interview he had with you, Ford. He said that you were bullying him, and frankly I did not find that surprising."

Perhaps the Master was less chastened than Ford had hoped.

"He wanted me to intervene to protect him from your excesses," Thornby continued. "I shall bring the matter to the attention of your superiors."

Ford nodded. "He was presumably upset because he admitted that he was in Trafalgar at the time of Callaway's death, sir," Ford told him. "He said he had seen someone entering the rhododendron bushes. These were obviously important facts he had withheld from Sergeant Croft. I cautioned him to tell me the complete truth and gave him the night to think it over."

The Master raised his brows in disbelief.

"Did he tell *you* that, sir?" Ford asked him. "Did he say anything about Callaway, or anything which might give me an insight into his own death?"

"He said nothing," the Master replied sullenly.

"Leaving aside imagined cats or other fairytales, sir, can you think of any reason he would climb to the Gymnasium roof?"

"I must admit that I cannot." This was the first polite answer the Master had given.

"Why did you go to his room and search it, sir, when the instinctive reaction would have been to hurry to see Trumpington's body, perhaps hoping that Mr. Robinson had made a dreadful mistake? What were you expecting to find in his room? A suicide note, perhaps?"

Thornby waved an evasive hand.

"I was very upset … I suppose I was seeking an explanation for this tragedy …"

"Did you telephone anyone yesterday evening, sir?"

"I may have done … My telephone calls, if any, are a private matter far beyond your scope."

The Master's haughtiness was beginning to reappear. Ford expected to be told any moment that he was being impertinent. Why, he asked himself again, are these people *so damned evasive and so damned hostile?*

"As you may be aware, sir, the telephone exchange keeps records of calls. I can certainly check with them—if your memory is incomplete."

"Very *well*, Ford," Doctor Thornby snapped, "I telephoned Lady Canderblank."

"Was that after you spoke to Trumpington, sir, or after Mr. Robinson told you of his death—or was it both?"

"I telephoned her to tell her that Trumpington was upset. She was not surprised."

He added, with withering sarcasm, "That was *after* I spoke to Trumpington, Ford. Anticipating your next inevitable question, the Trumpingtons and the Canderblanks are related; the General's late wife was her ladyship's sister. Trumpington was therefore their nephew. I asked her advice on whether to report your behavior to your superiors."

"Thank you, sir. And later?"

"Later, I naturally informed her of his death. One does not speak to someone about someone and then fail to tell her that immediately thereafter that person has been found dead. It was an *instinctive reaction*, Ford."

"What was the substance of the conversation, sir, apart from informing her of Trumpington's death?"

The Master snorted in annoyance but did not refuse to answer.

"We discussed whether or not to telephone his father in the middle of the night, and who should tell him. We resolved that I should be the bearer of bad news. Then there was the matter of whether this latest tragedy would affect the Prince's decision to send his son to Kings. You see, Ford, some of us have responsibilities beyond investigating accidents."

"Prince, sir?"

"Yes. One of Queen Victoria's grandsons. A Balkan prince. He's considering sending his son to Kings. It would be a great honor, but your involvement will certainly *not* help our cause."

He made it sound as if Ford's investigations were placing the decision in jeopardy, rather than the underlying crimes.

"I see, sir," Ford said. "I'll bear that in mind. Now, during the conversation, did Lady Canderblank suggest that you search Trumpington's room, sir?"

"Definitely *not!*"

"Have you informed his father yet, sir?"

"As a matter of fact, no. Perhaps I would have done so by now if you had not disturbed me with these repetitive and irrelevant questions."

Ford reflected that his own skin must be made of elephant hide to withstand the Master's endless barbs.

"May I borrow your key to the Gymnasium? It must be locked until we've finished searching the attics and roof in daylight."

For once Thornby looked defensive.

"I'm afraid I must have misplaced it. I know I had it before dinner yesterday, because I used it to attend a fencing practice."

He held up a large bunch of keys.

"But this morning it seems to be missing."

"That's very strange, sir! Who could have taken it?"

Thornby bristled. "Do you wish me to engage in guessing games, or do you wish me to inform General Trumpington of his son's tragic fall?"

Ford's spirits sank even lower. Now here was another complication to unknot. Was the Master lying? If not, who had taken the key? Where was it now?

"Thank you for your help, sir. I'll leave you to it. Incidentally, sir, have you heard from the Callaways in India?"

"No, I haven't, but the telegraph is very unpredictable over so great a distance, as you know."

"So I believe, sir."

Ford rose and then hesitated.

"Trumpington discussed nothing other than his complaints about me? No mention of Callaway? No mention of Connelly? No mention of black-mail, or its basis?"

The Master also rose and delivered a parting salvo.

"None, Ford. Let us be clear: that young man died because you brow-beat him. I hope God has mercy on your soul, because I certainly wouldn't! Good day to you."

◆          ◆          ◆

Colonel Percival Dagenham, formerly of the 17$^{th}$/21$^{st}$ Lancers, and now Chief Constable of Gloucestershire, lived twelve miles from Kings in a pleasant, rambling manor house. Ford met Dagenham in his study, a long low room with massive, ancient timbers supporting the ceiling, and a magnificent western view toward the Severn Valley.

"Ah, Ford, we meet at last," Dagenham greeted him. "Do come in and make yourself comfortable."

He waved Ford to a battered leather armchair standing before his desk and offered him a cigarette.

"I knew your father, by the by; a very decent chap, if I may say so, and his death was a sorry loss to all of us who knew him. How's your mother managing? I hope she's comfortable in the new cottage? I saw her a few weeks ago."

Ford felt a pang of guilt as he settled into the chair; he had been in Gloucestershire for several days and had not contacted his mother. He must at least telephone her.

Dagenham maintained a brisk but friendly conversation while a maid brought in tea and biscuits, and Ford warmed to him immediately. The Colonel was small and active, so that his movements were reminiscent of a bird's, and the illusion was strengthened by a habit of tilting his head to one side when listening. The room was lined with delicate watercolors of local scenery, which Dagenham shyly admitted were his own work.

"One daubs," he said, in modest dismissal of his talent, and then he turned to more immediate matters. "Now, Ford, what's happening over at Kings? I have to warn you that I receive daily, indeed almost hourly, telephone calls of complaint from Lady Canderblank, who is insistent that we declare the first boy's death—Callaway, I believe the poor chap's name was—an accident. Now we have another tragedy? Sir John Trumpington's boy?"

Ford summarized his progress, or lack of it, to date.

"Obviously, sir, it would be easy to conclude that young Trumpington killed Callaway to put an end to his blackmail, and then jumped to his own death in remorse. That may indeed be the correct analysis. But I'd prefer not to reach that conclusion just yet."

"That's very reasonable, Ford," Dagenham pondered. "Very ugly, and very hard for his father to bear, but reasonable nonetheless. Do you have any other suspects?"

"I have one other person with a clear motive, and means and opportunity as well; a younger lad who had the misfortune to be mistreated by Callaway."

"Mistreated?" The Colonel looked at Ford questioningly, then said, "Oh, I see what you mean."

"Then I have five others whose movements are not yet accounted for, sir, although they have no apparent motives—that includes the Canderblanks, incidentally. Canderblank Hall is my next stop this morning. Finally I have the Master, who's been unreasonably obstructive—not a sufficient ground for suspicion, but, at the same time, not to be ignored completely."

"So, it would indeed seem to be too early for any conclusions, Chief Inspector?"

"Yes, sir. I'll see the remaining people who are unaccounted for over the next day or two, and hopefully, I'll rule them out. However, I must admit I don't have a clear picture of Callaway ... Somehow I feel there may be more to this than simple blackmail."

He shook his head.

"I should have made more progress by now, sir. I must be missing the obvious."

"Nonsense, man," the Colonel replied. "You didn't start until Tuesday, and it's only Friday morning."

"Well, I assure you, it seems like three weeks to me, sir, rather than three days," Ford told him ruefully.

"Well, keep in touch, if you would," Colonel Dagenham said. "Don't hesitate to telephone at any time, day or night. I'll try to keep a lid on Deborah Canderblank, although that's a bit of a tall order. Have you met the lady?"

"I haven't had that pleasure yet, sir."

Ford glanced at his wristwatch.

"Speaking of the Canderblanks, I'd better get over there, if you'll excuse me."

"Ah, well, good luck. I'll lob a telephone call into John Trumpington, and ask him to let you alone to do your job. Poor man—what a shock this must be! The boy was the apple of his eye ... Anything else I can help with?"

Ford clambered to his feet.

"No, sir, thank you. That's all I need for the moment. Incidentally, I must say that Sergeant Croft is a pleasure to work with."

"Isn't he, though!" Dagenham replied enthusiastically. "Salt of the earth, and no country bumpkin, either. Have you sampled his wife's cooking yet?"

Ford laughed.

"I must have put on ten pounds this week, sir."

◆    ◆    ◆

Ford arrived at Canderblank Hall and reflected that it was indeed possible to build a truly ugly house out of beautiful Cotswold stone, provided one were sufficiently pretentious. A footman admitted him to an ostentatious entry hall dominated by an ill-proportioned fireplace.

"I'm a police officer," he told the footman, presenting his card. "I'd like to have a word with Lord and Lady Canderblank, if you please."

"His lordship's gone up to London," the footman said in tones that matched the ambience. "I'll see if her ladyship is at home."

And with Ford's card in hand, he stalked away.

Ford stood with his back to the fireplace until a saturnine man of indeterminate age, with shiny black hair plastered tightly against his scalp like a glossy ebony skullcap, descended the stairs.

"I am Lord and Lady Canderblank's private secretary," the man announced, inspecting Ford disapprovingly. His voice oozed like honey. "My name is Shipman. I regret it is not convenient for you to see Lady Canderblank at this hour. She is about to go riding, as is her custom."

"When will she be available, Mr. Shipman?"

"Alas, her ladyship's diary has many commitments, as one can appreciate ... If you would like an appointment, perhaps she will be available next month, after the family returns from Scotland."

"I regret the matter is somewhat urgent, and cannot wait that long."

"Then, if you provide me with a list of written questions, I'll see if her ladyship has time to address them over the next few days, and I'll give you her replies. I suggest you return at the end of the week."

He smiled falsely.

"When you do return, it would be better if you were to use the tradesmen's entrance," he added, gently chiding Ford for the effrontery of presenting himself at the front door.

But Ford had been insulted by better men than Shipman. "Here we go again," he groaned to himself.

"I do not wish to disrupt her ladyship's schedule, but I must speak to her in person at her earliest convenience."

"Then I fear you must wait until she returns from Scotland." He smiled again. "However, it is my understanding that she has already provided to the Chief Constable what little information she has on the unfortunate circumstances which bring you here, and therefore I am bound to say that I do not think it is necessary for you to see her yourself."

"Then we are at an impasse."

"So it would seem."

Now Shipman was positively beaming.

Ford returned his smile.

"I will send a police car and a woman constable to wait until it is convenient for Lady Canderblank to be driven to the police station for questioning."

Shipman's eyes widened. "Her ladyship does not go to police stations!"

"Then we are at another impasse, Mr. Shipman. I trust it can be resolved." He turned to leave. "I bid you good day. The police car will arrive in an hour or so, and wait in the forecourt."

Shipman shuffled his feet.

"Wait," Shipman called after him, "I'll see if Lady Canderblank's arrangements can be adjusted."

For the next ninety minutes, Ford waited in the ugly hall. A foolish, self-defeating obstinacy prevented him from sitting down.

Upstairs, meanwhile, Lady Canderblank twice telephoned the Chief Constable to complain of police harassment.

"Just see him, for God's sake, Deborah," he told her in exasperation. "Ford's only doing his duty. He's a perfectly decent chap, and he's well within his rights. Just get it over with!"

Eventually she descended the stairs and stood on the second step, looking down at Ford. She arranged herself so that the sun, streaming in through a large stained glass window behind her, was in his eyes. She had changed into a formal afternoon gown with a matching hat of improbable dimensions.

"Your name is Morris, or Austin?" she asked, in a querulous falsetto.

Ford looked up at her. She stood with regal grandeur, and yet Ford realized she was considerably shorter than she appeared to be. He surmised that she had been a plain girl, whose craggy features had doubtless been softened by the arts of skilled beauticians; now, in middle age, decades of vindictiveness and hauteur had set her mouth into a permanent sneer, and she carried her head so that she perpetually stared down at the world.

From the inflexible way she was holding herself, Ford guessed she was trussed up in ruthless corsetry, and that perhaps this constant discomfort lay at the root of her irascibility. The lines of her forehead suggested that the scornful set of her eyebrows was habitual.

"Ford, madam."

"Ah, I was sure it was the name of a cheap little car … Ford isn't even English, is it?"

She stared at him down her aquiline nose, and Ford guessed she was incapable of self-doubt.

"I fear not, Lady Canderblank," Ford replied. "I understand you were at Kings this weekend?"

"Why ask me questions for which you know the answers? Is this the reason you have intruded upon us?"

"What did you do after the play was over, Lady Canderblank?"

"You have no right to ask such an impertinent question."

"I regret that I do."

She stood gazing down at him, and he waited silently. He guessed she was coiled up tightly like a spring, and could snap at any moment.

"The room was stuffy," she said, evidently deciding to humor him, for the moment at least. "I took a turn through the grounds."

"Were you alone, Lady Canderblank?"

"My husband came with me to smoke a cigar, if you must know," she said in brittle tones.

"Did you return to your room at the Master's Lodge together?"

"He may have gone back first; I really don't recall."

She evidently decided her cooperation had gone on long enough. Her falsetto strengthened and took on a harsher tone.

"Really, Chrysler, this is quite intolerable. I shall speak to the Chief Constable in the strongest terms. I also wish to have the name of your immediate superior."

"That would be Superintendent Brownlee, Criminal Investigation Division, New Scotland Yard," Ford replied dispassionately. "The telephone number is Whitewall 1212. Here, let me write his name down for you on the back of my card, Lady Canderblank."

He took a pen from his inner vest pocket and wrote.

"Did you see anyone else while you were walking?" he asked as he handed her the card. "Oh, may I have it back? I forgot to include the telephone number."

She thrust his card back with a snort of annoyance.

"I refuse to answer any more of these ridiculous questions."

She gathered herself for a tirade.

"The purpose of the police force is to control the lawlessness of the lower classes, not to disrupt the lives of its betters by making mountains out of molehills. I recommend you take care to remember that. It is my understanding that the poor boy, Calhoun or Carter, or whatever his name was, had an accident, just as there has now been another tragedy, brought on, I understand, by your threats. I suggest you let them both rest in peace. Good day, Officer."

She turned to re-ascend the stairs.

"Thank you for your time, Your Ladyship," Ford replied. "I must advise you that, since you have chosen not to answer my questions with regard to young Callaway's death, I shall note in my report that your time is unaccounted for. It may therefore become necessary to conduct additional interviews."

She stopped, turned back, and appeared too stunned by his effrontery to reply.

"As you will appreciate, Lady Canderblank, solving a case of this nature consists largely of eliminating those who could not have committed the crime, leaving the remainder as suspects. You have chosen not to answer my questions, and I shall therefore place you in the latter category. Good day to you, Lady Canderblank."

"Of all the *in*solent ...!" began her ladyship, but Ford had already sketched a bow, and she was speaking to his back.

# Saturday

On Saturday morning Ford rose early, dressed in his tweed golfing clothes, and caught the exact train from Paddington Station to Oxford that Victoria Canderblank had specified. He carried his battered golf bag. He promised himself, as he often did, that soon he would discard his random array of ill-matched clubs and invest in a splendid new set that, he assured himself, would add twenty yards to every stroke.

In the forecourt of Oxford Station stood the splendid Canderblank Rolls Royce which conveyed him elegantly to Lord Canderblank's golf club. He wondered if Lady Canderblank was aware of these arrangements—he somewhat doubted it. As the car pulled up, he saw his hostess standing on the steps of the clubhouse in the sunshine, waiting to greet him. He alighted and was immediately drenched in a torrent of bright conversation.

"I was almost certain you wouldn't come," she exclaimed. "I'm so glad you did. It's this way—let me show you. Thank God, it's not raining; golf is simply too dreary in a drizzle, although that doesn't deter the diehards. Isn't alliteration fun? Let me introduce you to our caddies: this is Campbell, and this is Ross. Ross, this is the gentleman you'll be assisting. I see you found my clubs, Campbell; thank you. Can you guarantee this sunshine? Now, let's get over to the first tee before the crowds arrive. I hate waiting around for the doddering old duffers."

She led the way.

"Here we are; it's a slight dogleg to the right. The green is out of sight behind those trees. You'll have to give me a moment to warm up."

Ford took off his jacket and stretched to loosen up while Miss Canderblank swayed prettily through her own exercises, chatting all the time.

"Are you ready to start, Mr. Ford? Excellent! Please begin, and then I'll start from the ladies' tees. Goodness, are you left-handed? It seems so unnatural!"

Ford positioned his ball, and Ross handed him his elderly driver.

His wartime injury had ruined what little grace his swing might once have had, for he found it impossible to put his full weight on his rear leg during his backswing. These days a long drive was out of the question, and the important thing was to keep the ball in the fairway.

"Threehunnetfifteen yards to the pin, sir," said Ross in a bored staccato. "Out of bounds to the right. Best keep it leftish, sir, but not too far left. That there fairway bunker is twohunnetthirty from the tee."

Ford took a practice swing, pulling the club back slow and low with his right shoulder, keeping his right arm rigid, and his left loose, and with the elbow tucked down and in to his side, turning away from the fairway, cocking his wrists as he did so, picturing the trajectory of the club on the downstroke, and keeping his head as steady as he could.

He reached the natural limit of his back swing, a little short of where his left leg would complain, paused for a moment, and then let the club head fall as his hands accelerated and his body uncoiled and his hips opened, and the club head was through the imaginary ball.

"Now do that with the ball, and forget how much you hate the first tee," he ordered himself, and addressed the ball before his mind could wander.

He drove the ball with a respectable *whack*, although without the infinitely satisfying tremor through the shaft that meant he had hit it well. The ball sailed into the air, a little to the left of where he would have liked it, came down and bounced in the fairway, and bounced again, headed for the fairway bunker, but trickled into the first low cut of rough some twenty yards short of the sand.

"Safe enough, sir," said Ross without enthusiasm. "You'll be able to see the green from there."

Miss Canderblank had fallen silent for his tee shot, but now she burst into full voice once more as she walked forward to the ladies tees some sixty yards ahead.

"Not too bad, Mr. Ford. You're only just in the rough. God, I hate the first tee! I'm sure I'll slice it into those trees or duff it completely; I always do. I'm the only person in history to break a window in the clubhouse at Lytham off the first tee, which is impossible to do, since one is driving in the opposite direction. It's two hundred and fifty from these tees ... Now, ball, you know where you're supposed to go. That short green grass out there is called the fairway, and that's where you belong. Don't make an ass out of me!"

Scarcely pausing her flow of commentary to drive, she took a compact, quick swing, and her ball flew beautifully above the middle of the fairway to come to a rest perhaps twenty yards beyond Ford's ball, and dead center.

"That was a fluke, I assure you," she laughed gaily, marching smartly down the fairway with Ford at her side.

Ford stole a covert glance at her. Her hair was drawn back tightly into a ruthless bun, revealing her graceful neck and strong cheekbones. Her face was animated and lifted a little to catch the full warmth of the morning sun.

Is she beautiful, Ford asked himself, or is it her exuberance that lights up her face?

"I hope you like this course, Mr. Ford. It's a bit challenging, but it's not impossible, like some of the Scottish links. Troon, for example; whatever I do there, I know I'm going to lose a dozen balls in the gorse bushes—it's too frustrating."

They reached Ford's ball, which lay in the short cut of rough two feet from the fairway.

"Sitting up all right, sir," said Ross. "Onehunnertwenty to the center of the green, onehunnertthirty to the pin. Eight iron or nine iron, sir?"

The oval green lay below him, guarded by two bunkers at its throat. The ground around it sloped from left to right. The flag stood to the right side of the green as it sloped away, protected by the right-hand bunker. A close shot would have to clear the bunker but then stop quickly to avoid running down the hill and escaping into the rough.

"Better give me the seven, please, Ross."

Ross jerked the club from Ford's bag, clearly contemptuous of this sign of weakness. Ford took a practice swing to gauge the resistance of the rough and stood back to assess his shot.

"For goodness sake, don't go right," Miss Canderblank advised. "You'll never get it back up the hill. I do that all the time, I'm afraid. For some reason I find that scrub irresistible, and then I'm stuck in the briars and brambles down there."

Ford addressed the ball. The important thing was to hit it cleanly and to keep the club head moving through it, and to keep his head down to avoid snatching at it. By selecting a longer club, he hoped he'd need less muscle and that the club head would do the work.

Miss Canderblank fell silent.

Ford waited five seconds until he felt completely confidant, and then swung. The ball released sweetly from the rough and soared high into the air on a perfect line for the pin but almost certainly too short.

"Get up, ball," yelled Miss Canderblank.

The ball fell almost vertically not five feet from the flag, and came to rest three feet past it.

"Oh, excellent shot! Perfect! I wish I could do that! I'm tempted to lay up; I'll never clear the right bunker. Still, what the hell! You're only young once. Do *not* find the sand, ball. Do *not* go right. Please try to behave, for once. I'm sure this is the wrong club, Campbell. Ball, don't make a mess."

Clearly Miss Canderblank had a particularly obedient ball, for it flew high before plummeting back to finish a mere two feet from the pin.

"That was an excellent recovery out of the rough, if I may say so, Mr. Ford. God, I hate putting—it's positively the worst part of my game, particularly on those rare occasions when I have a chance at birdie. I'm usually trying to save a double bogie. Perhaps you'll be gracious enough to give me a *gimmie*, although that's cheating. We didn't settle the stakes, Mr. Ford; is a shilling a hole all right? Is the green going to be fast or slow, Campbell? Is it still wet with dew? Perhaps it will break a little to the right? Still, I'm getting ahead of myself—you're away, Mr. Ford."

They putted out. Ford almost left his putt short, but it trickled in at the last moment, while Miss Canderblank rolled her ball straight into the hole with smooth authority.

"Birdie-birdie, an excellent start! God, I love golf—it's my favorite thing. I've never really enjoyed riding. Oh God, now it's the second hole. This hole is longer than the Great Wall of China, and the green's totally impossible. Number one handicap hole on the course. Uphill for a mile and then downhill for another; out of bounds all down the left, sand all round the green. Ugh and double ugh!"

"Fourhunnerteighty yard par five, sir, uphill then down," Ross announced. "The top of the hill is threehunnertforty, so you can't see the green on this shot nor the next. The green is on a line behind that bunker to the right, sir, but it's twohunnertthirty to clear it. Best aim for that sand on the left, sir. That's threehunnertten yards away from here."

A pattern had developed.

Miss Canderblank kept up a steady flow of chatter, a mixture of amusing, self-derogatory anecdotes and stern instructions to her ball so dominating the conversation that neither Ford nor her ball needed to say anything in reply. She stopped talking only when he or she took a stroke.

In spite of her cheerful self-criticism, she was an excellent golfer, with a quick, compact, and efficient swing, which she executed in exactly the same manner for every shot, as if she were an automaton.

Her putting combined judgment and courage. Her few errant shots produced a colorful string of epithets, but were invariably followed by an excellent recovery.

Contrary to his normal preferences, Ford found her chatter soothing. He and his usual partners probably spoke no more than a hundred words in an entire round, and those words were limited to expressions such as, "That's a gimme," or "Your honor," or "Who's away?" with the occasional "Good shot," and "Oh shit!" thrown in. Social conversation ran to, "How's business?"—"Fair-to-middling, thanks" or, "How's the wife?"—"So-so." "Same time next Saturday?" et cetera.

But on this occasion, he was content to bask in the sunshine and her presence, and the more relaxed he became, the better he played, as was inevitable. Ross' early doubts of Ford's game fell away. The gentleman could not hit the ball very far, but from inside *onehunnertfifty* yards of the green he was deadly, bombing the pin with huge, high, arcing approach shots with plenty of spin to stop them dead on arrival. His putting was a little tentative for Ross's taste, but he did not make mistakes. An eight-to-ten-handicapper, Ross decided, and nothing wrong with that.

At the turn they gulped a sandwich and washed it down with lukewarm sweet tea.

"I need all the energy I can get, Mr. Ford," said Miss Canderblank. "Otherwise I will whither away on the back nine. Good, it's only ten thirty; we'll be done before lunch. Actually it's a bit ridiculous for us to be calling each other 'Mr. Ford' and 'Miss Canderblank.' I hate 'Victoria;' it's either too imperial, or it reminds one of railway stations ... Let's begin, incidentally. This is another very long hole, but it's wide and open. Just whack it down the middle ... Nice shot! I usually slice it into those trees. Anyway, the problem is that I hate 'Vickie,' too; so, anyway, my friends just call me 'V.' Ball, I want to make a good start on the back nine. Something to get my confidence up. *Not* those trees, please, and *not* those bunkers on the left, either ... Well, *that* was lucky! Anyway, I believe your name is Thomas? Are you a 'Thomas' or a 'Tom' or even a 'Tommie'?"

Ford had a rare opportunity to speak.

"I really don't mind; whichever you prefer, Miss Canderblank."

"V!" she insisted gaily.

"V."

"Very well, let's see. 'Tommie' is certainly cheerful, but perhaps a little too trivial for your persona, if I may be so bold ... We're still miles from the hole, just aim for that tree, I suggest, with a long iron or a wood. Campbell, we're still more than three hundred yards away, aren't we? Gosh, I wish I could hit a fairway wood like that; it has to be the weakest part of my game ... Anyway, we're down to 'Thomas' or 'Tom.' 'Tom Ford'—monosyllabic and dependable—no nonsense and no wasted energy. But could it be too prosaic? ... *Shit!* How could I be such an idiot? I'll never reach the green from there; this will be your hole for certain. *Thomas*, on the other hand, has balance ..."

And so it continued, while Ford kept playing exceptionally well and Miss Canderblank mesmerized him with her chatter. Between shots they marched the fairways side by side. Ford told his leg it could hurt as much as it wanted to once the round was over, provided it didn't betray him now; beside him she strode effortlessly, loose-limbed and lithe. They were off the course by half past eleven, and Ross was moved to say, "A very nice round, sir," as he accepted Ford's tip.

They returned to the clubhouse for sherry before lunch, and ate—at Miss Canderblank's suggestion—the poached Dover sole. Ford felt mellowed by the exercise and the food, and he wisely refused a second glass of wine.

He knew she was flirting in order to gain his confidence, but being flirted to, or *at*—Ford wasn't sure which was correct—was a very unusual and welcome experience, particularly with someone of Victoria Canderblank's exceptional attractiveness and social standing. The contrast between Lady Canderblank's pugnacious hauteur and her daughter's gaiety could not have been greater, and it was inevitable that her mother would forbid any further contact between them.

"Listen, Thomas, there's something I have to say. I know you can't discuss the case, but I think my mother's behaving like a complete pig. Frankly, she's an old fashioned snob, pure and simple. Actually she's just trying to keep Kings out of the scandal sheets, which is a very reasonable thing to do, but she's doing it in an idiotic manner."

She raised her hand to silence him, as if he had been about to speak, even though he hadn't.

"She telephoned me yesterday evening and was beside herself with fury. She said you'd threatened to arrest her, which I'm sure you hadn't. She'd be spitting bullets if she knew we were playing golf and having lunch together."

Again she held up her hand.

"I don't want to discuss it. I just want you to know that she won't influence my opinion of you."

"I'm very sorry to have upset her," he replied, finding it hard to believe Lady Canderblank was capable of any form of human feeling. "It certainly was not my intention. I didn't want to get this case in the first place, and the sooner it's done, the happier I'll be."

"Why? Because you won't have to see me any more?" she asked him with a coy smile.

"No, of course not, Miss Canderblank—*V*, I mean. It's just that …"

Ford was not sure what to say, and so he said nothing.

"Oh, Thomas, I didn't mean to embarrass you! We'll change the subject."

And so she did, until she noticed the time and bundled them both into the waiting Rolls Royce so he could be whisked into Oxford to catch the express train back to London and be home before three o'clock.

"Grin and bear it, Thomas," she said as she shook his hand in the station forecourt.

She regarded him gravely, and his heart turned a summersault.

"You know, I find stoicism very attractive. It's a quality I admire but am not capable of exhibiting. Now, hurry before you miss your train."

◆    ◆    ◆

Ford daydreamed his way back to London, but his pleasant memories of the morning's golf and subsequent luncheon were periodically interrupted by the words of Callaway, like sudden unwelcome squalls on a beautiful summer's day.

*"Dearest Mummy, why do you deny me …"*

*"For starters I want a fiver …"*

Deny him what? A fiver in return for what?

The train fussed into Paddington, and Ford went to the left luggage office where he had deposited a suitcase that morning. In the men's convenience, he changed out of his golfing gear, pulled on a suit and tie, and redeposited his sporting clothes and his golf bag.

Then he took the tube train to Camden, and found his way to Walnut Crescent.

"Good afternoon, Mrs. Markham. I'm sorry to bother you, but I need to see your nephew's room again. Then perhaps I'll be able to return the key."

"I'm not sure." Mrs. Markham hesitated, staring at him through her half-opened front door. "Mr. Markham's not here."

"Don't worry, Mrs. Markham. I can find the way."

He slipped past her and climbed the stairs before she could form a firm objection.

The sterile room was dusty from disuse. Where would a boy hide something? It depended on what he had to hide. Ford went through all the furniture again, removing drawers and feeling beneath hidden surfaces. He went through every book, opening each one and shaking it out to see if it would reveal hidden treasures. *David Copperfield* released a ten shilling note, and *Pride and Prejudice* gave up an obscene limerick—clearly not the work of Jane Austin—but that was that.

He struggled to move the bed to one side and lifted the carpet, but only the bare boards stared back at him.

By the window, a hole had been cut in the floorboard beneath the radiator to admit the hot water pipe. Ford knelt awkwardly in the dust and found that the board was loose.

Beneath it lay a cache of papers, a small leather bound book, and over thirty pounds in notes and coins. Ford set the money, the book, and the papers to one side, and continued to search, but there was nothing else to find. When he had returned the room to normal, he sat down at the desk to read the cache.

Some fifteen pages of carefully written text represented the beginnings of a novel entitled, *The Secret Hero,* By Michael Callaway,.

The novel's hero was a young man brought up as an orphan. Although the protagonist had many virtues—intelligence, athletic skills, bravery, charm, a commitment to worthy causes in the *"best interests of mankind"*—he was continuously rejected by society and never given the recognition and rewards he richly deserved. He was by far the most meritorious boy at his school, but failed to be appointed Head Boy, passed over in favor of the son of the Chairman of the Governors, who was unworthy of the position because he was a cheat.

At Oxford, the hero won his Blue at cricket, rugby football, rowing and fives, and was a brilliant student. On several occasions, he was invited to sing the leading role at the Royal Opera House in Covent Garden. However, though he was on the verge of winning First Class Honors, unknown forces intervened just before final examinations, and he was sent down on trumped up charges and declared *persona non grata* at the opera.

Friendless and penniless, he joined the Army at the outbreak of the war as a humble private soldier, yet his bravery and general military prowess propelled him rapidly through the ranks, and he rose to become a Colonel while he was still only nineteen.

Single handedly, armed with only a bayonet, he stormed an enemy machine gun post, killing the Germans manning it and rescuing a captured English Lieutenant General. He escaped from behind the German lines by stealing a Fokker fighter plane, and, despite never having flown before, was able to pilot himself and the General back to freedom. On the way, he encountered several German aircraft, all of which he shot down, although, alas, the General was fatally wounded in the dogfight.

Upon landing, the dying General revealed that the hero was, in fact, the illegitimate result of a noblewoman's transgressions, and heir to a great fortune. It was the noble family who had conspired to frustrate his every achievement.

Before his wounds overcame him, the General was granted sufficient time to recommend the hero for the Victoria Cross.

The young man confronted the noble family and was repudiated. Further, the General's recommendation for the Victoria Cross was denied. At the noble family's instigation, he was cashiered and discharged from the Army with dishonor.

Alone and friendless once more, the young man made his way to Switzerland, where, because of language difficulties, he found himself in a bordello rather than a hotel. Such was his obvious virility, however, that three of the prostitutes fell in love with him on first sight and took him in, and he spent his days gratifying their boundless appetites.

Although now finally appreciated and loved, such an existence could not satisfy his inherent nobility of spirit. Restlessly he boarded a train, uncertain of its destination. His fellow passenger was a Russian Bolshevik named Lenin. Lenin intuitively recognized the youth's many qualities and begged him to join the Revolution. The hero therefore accompanied Lenin to Russia, where he joined the Red Guard in its righteous quest to crush the aristocracy and establish a Worker's Paradise.

At that point the story ended. A page of notes gave hints of the future plot: *"kills Czar but saves Anastasia," "goes to Africa and discovers city of gold," "fights tiger barehanded," "secret island populated by naked black women," "returns to England with horde of diamonds and becomes Duke after all."*

Ford set aside this document with some relief and turned to the other, a brief letter dated the previous December.

> Dear Dickie,
> The essay questions are: (1) How was the British Navy able to neutralize Napoleon's superior military resources? Discuss with examples. (2) Who was the greater general, Marlborough or Wellington? Why? (3) "C'est magnifique, mais se n'est pas la guerre." Discuss.
> That's it: good luck. P"

Ford stared unseeing through the window; for a moment he stopped breathing. The room seemed colder. Then he let his breath out slowly.

"Oh my God ..." he sighed, reluctant to accept what he had just read.

Trumpington, the dogged but indifferent student, had surprised everyone by winning a scholarship to Oxford. Now the reason was apparent: Sir John Trumpington had secured an advance copy of the questions so that his son could prepare his answers. Ford recalled the heavily annotated lives of Marlborough and Wellington, the studies on Napoleonic France, the naval history, and the two volumes on the Crimean War.

Somehow Callaway had found this letter and begun to blackmail Trumpington, demanding silence for his own transgressions and cold cash. Judging by the considerable pile of money he had amassed, he must have bled Trumpington dry. Callaway, unlovable and unloved, had become an extortionist.

The novel was all about rejection by society; Callaway was having his revenge upon society by preying on it.

*"Remember, I'm just as good as you,"* he had written to Trumpington.

Still shaken, Ford turned to the hidden book. It was not, as he'd expected, a salacious work, but a thin tome entitled *In the Service of the Raj.*

Callaway must have found it in a secondhand bookshop, for the inside cover had a price of 3d and the inscription, *"Happy Birthday, Charlie, Love, Aunt Maude. 1916."* Callaway had written: *"Ex Libris Michael Callaway, April 15, 1920,"* beneath.

Ford riffled through it. Each chapter seemed to be devoted to an aspect of British military life in India: "The Garrisons of the Northwest Frontier," "The Army at Play," "At Home in the Punjab," and so on.

Unlike Callaway's other hidden materials, all the people in the photographic plates were fully clothed. Presumably the book reminded Callaway of his parents and his early life, but why would he hide it?

Ford found that he was not concentrating on the book, but that he kept coming back to Trumpington's letter. If the Master and Lady Canderblank regarded Ford with disfavor now, how would they react when this ugly little secret was revealed? *Shit!*

Ford stuffed his pockets with Callaway's secrets and went downstairs to find Mrs. Markham hovering nervously in the hall.

"Thank you very much, Mrs. Markham. I'm taking a few odds and ends, just to make sure I don't have to disturb you again. Examples of his handwriting, mostly. Here's the key to his room. Have you heard from your sister?"

"Mr. Markham will be back shortly," she responded, as if unwilling to communicate anything without her husband's approval.

"Ah," replied Ford. The thought of cajoling or badgering a reluctant answer from her stuck in his craw.

"Well, thank you again, and good afternoon to you."

Ford walked slowly back to the main road—his leg was throbbing from too much exercise, and he was beginning to limp. He had to ask for directions to the nearest police station. Once he arrived, he identified himself to the desk sergeant and asked to use a telephone. His first call was to Superintendent Brownlee. "I found a number of letters, sir, and a novel that Callaway had started. But I also found something of an extremely sensitive nature—something I must put in your hands right away."

"You'd better come for supper this evening, old chap, if you will. Do you remember my address?"

Ford did.

"We always have fish and chips on a Saturday night; is that all right?"

"Of course, sir."

"Cod or plaice?"

"Er ... cod, please."

"Half past seven all right, Ford?"

"That will be fine, sir. I'll try to see Doctor Waggoner on the way, and ask him to look at Callaway's novel."

"Good idea. I'll see you later."

His second call was answered by Doctor Waggoner.

"Come at any time, Chief Inspector. I'm always happy to assist Scotland Yard."

◆　　　◆　　　◆

Dr. Waggoner suffered both from his Swiss origins and from his profession as a psychoanalyst. He had settled in England in 1900 and found employment in Broadmoor, an institution for the criminally insane. Unfortunately, his origins had made him highly suspect during the war, when national xenophobia turned all foreigners into spies. The fact that he was not German was irrelevant.

In addition, his profession was regarded by many as quackery, indeed as morally subversive, since he was a disciple of the notorious Doctor Freud of Vienna. Freud, in the popular imagination, ascribed all human behavior to suppressed Oedipal desires whose true nature found expression only in the form of salacious dreams.

He had changed his name from Sigmund Wagner to St. John Waggoner, with the "St. John" pronounced in the English manner "sin-gin."

Scotland Yard was one of the few places in England where Doctor Waggoner was well regarded. He had been of considerable help during the war in interviewing suspected German spies—a secret irony, given his popular reputation. Further, Scotland Yard was populated by men whose profession brought them into constant contact with murderers and the violently insane, so the police valued the insights of a specialist dedicated to understanding deranged motivations.

Doctor Waggoner received Ford in his modest bungalow in the ugly suburbs of Kingston Upon Thames, and read Callaway's novel with painstaking attention. Ford was beginning to flag, and, by now, his leg was protesting strenuously.

His eyes, wandering around Waggoner's cramped, book-lined sitting room, grew heavy. The air was thick with the pungent smoke of Doctor Waggoner's tobacco pipe, which, as he read, he puffed with the regularity of a steam locomotive.

"Well, the story is obviously based on rejection, Chief Inspector," Waggoner said at last. "Although tasteless, I must say it's not badly written."

Ford noted that it was Waggoner's complete *lack* of accent, rather than a distinct accent, that marked him as a foreigner.

"What makes it interesting is the distinction between the clarity of some descriptions, and the vagueness of others," Waggoner continued. "Take the brothel scenes, for example: although they are extensive, they show a distinct lack of practical sexual experience—they're simple fantasies. The graphic depictions of the war indicate an interest in physical violence and brutality; the hero's objective is not merely to kill his enemies, it would seem, but to inflict pain and suffering upon them. I note that each victim screams and begs for mercy as the hero's bayonet strikes them repeatedly, and each successive wound produces a fresh torrent of blood."

He riffled through the pages.

"In contrast, the most realistic scenes are those in which he suffers rejection, particularly the scene in which his relatives deny his birthright—which is written with a simple stark reality, as if he had actually experienced it."

Waggoner found the text he wanted.

"Consider these two passages. In the brothel scene the boy writes: *He had his lustful way with each of them in turn.* It's as if he weren't sure of the practical details, and could not be more precise. In describing his rejection by the noble family, on the other hand, he writes:

> *She was quivering with rage, and her voice was filled with venom. "That's preposterous, you little hooligan," she spat. A vein throbbed at her temple and her hands were curled like claws.*

Ford reacted as if a bolt of lightning had struck him.

"*Of course!* Doctor, I've been a fool!"

Ford grabbed another page from his portfolio of Callaway's works.

"Look at this letter, Doctor."

He handed it to the psychiatrist.

"*Dearest Mummy, Why do you deny me ...*' Like an idiot, I've been assuming that the rest of the sentence would describe what it was he wanted. But in fact the sentence is complete; his mother is denying their very relationship. *"Dearest Mummy, Why do you deny me?"* How could I have missed it?"

"May I see the other correspondence, Chief Inspector?"

Ford handed the letters to him, and Waggoner turned the pages.

"Yes, the tone of the note is quite different from the others ... You will have observed, I'm sure, the rather cold formality of the other letters, filled with platitudes, and, in his case, demands for money ... And, of course, the sharp contrast between *"Dear Mum"* on the one hand, and *"Dearest Mummy"* on the other, written perhaps in passion or perhaps in irony."

"Would a boy like that be suicidal?"

"Oh no. He would have been sustained, indeed strengthened, by his fantasies; after all, his hero became a Duke in the end."

Ford shifted his weight forward in his chair.

"Doctor, I'm very grateful to you. This is *immensely* valuable! I'll intrude upon your time no more."

"I'm always glad to help, particularly on an intriguing case like this."

Ford noticed something in his manner.

"Would you be interested if I kept you up to date as the case develops?"

"I'd be immensely grateful," Waggoner replied, his eyes gleaming. "To tell you the truth, I'm usually asked to examine one specific issue, and I often wonder about the broader context; it's rather like examining one piece of a jigsaw puzzle without ever knowing what the overall picture turned out to be."

"Then, I keep you posted, Doctor. Now, if you'll excuse me, I have to see Superintendent Brownlee."

They both rose and shook hands.

"Let me show you out, Chief Inspector. And please give my regards to Superintendent Brownlee."

◆    ◆    ◆

A rich aroma of fried fish and chips enveloped the Brownlees' untidy kitchen like a warm fog. The family did not stand on ceremony, and the meal was served in its original newspaper wrappings. In Superintendent Brownlee's opinion, the soaked newspaper, transparent with grease, preserved the flavor and kept the food hot.

Bottles of beer and vinegar, a vast saltshaker, a jar of pickled onions, milk for the kids and a pot of tea for Mrs. Brownlee, competed for what little space was left on the tabletop.

The Superintendent spent time in extolling the virtues of their local chippie, Mrs. Brownlee provided an update on her sister-in-law's latest medical catastrophe, and the kids argued over whether their father should take them to watch the Surrey play at the Oval, or to the Science Museum for their next family outing.

Ford let himself be swaddled in the cheerful din, reflecting that a man who is free of pretensions, like Brownlee, is a man who is truly free. Ford had a sudden fantasy in which he was entertaining a junior colleague in his own noisy kitchen, and Victoria Canderblank sat at the table, surrounded by their children, crunching fried sole with her pretty teeth and discussing her latest round of golf.

Ford laughed at himself inwardly for having so improbable a pipe-dream, and joined the discussion of the relative strengths of the archrival Surrey and Kent cricket teams. After supper the kids were banished to play upstairs, Mrs. Brownlee popped out to visit her friend from next door, and Brownlee cleared the wreckage from the table so that he and Ford could talk over another bottle of brown ale.

The Superintendent settled to his ease and sat, wearing a misshapen grey woolen cardigan, a labor of love from Mrs. Brownlee's devoted but inexpert fingers.

"So, what do you have, old chap? Are the grounds of Kings becoming littered with fallen bodies?"

"I fear so, sir. Death by falling from a roof under unknown circumstances. No witnesses."

"What do we know about either death, so far?"

"We have no witnesses and no material evidence to rule out an accident or suicide or murder in either of the two cases, sir. We have no evidence to tie the two cases together—at least nothing beyond the obvious coincidence. There is at least one powerful explanation for the whole thing, but I'd like to leave that to the end, if I may, and get your opinion."

"Fine, let's start with the facts."

"As far as the first death is concerned—young Callaway's death—which occurred one week ago this evening, there is no indication that he was suicidal. There's no hint of it from the people who knew him, although he was extremely secretive, and Doctor Waggoner, who read a piece of fiction that Callaway wrote, says that he was not the suicidal type. Therefore I'm assuming his death was accidental or murder."

He lit a cigarette.

"As far as the circumstances are concerned, it appears that a person or persons unknown entered Callaway's room at about a quarter to eleven in the evening. Due to the unusual circumstances, with visitors about and people in costumes, it was possible for someone who was not a member of

Trafalgar to gain such access unnoticed—or, of course, it could have been a member of Trafalgar."

"Mmm," Brownlee muttered. He had closed his eyes in order to concentrate.

"During the confrontation, Callaway either fell from his window ledge by accident or was pushed. Doctor Pondsford is certain he died from falling, although his examination of the corpse was extremely superficial. It may be necessary to exhume the body to confirm it, although I tend to believe his diagnosis."

"His skills are widely acknowledged," Brownlee commented, opening his eyes briefly. "After your last report, I had someone look into his qualifications and reputation. At Guy's Hospital, where he consults, they think he walks on water."

"Very well, sir. I'll assume Callaway fell or was pushed," Ford said. "The unknown suspect descended to the kitchen, stole a knife, entered the bushes and stabbed Callaway, presumably to ensure that he was dead. The post mortem stabbing indicates that Callaway had a mortal enemy, and it's absurdly unlikely that someone else would wander into the bushes in the pitch black of night, find his body by accident, and decide to stab it. Therefore, whoever stabbed him was in his room when he fell, sir."

"Or was standing by the bushes when he crashed down into them."

"True, sir, although less likely."

"I agree. So, the stabbing was to make sure he was dead," Brownlee said slowly. "That sounds reasonable."

"Curiously, the unknown suspect was seen coming down from Callaway's room and then going back up again—either a woman or a man dressed in a woman's theatrical costume."

"Curious indeed. Perhaps he realized he'd left something behind, or he went back to make sure there was no incriminating evidence ... What about suspects?"

"There are two boys we know of who might have done it, sir. The Captain of the School, Trumpington, the boy who was killed on Thursday night, was present in Trafalgar at the time, and was being blackmailed by Callaway. The second, a fourth-former named Connelly, admits to having gone to Callaway's room at the relevant time, and of having been sexually abused by Callaway on several occasions.

"Callaway was an unpleasant and unpopular boy, and there may have been other pupils who wished him harm; however, Trumpington and Connelly are the only two who appear to have had a sufficiently powerful motive to murder him."

"Go on."

"There are five other people who were at the School at the right time whose movements haven't yet been corroborated: Lord and Lady Canderblank and their daughter, and the local publican and *his* daughter. I'm assuming the Bishop of Gloucester is innocent by definition."

Brownlee snorted in amusement.

"The sanctity of apostolic succession?"

"Exactly so, sir," Ford smiled. "Everybody else—over three hundred of them—have reasonable alibis. As far as I know, the Canderblanks and the Greens had no motive, so it's very likely that they weren't involved. However, based on the discovery I made this afternoon, I'll have to add Trumpington's father to the list."

Brownlee's eyes came wide open. "Indeed?"

"Yes, sir—although I have no knowledge of the father's movements and no evidence to suggest he was even at the School."

"So, the poor young chap Connelly could have killed Callaway in a fit of hatred or fear, and *either* of the Trumpingtons—father *or* son—could have killed Callaway to stop his blackmail. Is that correct?"

"Yes, precisely, sir."

Brownlee chuckled. "You know, Ford, as an aside, if Callaway fell by accident, and the fall killed him, and then after that, the stabber stabbed a dead body, I wonder if that's murder, or even attempted murder?"

Ford laughed.

"You'll have to ask the Crown Prosecutor, sir."

"I will. I tend to be confused by the finer points of *mens rea* and *actus reus*. Now, what about Trumpington's death, Ford? And what makes you consider the senior Trumpington as a possible suspect?"

"Trumpington fell to his own death on Thursday evening, sir—two days ago. He might have fallen by accident, he might have committed suicide, or he might have been the victim of another murderous attack. In any event, a note was found in his room which indicated that Callaway had been blackmailing him, and this afternoon I discovered evidence of the basis for the extortion."

From his inside vest pocket, he produced the letter he had found in Callaway's secret cache.

"It's in this letter, sir, which Callaway had hidden in his room at home in Camden. Trumpington's father, General Sir John Trumpington, habitually signed himself as *P*."

Brownlee read the brief letter slowly and carefully.

"*Oh!* Oh dear *me!* How did Callaway get a hold of *this?*"

"I've no idea, sir," Ford said, shrugging. "However, according to his pal White, Callaway was not adverse to a spot of breaking and entering, and he may have come across it in the course of burglarizing Trumpington's room. But regardless of how he acquired it, Callaway must have told Trumpington he had it."

"Very likely."

"You may recall that I interviewed Trumpington shortly before his death, and it was clear that he knew more about Callaway's murder than he was admitting at the time. It's possible, as the Master has claimed, that he expected I would accuse him of Callaway's murder, and that that is what drove him to his death."

"It's easy to imagine that the two deaths are tied together," said Brownlee, nodding. "It would be easy to imagine that Trumpington killed Callaway and then committed suicide in a fit of remorse ... Or fear of exposure ... Perhaps it's true, or perhaps someone else is trying to present us with a neat solution ..."

He chuckled again.

"I've never been much of a one for neatness," he added, glancing round the ample evidence in his own kitchen. "So, where do you go from here, Ford?"

"Well, sir, I have the following bits and pieces. First, I would prefer to rule out the other six suspects in Callaway's case, just for the sake of completeness. That means I have to be sure they had no motive."

"Makes sense," Brownlee muttered.

"Second, I'd like to understand more about Callaway, because there are some very strange things about the whole affair. For example, there's this whole conundrum about his mother; perhaps it's just delusional, but it's very odd. Then there's the fact that the Callaways haven't sent a telegraph to the School, or to the Markhams since learning of their son's death. That's simply not natural."

"You've lost me, old chap. Sigmund Freud was never my strong point—or Oedipus, for that matter. Is this about the letter he started to his mother before he died?"

"Yes, sir—sorry for the confusion."

Ford explained Callaway's literary efforts and Doctor Waggoner's interpretation of them, and the conclusions he had drawn.

"Last but not least, sir, why would he hide a book about military life in India? It makes no sense at all. Am I being ridiculous?"

Brownlee thought for a moment.

"No, I don't think you are," he replied. "There may be some perfectly reasonable explanation, but, on the other hand, someone thought that it was worth it to murder the boy. It short, it's a rum do, and you don't ignore rum do's in cases of homicide."

"Thank you! It's been nagging at me, sir."

"I propose we contact the police in India through the Colonial Office, and see what the Callaways have to say."

"Exactly, sir. I was going to request it."

"Good. I'll take care of it."

"While we're testing the limits of my sanity, sir, there's a third area of concern. Doctor Thornby and Lady Canderblank have been doing their best to hush up the whole affair. Lady Canderblank made sure there was no physical evidence following Callaway's death, and cowed Doctor Pondsford into writing a fraudulent death certificate. Doctor Thornby removed evidence of Callaway's blackmailing activities."

"Hmm," Brownlee grunted, his eyes closed once more.

"They've both been unnaturally antagonistic, and they've both been pestering Colonel Dagenham to close the case. Miss Canderblank has been inexplicably friendly, in direct contrast to her mother's hostility. Concern for the School's reputation is a reasonable motivation, but not to the point of outright obstruction, it seems to me. Oh, I should mention that Lady Canderblank complained about my questions and asked for your name, sir."

Brownlee opened his eyes.

"Lord Canderblank has political ambitions, as you may know, Ford. In my experience, there is no more dangerous beast in the jungle than an ambitious politician ... or an ambitious father, I'm sad to say, judging from this letter from the senior Trumpington ... Speaking of letters, in fact, her ladyship honored me with a note that arrived at Scotland Yard by messenger this morning, and was sent over to me at teatime this afternoon. You may find it amusing."

Brownlee found the letter beneath a pile of discarded fish and chip wrappings and handed it to Ford. It had been penned by the Canderblank's saturnine secretary.

Canderblank Hall
Glos.
June 8, 1920

Colonel Percival Dagenham, CB,
Dagenham House, Old Trundleford, Birdslip, Glos.

Detective Superintendent George Brownlee, CID,
c/o New Scotland Yard, Westminster.

Gentlemen:

Her Ladyship has instructed me to bring to your prompt attention the imprudent and inappropriate actions of your subordinate, Inspector Ford. By her instruction, you are hereby requested and required to remove the said officer from his present duties forthwith, and to replace him with another officer with a better appreciation for proper police conduct.

I am further instructed to advise you that any delay in your actions will result in a Question being asked in the House of Commons.

Very Truly Yrs.,
H K W Shipman, Esq.,
Secretary to Lord and Lady Canderblank.

"Do you want to stay on this case, old chap? Here's your chance to jump off the merry-go-round."

"I want to jump off, sir, God knows, but I can't," Ford replied with a shake of his head. "However, I certainly don't wish to cause any problems for you or Colonel Dagenham."

"I telephoned Dagenham after receiving this. He and I are in complete accord. I wrote out a response with his concurrence. Here it is. I'll send it off unless you don't want me to."

Metropolitan Police
Criminal Investigation Division
New Scotland Yard
Westminster

June 9, 1920

H K W Shipman, Esq
Secretary to Lord and Lady Canderblank
Canderblank Hall
Glos

Dear Mr. Shipman,

In re: Criminal investigation into the deaths of pupils at Kings School

I am in receipt of your letter of June 8th in regard to the above captioned subject. Please advise her ladyship that Colonel Dagenham and I are entirely satisfied with the conduct of Detective Chief Inspector Ford in this matter.

However, in view of her ladyship's allegations of police misconduct, I have forwarded copies of your letter, together with copies of this reply, to the Home Secretary and the Solicitor General.

Yr. Obed. Svt.,

George Brownlee
Detective Superintendent

Carbon Copies:

Colonel P Dagenham, CB, Gloucestershire Constabulary

1.   Permanent Secretary, Home Office

2.   Permanent Secretary, Solicitor General's Office.

"Tempest in a teapot, old chap," said Brownlee soothingly when Ford had finished reading. "Besides," he added, glancing at the kitchen door to make sure his wife could not hear him, "if she wants to be a bloody bitch, she'll find I can be a bloody bastard!"

Ford absorbed this uncharacteristic outburst with admiration.

"Thank you, sir, for your support." He paused. "Getting back to the case, there's one more thing I don't understand. If Trumpington was intent on committing suicide, why did he leave that note from Callaway lying around to be found? Why leave evidence tying himself to Callaway and risk bringing his father into all of this?"

"On the face of it, old chap, I think we're looking at two murders. Even if you decide you've solved one—Trumpington killing Callaway—we've still got another murderer on the loose."

# Sunday

G od rested on the seventh day, but God had no murders to solve. Ford
made himself a breakfast of tea and burned toast in his cheerless
kitchen, imagining the feast to which Croft was probably sitting
down—that is, if Croft had returned from his morning's mission.

Ford telephoned to the Canderblanks' London residence in Mayfair,
but was told that His lordship had returned to the country. A similar call
to the Trumpington residence informed him that Sir John was at Kings.

He then telephoned the Stroud police station to alert his driver. By now
he had memorized the relevant parts of the Great Western Railway schedule, and he dragged his aching leg to Paddington with ten minutes to spare
before his train departed.

In Lower Tuckscomb, the Kings Arms was crowded with cricketers pre-
paring for a Sunday match with a neighboring village. Ford waited until
the crowd had sorted itself out into players and spectators and had straggled across the road to the village green. It disposed itself on blankets and
deck chairs in easy reach of the tea urn that Mrs. Green had set up on the
grass, and play began.

Ford found Croft near the urn and helped himself to Mrs. Green's hospitality. He lingered a moment, enjoying the idyllic scene, and putting off
his moment of confrontation with Green. The visiting team had a fast
bowler with an improbably long run and a delivery which reached the
batsman at head height. The opening ball flashed past the batsman's left
ear, eluded the wicketkeeper, and kept going until it splashed into the
Coln. Apparently this was a common occurrence, for several small boys
were waiting without shoes and socks to wade in and retrieve it.

"Well, Croft, no peace for the wicked," Ford said, and they turned to
enter the Kings Arms. Mr. Green was resting momentarily from his labors
in the empty public bar.

"I'm sorry to bother you when you've got a crowd," Ford said, "but I've been waiting for a chance to speak to you."

Green acknowledged the inevitability of a police interview with a surly grunt.

"Them deaths up at the School? Well, you'd better make it snappy before I have to start on the lunches."

"I understand you were at the School last Saturday evening until about ten thirty, and then came home, Mr. Green? I just want to verify that for myself," Ford said.

"I already told Bob Croft that, and I also told him I don't know nothing."

He looked accusingly at the sergeant, as if Croft must have made a false report.

"Lucy was also at the School," Ford continued. "Why didn't you wait for her?"

"I looked into the kitchen at the Lodge, and she was still busy with the company. So I just came home."

"So, you left about ten thirty and got home a little after eleven?"

"If you say so," Green said sullenly.

"The question is, do *you* say so, Mr. Green?"

"Yes, I do."

"In your horse and cart, Mr. Green?"

"Of course."

"My problem is that nobody has reported seeing you, Mr. Green," Ford told him. "The School was still crowded at that time, and there was traffic on the road. No one has reported seeing a horse and cart. The charabanc driver, for example, is very certain, because it would have been difficult to overtake you on the hill. He left the School a little after ten thirty and arrived here ten minutes later to drop off the guests staying here."

"He must be wrong."

"I don't think so. He had to note the exact times he was waiting and when he left so the company could pay him. He wrote those times down in his book."

"Well, I came the back way," Green responded defiantly.

"You went three miles out of your way in the middle of the night, Mr. Green?"

"You can't prove I didn't," Green answered in the same tone as before.

"That's true," Ford said quietly. "You could have left the School by the lane behind the rugby fields, picked the lock on the back gate, driven out of it, and put the lock back on again—all without old Thompson, who lives in the cottage by the gate, hearing you; and, more to the point, without his dogs hearing you. Old Thompson told Croft he's absolutely certain that no one left by that route, so we'll have to see if we believe Thomson or if we believe that you took a wildly circuitous route."

Green looked mulish.

"Wouldn't it be easier to say that you left much later, Mr. Green?" Ford appealed to him.

"I don't know nothing, I tell you!"

Green's surliness was changing into truculence. Trumpington was the last witness to whom Ford had given a little time to reflect upon the absurdity of his testimony, and Trumpington had shown up dead within a few hours. It was not a mistake that Ford intended to repeat.

"Are you sticking to that story, Mr. Green?"

"It's the truth, and you can't prove otherwise. I know my rights."

"Very well, Mr. Green, I'll have to ask you to accompany Sergeant Croft to the Stroud Police Station for further questioning."

"In the middle of a cricket match? I've work to do!"

"Do you wish to change your statement? Do you want to stick to your version against the sworn testimony of Thompson and the omnibus driver?"

"Come on, George, don't be an idiot," said Croft. "Why waste my time and yours? What's the point if you've nothing to hide?"

Green considered his options.

"Well, maybe I am a little hazy on the times. Maybe I left a little later."

"Perhaps you left at eleven," Ford suggested. "That was when the Great Lawn was deserted and the main gate was still open and unguarded. According to all the witnesses, it's the only time you could have driven off without someone seeing you."

"Perhaps."

"Come on, George, for Christ's sake!" Croft said impatiently. "Did you leave the School at eleven bleeding o'clock, or did you not?"

"What's it to you, Bob? Who cares if I left sooner or later?"

"It seems you care, Mr. Green," said Ford. "You care enough to make up a story about riding round the back way in the middle of the night. You care because, if you left earlier, Callaway was still alive, and if you left later you were still at the School when he died, and well you know it!"

"You're wasting your time, sir," Croft said to Ford. "Let me take him down to Stroud so he can think about it in a cell."

"All right, all right, for God's sake!" Green finally conceded. "I left later, like you said. Now, get off my back and let me get on with my work!"

This admission was greeted by a round of applause from the spectators outside, as if they were somehow eavesdropping on the interview and were applauding Green's change of heart.

"What did you do between ten thirty and eleven, Mr. Green?" Ford asked.

"I just hung around and waited for Lucy," Green said sullenly.

"Outside the Master's Lodge?"

"Yes, that's where she was. I waited by the tradesmen's entrance round the back."

"Did you go anywhere else? Did you see anybody?"

"No, I just waited, that's all."

"You waited in the dark from ten fifteen until eleven, when Lucy came out and you gave her a ride?"

"Yes—what's wrong with that?"

"Nothing, if it's the truth, Mr. Green. You're sure you didn't see any-one? Not a single soul? There were still people about."

"Well, nobody special," Green replied ungraciously. "I suppose I saw the maid come out and put rubbish in the dust bins, things of that nature, and one of the guests, but no one who shouldn't have been there."

"Which one of the guests?"

"It was a woman. I couldn't see more in the dark."

"Was she leaving the house or entering it?"

"Going in; she went in through the French doors on the terrace. That's how I knew it wasn't the help."

He snorted in amusement, his ill temper momentarily set aside.

"It's funny, but when she opened the door to go in, I could hear that old bag Lady Canderblank yelling fit to bust."

"And then Lucy came out, Mr. Green?"

"Yes, and I gave her a ride. *Look,* what's wrong with giving my own daughter a ride home? I didn't see that boy Callaway. I wouldn't even have recognized him. I didn't see *any* boys. I just waited and gave Lucy a ride."

His truculence had returned.

"What's wrong with that?" he repeated.

"When you got home, Lucy wasn't with you—that's what's wrong with it, Mr. Green."

He glanced away sheepishly.

"Well, we had a falling out on the way."

"What about?"

"It's none of your damned business! It's a family matter."

Green would offer nothing more, and Ford had to remind himself that innocent witnesses usually offer nothing in such circumstances because they have nothing relevant to hide.

There was a sudden influx of thirsty cricketers, and Green escaped to serve them.

Ford sighed.

"Go and find Lucy, please Sergeant; we might as well get all the unpleasantness over with. We'd better interview her in my room—there's no privacy here. Did the policewoman come from Gloucester?"

"Yes, sir, she did; she's waiting by the car. They sent Sergeant Jackson, sir, she who's Sar'nt Major Jim Jackson's daughter. She's very good at her job, sir, but she's a bit pushy, if you know what I mean."

"Thanks for the warning. Send her up to my room, and then bring up Lucy, if you please."

◆    ◆    ◆

Sergeant Dorothy Jackson was a woman before whom even the bravest Amazon would quail. She was not particularly large, but she seemed overpowering, just as a short Sergeant Major can overpower a parade ground full of soldiers twice his size. She did not so much enter a room as occupy it. Yet her voice, when she spoke to Ford, was quiet and respectful.

"Perhaps, if I may suggest it, sir, a woman's touch? No offense, sir, but sometimes it's more direct, if you see what I mean? A woman can't lie to another woman the way she can to a man."

Ford remembered her father clearly, a rock of dependability and competence amid the squalor and insanity of the trenches, and he thought he recognized echoes of his features in her level gray eyes and square, no-nonsense jaw line.

"I don't mind at all if we get the truth out of her without wasting a lot of time, Sergeant. It's a question of whether she spoke to the boy Callaway on Saturday night a week ago, and if so, what happened."

"Thank you, sir. I'll do my best."

Lucy Green entered the room with Croft and flounced to the chair they had arranged for her. She sat down with what she obviously hoped was casual disregard. She was heavily made up and dressed in a manner she probably thought was provocative. Ford reflected that she might have been pretty, except for the makeup and affectation; instead, she had managed to make herself look cheap.

Ford nodded to the policewoman, who advanced until she seemed to tower over the witness. Out of the corner of his eye Ford saw Croft registering apprehension.

"Now, Lucy Green," said Sergeant Jackson, in a penetrating voice, "who put a bun in *your* little oven, then? First time unlucky, was it?"

Lucy Green's eyes widened in shock and narrowed again in anger. Her chin came up, and a look of mulish obstinacy appeared on her face.

Ford, as shocked as Lucy, considered intervening, but the sergeant was as unstoppable as a traction engine with a full head of steam.

"Come on, girl, you're not the Virgin Mary, and whoever knocked you up, it wasn't the Archangel Gabriel. We'll get the truth out of you sooner or later, so you might as well tell the Chief Inspector who's been in your knickers before you get yourself in more trouble than you're already in."

Lucy's expression changed to consternation. She stared up at the muscular policewoman and searched for a sign of sympathy or human kindness, but there appeared to be none.

"Do you want your baby born in a woman's prison?" Sergeant Jackson continued inexorably. "Is he worth protecting, whoever did the dirty?"

Lucy broke. She must have known, just as Ford and Croft knew, that her willpower was simply not strong enough to resist the sergeant's relentless force of personality. It was only a matter of time.

Lucy chose a tone of self-righteous indignation.

"It was him what was murdered. He sort of made me. But I didn't do it, I swear!"

"Didn't do what? Give him a quickie or kill him?"

"Kill him, of course."

"Did you see him on that Saturday night?"

"I needed money for that woman in Gloucester—you know what I mean. My friend told me about her. I needed five quid. He said he didn't have any money. He laughed and said I was on my own."

"Where did you see him? In the bushes or in his room?"

"In the bushes? Why in the bushes? In his room, of course. He wasn't there at first, and so I waited and he came back."

"What happened? The truth, now, or you'll be sorry."

"Nothing happened—I swear on the Bible. I asked him for the money, just like I said, and then he just laughed and threw me out like a bit of old rubbish. Then I saw Dad and came home with him. I was upset, like."

Her voice became shrill with self-pity.

"Dad made me tell him what had happened. He was so angry, he threw me off the cart, and I had to walk home. That's the truth, cross my heart and hope to die."

"You can go to jail for lying to a police officer, Lucy," the inexorable Sergeant Jackson told her. "And there's women in there you wouldn't want to be left alone with, a pretty little thing like you. But that's where you'll be, my girl, if you're lying, with nobody to lift a finger to help you!"

"It's the truth! It's the *truth*!"

"Six months from now you'll be behind bars with a bunch of hard cases, and I'll be down the boozer enjoying myself, and I won't even remember your name. Now, what else happened?"

"Nothing! I swear to God." Tears begin to flow as if a faucet had been turned on.

Ford could stand it no more.

"All right, thank you, Sergeant."

He took her place, finding a handkerchief for Lucy.

"You were waiting on the company at the Master's Lodge? Tell me what happened. Take your time."

Lucy explained between shuddering sobs that she had helped serve the refreshments until the company broke up. Lord and Lady Canderblank went out, Doctor Thornby went to his study, and Mrs. Thornby fussed over Lucy and the Thornby's maid until the room had been cleared and tidied to her satisfaction.

At the last moment, Mrs. Thornby had sent her upstairs to fetch a vase from the landing so that the flowers could be changed. As she was doing this, Lady Canderblank had returned and told her to run her a bath immediately. Lucy had told Lady Canderblank she was not part of the domestic staff, but that sent Lady Canderblank into a rage.

"The old cow was in a right royal state, ranting and raving. I kept saying it wasn't my job, but she wouldn't hear it."

"How did she look?"

"She looked a bloody mess," Lucy said maliciously. "Like she'd been dragged through a briar patch backwards. She said she'd slipped over and tore her dress. That's why she needed a bath. If she'd been nicer, I might have helped, but not with her in that bitchy mood."

"What time was this?"

"It was a quarter to eleven, because as I was going down the stairs, the grandfather clock started chiming, and I jumped out of my skin and almost dropped the vase."

"Then what did you do?"

"I sent Ethel—that's the maid—upstairs to help Lady Canderblank, God help her, and then I went out and went to *his* room."

"Did you see anyone on the way?"

"No. The door wasn't locked, so I waited, and then he come back, like I said, and he threw me out. I'm glad he's dead, but I never touched him, I swear. Then I saw Dad, and we went home in the cart, and Dad made me tell him I'm in the family way, and needed a you-know-what, and he got so pissed off, he made me get off."

Lucy's voice was full of resentment.

"First that bitch yells at me, then *he* throws me out, and then Dad yells at me and throws me off the cart. It's not fair; it's just not bloody well fair at all!"

Self-pity took over and she was engulfed in a fresh wave of tears.

"Now he's dead, and Dad refuses to help. Who's going to look after me?"

This time the tears had set in for good, and there was no point in trying to continue.

Ford stood back and Sergeant Jackson gently helped Lucy to her feet. Ford realized her bullying interrogation had been an act.

"There now, Lucy my girl, no more questions. You'll feel better if you wash your face in cold water. I always do, after a good cry. Come on, show me the way."

Lucy led her off obediently. At the door Sergeant Jackson turned back to Ford.

"There're occasions when you have to be cruel to be kind, sir. It's like a dentist pulling a tooth—you just get it over with. This way it's out in the open, and she can concentrate on getting her life back together. There's a home for girls in trouble in Gloucester; I'll speak to them about her."

She disappeared through the door.

"Holy mackerel, Croft!" Ford gasped. "I've never seen anything like it. I wouldn't last two minutes with her."

"I was trying to warn you, sir," said Croft. "She puts Lady Canderblank in the shade, and that's the truth, when she's in that mood. The funny thing is, sir, she's a big softy, not that you'd believe me. The missus is a great pal of hers, like she was our niece or something, and my missus wouldn't give her the time of day if she wasn't decent."

Ford didn't know whether to think about the policewoman's remarkable interviewing technique or Lucy's revelations.

"Oh, I believe you," he laughed. "Let's get a breath of fresh air, Sergeant, and make notes before we forget the details."

◆    ◆    ◆

The cricket match was proceeding at a leisurely pace, as befitted country cricket on a sunny Sunday, and Ford and Croft paused for a moment. The fiery fast bowler had been replaced by a short, fat, leg spin bowler with a wristy action.

"That's Dave Thompson," the Sergeant commented. "When he's having a good day, he's a killer. I still play for the village, time permitting—wicket keeper."

The batsman drove the next ball to the long off boundary.

"Of course, sir," he added with a glance at Ford, "Dave's not in *your* league."

He clearly wanted to ask Ford about his own cricket, but was held back by politeness. Ford relented.

"I might have been good enough to play for the county, Sergeant, but I couldn't afford to be a gentleman. Players earn next to nothing, and when you're too old, you have no way of earning an income. So I faced the economic realities and gave it up."

Ford didn't have to explain to Croft that England's social class system had engulfed the game of cricket. *Gentlemen* were amateurs, and *players* were professionals. The gentlemen were cloaked in nobility of spirit, playing for the love of the game, while the players were a lesser breed, almost on the borders of venality. Had most of the gentlemen not had private incomes and sales jobs provided by firms that wished to take advantage of their fame, the image of amateur nobility might have reflected reality.

"Then I got my leg banged up in the war, and that was that," Ford concluded.

It wasn't entirely true, Ford thought, but it wasn't entirely false, either. It was more a question of—well, enough of that; the Greens' testimony had to be sifted through.

"Let's get back to Green," Ford said. "The long and the short of his statement is that he was alone and unaccounted for from ten thirty until eleven. His only lie, once he had stopped lying, as it were, was that he had waited until his daughter came out of the Lodge, and then he picked her up. But in fact, she'd gone to Callaway's room, and he followed her and picked her up from there. So he was lying to protect her."

"That's what I thought, sir, assuming she was telling the truth."

At that moment, Sergeant Jackson joined them. She had discarded her aura of severity, and grinned infectiously. Ford found himself smiling back.

"Lucy's in her room sobbing her heart out," she told them. "I left her to cry it out. The sooner she gets away from here and faces her responsibilities, the better off she'll be."

There was a sharp crack of bat on ball from the cricket pitch, and a well-struck cover drive flew toward them. Sergeant Jackson caught it expertly and tossed it back effortlessly to the nearest fielder, who was at least one hundred feet away.

"We could use you on the village team, Dotty," said Croft admiringly.

"But I'm only a little girl, Uncle Bob," she said mockingly. "I'm not strong enough to play. I might burst into tears if I got hit by the nasty hard ball."

The men chuckled and she grinned.

"Talking of tears," said Ford, turning the conversation back to the case, "do you think Lucy Green was telling the truth, Sergeant Jackson?"

"It had the ring of truth about it, sir. She admitted being in the boy's room. She could have pushed him out."

"Connelly saw a female figure coming down the stairs as he was going up," Ford pondered. "He didn't pay close attention, and he assumed it was one of the boys dressed up as a girl for the *Pirates of Penanze*. It could have been Lucy."

"That's true, sir," said Croft. "The timing just about fits. She was in the Lodge until a quarter of eleven, and then she went straight to Trafalgar, went up to his room, pushed him out, came down, passing Connelly, got the knife, stabbed the body, and was still in time to join her father and leave by eleven."

"Suppose she didn't kill him?" Sergeant Jackson asked. "I'm not sure she's sharp enough to do all that in five minutes. Her father could have followed her up and killed him after she left. She might have started walking to the gates, and he could have caught her up."

Ford groaned. "That's very true ... Well, either way, we have two clear suspects. Both Greens have a motive, in Lucy's case because Callaway was abandoning her, and in Green's case the motive was simple fury at the boy for having his way with her. Both Greens lack an alibi for the vital ten or fifteen minutes. So, now we have four suspects with motives—the Greens because of the baby, Trumpington because of the blackmail, and Connelly out of fear."

"Shall we take the Greens in, sir?"

"No, I don't think so, Croft. At this stage we can't tell which suspect is the most likely."

He scratched his head in frustration.

"Besides, I still don't think we know enough about either Callaway's killing, or Trumpington's, to be certain. I mean, it's plausible to suppose that either of the Greens decided that they might have been spotted by Trumpington, and waited a few days for the right moment to kill him—and the same goes for Connelly."

He shook his head.

"It's all still very confusing," he said. "I feel we're somehow missing the point. For example, there's Lucy's fascinating evidence that Lady Canderblank was dirty and disheveled, and that Green saw a woman entering the Master's Lodge. There are still plenty of loose ends, I'm afraid."

He stood gazing into the bickering Coln, until Croft's stomach rumbled and compelled him interrupt Ford's reverie.

"What's next, sir?" Croft asked. "I did alert the missus that we might have guests for Sunday lunch, if roast beef and a spot of Yorkshire pudding is to your liking?"

"That sounds wonderful, Sergeant," discovering that he was starving. "On the way, you can bring me up to date on what we know about the Trumpington case. What have you been able to establish so far?"

As they strolled back along the banks of the Coln River, Croft extracted his battered notebook from his tunic.

"Well, sir, unlike the Callaway case, there weren't a lot of people gadding about, sir. I took the same approach as last time, sir, and this is who's unaccounted for. Incidentally, I took the liberty of getting Sergeant Jackson's help, sir."

He consulted the notebook.

"First off, there's Miss Larue and Mr. Bottomly, sir, and old Mr. Jaspers. The three of them seem to have schedules like clockwork, sir, walking the dog and so forth, and as luck would have it, Mr. Robinson was on duty again. It's Sergeant Jackson's opinion that Miss Larue has developed a strong interest in Gymnastics, and Mr. Bottomly in French, if you take my meaning, and it's dark and deserted around the back of the gym."

"Goodness me, on the School grounds! The powers that be would have a fit!"

"More than likely, sir," Croft grinned.

His face darkened as he looked at the next name on his list.

"Young Connelly is a question mark again, I'm afraid, because Mr. McIntire caught him out of bed. He told Mr. McIntire he'd decided to make a bunk for home, but changed his mind when it started raining. Mr. McIntire had caught him climbing in through the kitchen window at about eleven thirty, sir, so he's unaccounted for. In addition, there's two or three witnesses say he had an argument with Trumpington about nine o'clock that evening."

"Do we know why?"

A smattering of applause rose from the direction of the Kings Arms. It was really far too nice a day to be discussing a death that had occurred on a rainy evening, Ford thought. He watched the white-garbed cricketers for a moment, wondering, as he sometimes did, whether he should have taken his chances and played for the county, instead of joining the police force.

Croft's voice brought him back to reality.

"Connelly says it was because Trumpington was going to cane him, sir, for being late for band practice, or some such. Connelly said that wasn't fair. Trumpington said that anyone associated with Callaway probably deserved twelve of the best—just on principle."

"Why didn't Connelly go to Mr. McIntire, if he was being treated unfairly?"

"I asked him that, sir," Sergeant Jackson said. "Apparently Trumpington told Connelly that if he did, he'd make his life a living hell, sir."

"God, I hope Connelly's not our villain," Ford groaned. "I hope it's all bad luck."

"Me, too," Sergeant Jackson said. "It's outrageous how he's been treated, poor little tyke."

"I know," Ford replied. "However, he certainly seems to have a knack for getting himself into impossible positions. I keep hoping we can take him off the suspect list, but he just keeps jumping back onto it again. Who else is unaccounted for?"

"Lucy Green also went out for a walk that evening after closing time, so she left the Kings Arms at ten, and she could have been up at the School by ten thirty."

Ford shook his head.

"We have absolutely nothing to connect her to Trumpington. We don't even know if they ever met each other. I'm sure that either Trumpington died by his own hand out of remorse for killing Callaway, or Callaway's killer killed him because he knew too much. He sees me, he sees the Master, he sees Connelly, and then he falls to his death. It's got to be because of that chain of events …"

Ford clutched his forehead with his hand and laughed. "My head's beginning to spin … Trumpington becoming convinced that he was going to be exposed, or someone becoming convinced that Trumpington was going to expose *him* … or even *her*. Connelly could be lying about his talk with Trumpington, for example. He could have told Trumpington he knew about the blackmail and intended to keep up where Callaway left off. Trumpington had a five pound note on him, let us not forget. Anyone else on your list?"

"Well, sir, Miss Canderblank visited the Master's Lodge to drop off a library book a little after ten, so she was in the general vicinity."

"It really is *deja vu*! Trumpington's suspect list is almost the same as Callaway's."

They reached the end of the green and crossed the road to Croft's radiant cottage garden.

"What do we know about each one's movements?"

"Trumpington was last seen alive by Mr. Bottomly at ten thirty, just when he was starting his run," Sergeant Jackson replied. "Trumpington was walking in the direction of the gym. Let's say that Mr. Bottomly sneaked around to the back of the gym to meet Miss Larue. Mr. Jaspers left his house and walked round the Great Lawn. It takes him fifteen minutes, sir, and he didn't see anyone."

"He might not have seen anyone entering the gym when he was at the far end of the Great Lawn by the Gatehouse."

"True, sir, but he says—and I've got other witnesses who agree—that his dog has a nervous disposition and reacts to anyone it sees, even at that sort of distance."

Delicious aromas of Sunday lunch emanated from Croft's front door.

"Let's try to finish up so we don't spoil lunch," Ford suggested. "As I understand it, we've got Mr. Bottomly and Miss Larue inadvertently guarding the back of the Gymnasium, and Mr. Jaspers and his faithful hound doing the same in front. The only unguarded door was the staff door. That would mean that Trumpington's killer was already in the gym, or had a key to the staff door, because otherwise, he would have been seen entering. And *that* means that Trumpington was there to keep an appointment. Unfortunately, there's no neat little entry in Trumpington's note book recording *'Meet X at 10.30 on roof of gym.'*"

"Yes, sir," said Croft, "And we have Lucy Green and Connelly unaccounted for. Miss Canderblank left the Lodge to return home at half past ten, according to Mrs. Thornby, but she could have left the grounds and sneaked back in, and, to tell you the truth, sir, I haven't attempted to interview her, sir. I don't exactly relish going to Canderblank Hall, sir."

"That's very understandable, Sergeant. I'll do that this afternoon, after I've been up to the School."

If Victoria was there, he thought, then he would relish the visit very much. If, on the other hand, her mother was there …

"Then you'll need a good lunch to fortify you, sir," Croft said, as if reading his second thought.

Lunch—grilled brook trout caught by Croft the previous day and kept on ice in the stone lockup; rare roast beef with Yorkshire pudding, roast potatoes and cauliflower; and apple pie and cream, fresh baked and hot out of the oven—left Ford longing for a good afternoon nap in Croft's battered leather armchair, rather than a trip up the hill to Kings. But up the hill he went, with only his driver for company, leaving the Croft to claim his armchair and Sergeant Jackson to look in on Lucy at the Kings Arms before returning to Gloucester.

◆     ◆     ◆

Ford's usual depression at entering the School was made worse by the prospect of interviewing General Trumpington. What on earth could he say to a man would had conspired with his son to cheat, leading to a chain reaction of blackmail, murder and suicide? *Let this be a lesson to you?*

And there were other questions. Why hadn't the Callaways sent a telegraph from India to Thornby or the Markhams? Who was *"Oh, it's you?"* Lucy? Trumpington? Who did Green see entering the Lodge—if he wasn't lying? Why had Doctor Thornby rushed to Trumpington's room? Why had Trumpington left that incriminating note waiting to be found? Who had he agreed to meet in the Gymnasium attic? Why would the arrogant Trumpington agree to meet *anyone* in the attic instead of his room? Why the hell did Callaway hide that innocuous book about the Army in India?

"We're here, sir," said the driver, interrupting his thoughts, as they rattled beneath the massive stone pillars of the Gatehouse.

"What? Oh, sorry. I was miles away. Take me to the Master's Lodge, please, Constable."

Sir John Trumpington was not at the Lodge. Mrs. Thornby informed Ford that he and her husband had left an hour before for Canderblank Hall.

"Perhaps I'll be able to catch him there," Ford said. "Mrs. Thornby, if I may, do you recall just what each of your guests did after the *Pirates of Penzance*? They all came back here for refreshments, and then everyone turned in, I believe?"

"I'd prefer to wait until my husband returns before answering any questions, Ford," she responded, unconsciously duplicating Mrs. Markham's reply in similar circumstances. "Besides, the Sergeant took our statements."

Ford realized he had never considered Mrs. Thornby as an independent person, but merely as an extension of the Master. And yet she stood before him in a floral summer dress, regarding him calmly, sure of her footing in her own home.

"I have no doubt that the statements were full and complete, ma'am. But, as I'm sure you'll appreciate, Trumpington's tragic death has caused us to revisit our earlier information. I'm trying to corroborate a statement we've just taken from Lucy Green. I doubt the Master gets involved in the minutiae of domestic arrangements?"

Mrs. Thornby hesitated, then seemed to reconsider. "You'd better come in for a moment," she said reluctantly, and led him into the sitting room.

The room had that special kind of neatness and order that betrayed a constant stream of visitors. Mrs. Thornby had been unable to give it personality, and it reminded Ford of a doctor's waiting room.

Mrs. Thornby raised her eyebrows.

"Yes, Ford?"

"Let's see—the Canderblanks went out for a walk, and your husband went to his study," Ford recounted. "The others went to bed. You took the opportunity to get Ethel and Lucy to clean up after the party. Lord and Lady Canderblank came back, and Lady Canderblank had an altercation with Lucy, I believe. Were you aware of it at the time?"

"I was not; I went down to the basement with Ethel and heard about the argument afterwards. That stupid girl Lucy must have mishandled the situation, although I must admit that Lady Canderblank can be difficult at times. She had slipped and fallen, I believe, and needed a bath. Unfortunately, the wretched boiler decided to break that very day, and there was no hot water."

"Lady Canderblank came in by the veranda doors?"

"Of course not! Why would she do a thing like that? She came in by the front door."

"Did you happen to notice if she returned with his lordship, ma'am, or did she come back later?"

"He returned before her, as I recall, but I really do not see why you are so concerned with the comings and goings of my guests." She had begun to sound like her husband. "Surely, poor Trumpington's death has tragically laid this matter to rest? I hope you're not going to pick at a scab before it has time to heal?"

"I hope so, too, ma'am, and I'm sorry to bother you with these old details. And so, of course, you didn't leave the house yourself?"

"As I have previously reported, the stupid boiler had broken. I was downstairs in the basement with Ethel in a vain attempt to mend the water heater. Lady Canderblank came down into the basement with us, and she was not pleased, to put it mildly. The Wimbletons tried to help ... Even the Bishop, up in his room, was disturbed and descended in his dressing gown. There was water all over the floor. Lord Canderblank complained that it had soaked his slippers ... Victoria was woken up and arrived, thank God; she finally calmed her mother down. It was extremely embarrassing."

The memory of her domestic disaster made her blush with shame.

"I was subsequently informed by the repairman that it was—I believe I have the correct terminology—a ruptured gasket."

"Ah," Ford said, as if he knew all about ruptured gaskets. "I thank you for your time, Mrs. Thornby, and I'm sure you won't be bothered again, at least in this matter. Please tell the Master that I had hoped to see him to sign his statement with regard to Trumpington. In the meantime, perhaps

I'll catch him at Canderblank Hall and save you the inconvenience of another visit to the Lodge. Thank you, ma'am."

She did not move as he departed.

Ford left the house and walked round to the rear. There were tire tracks aplenty in the gravel driveway that ran beside the house, and nothing to suggest that Green had waited—or not waited—there in the dark. He looked back at the house. Beside the back door stood a row of dustbins discreetly positioned behind a row of azaleas, and farther along the rear wall was a pair of French doors opening to a paved veranda that was surrounded with rose bushes. An extensive trellis stood at the end of the house, thick with ancient ivy.

If Green had waited here, he would have seen Ethel running in and out with the refuse of the meal, and he could well have seen someone entering the French doors. It would have been too dark to identify the person, but the light through the doors would have been sufficient to see whether it was a man or a woman.

When Ford returned to his car, he found Mr. Jaspers waiting patiently while his dog inspected one of its rear tires with close attention.

"This is all very, very sad, Ford," said Mr. Jaspers as Ford approached him. "The Master called me in to see Sir John this morning. Of course we did not mention Callaway's note. A general can vanquish an army, but be felled by a simple tragedy."

Mr. McIntire joined them. Both he and Jaspers had suffered the death of a member of his own House, and there seemed to be a bond between them.

Ford realized that he knew nothing of the relationships between the masters, some of whom had lived in Kings and worked together for twenty years or more. Perhaps Jaspers and McIntire had always been friends.

"I realize that you may not be able to tell us anything, Ford, but what is your assessment?"

At least these two masters recognized that Ford had a professional duty, however distasteful, and was not an inconvenient, meddling bureaucrat, as the rest of Kings seemed to consider him.

"Well, sir," Ford said, "Trumpington's fall certainly suggests an explanation for Callaway's death. In the circumstances, one might conclude there was no further need to investigate Callaway, and that Trumpington had a tragic accident."

Mr. Robinson, who had been on duty during both deaths, joined the group. On Sunday afternoons, many of the masters could be expected to be out for a stroll, and Ford wondered if the entire staff would soon be assembled. He could well imagine the intense curiosity and apprehension permeating the Senior Common Room.

"If that is your conclusion, Ford," said Mr. Jaspers, "the matter could be laid comfortably to rest and we could all focus our attentions on rescuing what is left of the summer term. The boys will soon put it to the back of their minds; there's Field Day coming up, and then the final examinations. Without offense, Ford, your presence keeps us all too conscious of these ugly tragedies."

"It's a bit too much like Richard II," said McIntire, and the group looked blank.

"Act 3," McIntire prompted. "It's a pun."

*"For God's sake let us sit upon the ground, and tell sad stories of the deaths of Kings'*—is that what you meant?" Ford asked.

"No wonder you won the Falmouth Prize, Ford!" Jaspers commented in admiration.

Ford glanced back at the Lodge and saw Mrs. Thornby peering through her lace curtains at the gathering outside. He had the bizarre notion that they might be guilty of some abstruse infraction of Kings etiquette.

Ford looked at his watch and saw that it was now three o'clock. Fearing he might miss Sir John yet again, he made his farewells and requested the driver to take him to Canderblank Hall. As they passed through the village, he could see that Croft had roused himself sufficiently to carry a deck chair to the green to watch the cricket match, and from that vantage point had relapsed into his postprandial slumbers.

◆    ◆    ◆

At Canderblank Hall, Ford received the same chilling reception as before. After waiting some thirty minutes, he was informed that Sir John Trumpington had returned to London in Lord Canderblank's company, that the Master had returned to the School, and that Lady Canderblank was not at home.

Mr. Shipman, the private secretary who delivered this message, had one other point that he wished to make.

"I am finding it hard to descend to some level of communication that is sufficiently basic that you can comprehend it, Officer. I will try once more. Rest assured that his lordship and her ladyship will *never* be at home when you call, and that the footmen have been given instructions that they are *not* to admit you through the front door again. Is there anything that I have just said that you do not understand?"

"Indeed, I understand you very fully, Mr. Shipman. I am *persona non grata.*"

"Ah, Officer, I am gratified that you finally appreciate the situation. I congratulate you! We seem to be communicating at last."

Ford paused to consider his options. His range of authority was very broad. He had, for example, the right to enter Canderblank Hall against the owner's consent; he could detain the self-congratulatory Mr. Shipman; he could telephone ahead and have the motorcar carrying Lord Canderblank and Sir John halted on the road to await his arrival.

He had, in short, an extensive number of ways in which he could wipe that smug smile from Mr. Shipman's face. But any such actions would have demeaned himself far more they would have demeaned the Canderblanks or their secretary.

"Good afternoon, sir," said Ford, and he returned to his car.

"I have to go back to London, Constable. I'd better go the station and try to get a connecting train."

"That's a bit dodgy on a Sunday, sir. Best go to Swindon or Oxford, sir. I'll be happy to drive you; to tell you the truth, I've never driven as far as Oxford."

"That's very good of you, Constable."

"Begging your pardon, sir, it's a fine afternoon, and perhaps I could take the top down?" He had brought, to Ford's secret delight, a pair of rakish goggles to accompany his gauntlets.

And so Ford leaned back against the leather upholstery of the plush seat in the sunshine, closed his eyes, and let himself be lulled by the breeze and warm sunshine.

Callaway had fathered Lucy's child, Ford thought, and refused to accept accountability. Perhaps, *"Oh, it's you"* was Trumpington, and, *"you-know-what"* was Lucy's condition ...

Green had watched an unidentified woman enter the Master's Lodge a little before eleven—if he could be trusted ... Who was she?

How did Trumpington manage to have five pounds if Callaway was bleeding him dry? Why had Callaway hidden that book? It might not be a bad idea to see the details of Green's police record, if any ... It was a wonder that that wild, fast bowler had not taken someone's head off ... Victoria Canderblank played an excellent all-round game of golf ... It was a great pity she hadn't been at Canderblank Hall ...

"Oxford Station, sir."

Ford jerked awake, lit a cigarette and passed it to the driver, lighting a second for himself.

"When you get back, would you ask Sergeant Croft to come up to London tomorrow? I'll meet him at the Yard at noon. Tell him to pack for an overnight stay, just to be on the safe side. Did you enjoy the drive?"

"We averaged twenty-one miles per hour, sir," the constable grinned. "Now I've got a record to beat."

# Monday

I t was past midnight when Ford wearily returned to his flat and found
that a letter had been tucked under his door.

Cassius:
I demand my rights as a citizen: you must interview me without further
delay. I shall appoint 7 p.m. on Monday and Luigi's in Wardour Street as
the appropriate time and place. You may indicate your availability either
by a puff of the appropriately colored smoke from your chimney, or by
leaving a message for me c/o my father at the United Services Club.
V.

This missive had been written on Saturday, and Ford wondered how
she had managed to discover his home address. However she had done so,
the letter had the beneficial effect of banishing the usual nightmares from
his dreams, and he awoke early and in an unusually optimistic mood that
even the prospect of interviewing Sir John Trumpington and Lord Canderblank could not dispel.

He dressed with unusual care and set off for Sir John's address in Mayfair, stopping at the United Services Club on his way to deliver his reply.

Ford found that Sir John Trumpington occupied the first three floors of
a narrow townhouse near Berkeley Square. The residence was a male bas-
tion that made Ford's tiny flat pale by comparison. While Ford's flat contained only the minimum amount of elderly furniture necessary to support
his existence, and the kitchen demonstrated his lack of interest in cooking,
General Trumpington lived in masculine opulence. There were deeply
cushioned leather armchairs at every turn and walls lined with hunting
trophies and military paraphernalia as far as the eye could see. Ford

glimpsed a billiard room through a half-open door as he was escorted into Sir John's presence.

When Ford saw him, Sir John was standing before the fireplace of his study, rigidly straight-backed, with a short military haircut and a severely clipped moustache. He was dressed in a morning suit as if he had an appointment in Whitehall or at the House of Commons. A black crepe armband of mourning encircled one sleeve.

A lifetime of holding his emotions strictly in check had given him a wooden expression, as if he were an automaton passing through life almost without experiencing its joys and woes.

The walls abounded with the stuffed heads of wild animals unfortunate enough to have encountered Sir John on his hunting expeditions. The head of a Chinese panda bear above the fireplace seemed to be asking, "Why me?"

Ford began by extending his condolences, which Sir John accepted with soldierly fortitude, and then Ford hesitated, not knowing quite how to proceed without intruding too far into the grief Sir John was obviously trying to control.

"Look here, Chief Inspector," Sir John said, "I appreciate that you have a job to do, and this must be damned awkward for you. So I suggest you spit it out and have done with it. I'm not a man to stand in the way of an officer trying to do his duty."

Ford sighed in relief.

"I appreciate that, sir. I understand this must be very difficult. Have Doctor Thornby or Mr. Jaspers advised you of the circumstances, sir?"

"They have told me that the other boy who died—who, I understand, was a complete cad—had managed to gain some sort of hold over my son and was blackmailing him. Obviously it is a profound shock to hear that my son was in this position, and, frankly, it's simply incredible that he would have done anything dishonorable."

Ford had brought Sir John's letter with him, and it was burning a hole in his breast pocket.

"I believe you met my son, Chief Inspector, but did not *know* my son. He was an exemplar of the principal that hard work, honesty, and fair play will be rewarded. He took his mother's death from a Zeppelin bomb very hard, but he had the fortitude to carry on. There can be no doubt that he would have been successful; I was looking forward to watching him far exceed my own accomplishments."

Ford nodded. "You will realize, sir, that in the circumstances, I must consider every possibility. I am afraid that, while your son's death may have been an accident, there are other possibilities, and I must look into those as well."

"I completely understand, Chief Inspector, and in your shoes I'd do precisely what you're doing."

Sir John squared his shoulders manfully.

"I accept it that, in view of the boy's note, the events could be interpreted as suicide. I am not a fool, Chief Inspector. I am sure you have considered the possibility that my son caused the other boy's death and then his own."

Ford squared his own shoulders. He could delay no further.

"Sir, I have searched the effects of Callaway, the first boy who died, and among them I found a letter written last December in what police experts have confirmed is your handwriting. I believe that letter forms the basis for the extortion."

Sir John blinked and swallowed.

"I have not formed a firm conclusion, Sir John, since I am not yet in possession of all the facts. However, the letter in Callaway's possession indicated that you had arranged for your son to have advanced notice of the questions in his scholarship examinations at Oxford."

Sir John's shoulders sagged. His rigid self-discipline had cracked, and for the first time Ford saw the play of strong emotions across his features. Ford continued.

"Callaway was therefore in possession of information that could ruin both your reputation and your son's. Your son did unexpectedly well in the exam. Callaway had a reputation for snooping into other people's property, and he may well have found your letter by searching your son's room."

Ford was struck by such a sudden, ugly realization, that a huge chasm of doubt opened in his mind, and he almost missed the General's response.

Sir John's voice was a whisper, ragged with despair. "You are suggesting that my son killed that boy to protect me, and then took his own life in remorse. He did it to preserve my reputation ... He did it to redeem our family honor."

"Sir," Ford said, wishing he were anywhere but here, "in the event that this becomes my firm conclusion, I shall recommend to my superiors that your son's death be reported as an accident, and that the investigation of Callaway's death be terminated without an official conclusion. The case will go unsolved."

Sir John squared his shoulders once more.

"That's very generous, but I require no special favors. I have always believed in taking responsibility for one's own actions. You must do your duty, Chief Inspector."

"My duty, Sir John, is to do what is in the public interest. There is no public interest in needlessly exposing you or your son. And I must repeat, sir, I have not formed any such conclusion; both cases are still open." Ford paused. "There is one other detail, sir. Did you send your son money recently? He had a five pound note in his possession."

"A fiver? Good Lord! No, I didn't send him anything. He had his allowance, of course ..."

"Well ..." Ford said, "the boy Callaway had been blackmailing him, so I was surprised to find that your son had so much money on him. It opens up a variety of unpleasant avenues. However, if it is not germane, it need not be mentioned."

The General stared at him.

"I think that's all I need, sir," Ford said. "Again, I apologize for intruding on you in very difficult circumstances."

Sir John continued to stare.

"Ford ... Ford ...," he mused half under his breath. "We have met before, I think, Chief Inspector?"

"Yes, sir," Ford answered. "We have."

"I thought as much. If there's anything I can do ..."

Ford said softly, "Nothing, sir; I'll find my own way out."

Under other circumstances, Ford would have asked the General to account for his movements at the time of both deaths; he would have searched young Trumpington's room; he would have asked the General to write out and sign a statement immediately so as not to give him time to concoct an elaborate and fictitious account of the letter in Ford's pocket. But he did none of these things.

As the front door closed behind him, he was already regretting that he had not done so. God knew, he thought, that he had made enough mistakes on this case and failed to do enough obvious things to fill a textbook on how *not* to investigate a murder. He stood on the front steps of Sir John's residence, silently berating himself in the bright morning sunshine.

◆     ◆     ◆

"If we're able to take this village," said the Brigadier, stabbing at the map with his cane, "We'll be able to knock out their artillery and bring up reinforcements. A small force—perhaps two companies—should be able to get the job done. Then we'll bring up more infantry and field artillery under cover of darkness and establish a salient before the enemy has time to react."

"An excellent plan, sir, if I may say so," said a Staff Major who then turned to Ford. "It looks like it's time for you to earn your keep, Captain" he said.

Ford moved uneasily in his field chair. He was disheveled, unshaven, and his boots and legs were thick with mud. His uniform was soaked from the endless rain that had turned the entire sector into a noxious bog. He hadn't slept for two days.

"My chaps have been on the line for two weeks," Ford said, "and we've done sorties the last two nights. They're exhausted. I suggest we ..."

The staff officer cut him off. "Nonsense, man, you must pull your weight, just like the rest of us."

He flicked a thread from his impeccable uniform.

Ford appealed to the Brigadier. "The mud is knee deep, sir. It's like wading in glue; it will take a very long time to cross no-man's-land. We'll be defenseless until we reach their lines."

"Come, come, Captain; you have to accept that a few odd casualties are inevitable," the staff officer said with irritation, saving the Brigadier from needing to reply.

Life is full of injustices, Ford reflected, and nowhere was this truth more apparent than the ability of staff officers, in comfort and security miles behind the lines, to send less fortunate men into battle.

There were two wars, one represented by maps with neat little flags and pieces of ribbon stuck into them, and a second that consisted of mud, rain, barbed wire, shell holes, waterlogged trenches, stammering machine guns, whining mortar shells, ear-splitting artillery barrages, hunger, pain, fear, exhaustion, and screaming death.

In the first war, the prevailing logic was that the enemy must have a weak point somewhere, and that one must constantly push one's own little flags against the enemy's little flags, until one was lucky enough to strike a point of vulnerability, in which case one's own little ribbon could be moved forward half an inch.

Brigadier Trumpington listened to the discussion with some sympathy for Ford. Unlike the Staff Major, he had been in combat in the Boer War, and he knew the horrors of battle at first hand. However, his superiors had demanded action, and his career depended upon the flags and ribbons rather than on the suffering they represented.

He spoke to terminate the discussion.

"You'll attack tonight at ten, just as planned. Good luck! Er, I've forgotten your name, Captain?"

"Ford, sir."

"Very well, Ford. Carry on."

The attack was successful, and the little ribbons and flags were duly adjusted. Brigadier Trumpington and the Staff Major were promoted. Ford was wounded, and half of his men were either killed or injured so badly that they would never fight again.

Two weeks later, the enemy counterattacked, and the ribbons and flags were returned to their original positions.

Ford spent three months in a field hospital where his thigh was periodically probed for shrapnel. The doctors feared fragments were lodged against the bone, and they cut deep. Due to an unfortunate miscommunication in the supply lines, morphine was seldom available.

◆    ◆    ◆

When Ford arrived at Scotland Yard, Croft was standing outside the courtyard entrance talking to the constable on duty. He had put on his best uniform and shined his boots to mirror-like perfection. He was carrying the files that contained the statements he had taken at Kings, accounting for everyone's movements on the nights when Callaway and Trumpington had died.

"My Lord, sir! The Yard! I've never been here before," he said fervently.

He entered the building in the manner that Ford imagined devout Roman Catholics would enter St. Peter's Basilica in Rome for the first time. Ford took him upstairs to the rabbit warren of scruffy offices occupied by the CID, introduced him to Superintendent Brownlee, and then sat him down at his own desk.

The prosaic surroundings did not seem to diminish Croft's enthusiasm.

"Sergeant, I've been a complete idiot!" Ford told him without preamble. "I need you here to straighten me out and keep me on the straight and narrow henceforth. Order, discipline, and common sense; these are what you're here to supply, and they're badly needed, believe me!"

"Don't be daft, sir! I think you've got the two of us mixed up!"

"Oh, no I haven't, I'm afraid, Croft. Let me bring you up-to-date, and then we'll move forward."

Ford summarized his meeting with Sir John, and the realization that had come to him as they had talked.

"Oh Christ, sir! You're right! I'm at least as big an idiot as you!"

"It changes our understanding, does it not?

"Completely, sir."

Ford went to the antique blackboard that occupied much of one wall. He began to clean away the inconclusive remnants of the Durham case, setting loose a fine cloud of chalk dust that distributed itself to every available surface, most of which consisted of piles of papers and files that Ford had never quite got around to clearing up.

In the top left-hand corner of the board, he wrote the word *Time*, and then constructed a timetable below it, starting with *10.15*, and marked off in five-minute intervals until *11.00*. Next to the word *Time*, he wrote *Callaway*.

"Callaway was in the crowd outside Old School until a quarter past ten, or thereabouts. Then he went off to the bushes for a smoke."

Next to *10.15*, he wrote *Enters bushes*.

"There he was joined by White and Connelly."

Ford made the appropriate notations.

"White went back to Queens and signed in at ten thirty. As he was leaving, he heard Callaway saying, *"Oh, it's you."* Therefore, whoever *"Oh, it's you"* is, that person probably entered the bushes at ten twenty-five."

Ford continued to write.

"At ten thirty-five, Callaway signed into Trafalgar and was seen at his window by Mr. Jaspers at ten forty. Do you agree so far, Sergeant?"

"Exactly, sir."

"Now, regarding what happened on the stairs—according to the list of activities which you and Mr. McIntire constructed, what do we know about who was going up and who was going down?"

He wrote another column headed *Stairs*, and gave Croft the chalk.

"I suggest you remove your uniform coat, Sergeant, or it'll get covered in chalk, and you and I will be in trouble with Mrs. Croft."

Croft heaved himself out of his chair, slipped out of his coat, and took the chalk in hand. It took a while to transcribe his notes, but at last the job was done.

A constable entered the room.

"Have you had lunch, sir?" he asked, and then added, "There was a telephone message from a Miss Canderblank, confirming a meeting at seven this evening in Soho, and another from the British Museum saying they have the copies you requested, sir."

Croft managed to give no visible reaction to the news of Ford's evening plans, and Ford dispatched the constable to purchase pork pies and to bring tea. Ford sat back in his chair to review the sergeant's handiwork.

"We appear to have a blank spot on the stairs from ten thirty-five until ten forty-five, during which, presumably, Callaway went up, and Trumpington was moving about. You will recall that he said he saw no one. Then, at ten forty-five, we have Connelly going up, and, according to him, a 'Major General's daughter' coming down. Let us assume that either Connelly or this 'daughter' shoved Callaway from his window. Connelly admits to being in Callaway's room, but claims it was empty."

"However, he could be lying, sir," Croft grunted. "He had a strong motive for wanting Callaway dead."

"True. But, if he's telling the truth, 'twas the Major General's daughter 'what dunnit.'"

The constable returned with pork pies and tea.

"The Major General's daughter was either a man or a boy in disguise, like, or actually a woman, sir," said Croft, his mouth full of pork pie. "It wasn't one of the boys who played Major General's daughters, because all of them were in other houses and accounted for. Of course, Connelly's not a good witness; he doesn't even know how tall this person was."

"True, Sergeant. Please go on."

"If we take the people that aren't accounted for, there's the two Greens, sir," continued Croft, going to the chalk board with a stick of chalk in one hand and a half-eaten pork pie in the other, and writing up their names.

"Then we've got young Connelly, of course, sir, and Trumpington, and then the three Canderblanks—Lord and Lady Canderblank, who were out walking, and young Miss Canderblank, who was in her room but can't prove it."

Croft glanced over his shoulder and asked coyly: "Do you want me to include her, sir?"

"Yes, she's still on the list. I'm taking her statement this evening."

"Right, sir," said Croft phlegmatically, as if taking statements from attractive young ladies over dinner were a completely humdrum aspect of police work.

They spent the next hour filling in the details of all the movements of their suspects, so that they could look down a column and track an individual's movements, or across a row to see where everyone was at any given time.

"Well," said Ford, "it appears from this that any of them could have done it, at a pinch. However, it doesn't seem likely that it was the Canderblanks, unless they're lying to protect each other, and, in any case, they don't have a motive. That leaves the Greens, Trumpington, and Connelly, and they all have some sort of motive."

"What do we do now, sir? Go back and grill 'em all again?"

"No, we go and get another blackboard and some more tea."

The young constable supplied both. The second blackboard stood on an easel and could only be arranged in the room if the doorway were partially blocked off.

"Did you find digs for Sergeant Croft, Constable?"

"Yessir, at the police hostel in Lambeth, sir." He turned to Croft. "It's not bad, Sarge; it's on my way home, so I'll show you the way, if you like. And there's a pretty fair boozer on the corner."

"Good," Ford said. "Now, we'll use this board to write a list of everything we don't have answers for; anything that strikes us as odd. I'll go first." He rose, stepped to the board, and picked up a stick of chalk. "Why did Callaway hide the book about India? I've read it twice now, and it contains nothing worthy of making it a secret."

He wrote: *Why hide book?*

"Next, who is *'Dearest Mummy'*? Next, who is *'Oh, it's you'*?"

"Who's the Major General's daughter on the stairs?" Croft offered. "Who did Green see going into the Lodge?"

"Good," said Ford, writing busily.

At that moment the door swung open and sent the blackboard crashing to the floor. Ford jumped back to avoid being struck, while Croft found himself engaged in close combat with the easel.

"Am I disturbing you, old chap?" Brownlee asked mildly. "Are you sure you have enough blackboards? I have another if you'd like to nail it to the ceiling?"

"We're summarizing our facts, sir," Ford grinned.

"Excellent! May I join you?"

He leant backwards into the corridor.

"Cartwright!" he yelled. "Three teas!"

He turned back into the room.

"Here, Sergeant, let me help you with that easel before it gets the better of you … Good Lord, it's a feisty devil, isn't it!"

Brownlee assisted in setting up the blackboard again, dusted himself off, and then settled into Ford's office chair. Ingrained habit caused Croft to stand at attention in his superior's presence.

"Oh, do sit down, Croft," Brownlee protested. "We don't stand on ceremony, literally or figuratively. You know, Mrs. Brownlee and I honeymooned in the Cotswolds … We stayed at an inn in Lower Slaughter and bicycled about from there … I've never been so exhausted in my life."

Constable Cartwright slipped sideways through the door with three teacups and saucers arranged expertly upon one another in one hand and managed to make himself sufficiently inconspicuous in the corner behind Brownlee that he could remain to listen.

Ford explained the list of questions.

"Handwriting experts," Brownlee suggested. "Callaway's signature, Sir John's letter, Callaway's ransom note—we've got to be sure. Possible fingerprints on Trumpington's five pound note."

"I have the Master's fingerprints on Callaway's ransom note also, and I also have Lady Canderblank's on one of my cards."

"Do you, by Jove! Let's see, what else? The smoking French lady and the running gym teacher—I seem to remember them; why aren't they on your list? Good Lord, Ford, you have suspects coming out your ears! Isn't it about time you started narrowing them down?"

"I would if I could, sir," Ford said ruefully.

"What did the undertaker fellow say about Callaway's body?"

"Yes, sir," said Croft, with a preliminary clearing of his throat. "Tobias Jones, or 'Jones the Coffin' as we call him in the village. He was sent for by Doctor Thickett on Monday morning, and told to bring a coffin. When he got there, the London doctor was just leaving. Jones and his man placed the boy's body in the coffin and took it to his workshop, where they undressed him."

He looked up from his notes.

"Jones said his neck and back were broken, and the back of his head was bashed in. He's seen more bodies than I've had hot dinners, and I'd take his word over any London doctor, if I may say so, sir. The stab wounds were clean with almost no blood. Doctor Thornby himself came with a shirt and tie and a suit to dress him in, and took the theatricals away."

"The Master?" Brownlee asked sharply. "Why the Master on so trivial an errand? If I recall your notes correctly, it was Mr. McIntire who took Callaway's clothes from his room."

"Good point, sir," Ford said. "That hadn't struck me."

"What did the Master say to Jones about Callaway?" Brownlee asked Croft.

"Doctor Thornby wouldn't look at the body," Croft told him. "He was squeamish, like. He asked Jones for the knife. Jones said that he should give it to me, but the Master insisted, on account of it being school property. That's about it, sir."

"Have we questioned Doctor Thornby about the knife?"

"Not yet, sir," replied Ford. "Trumpington's death overtook us, and we know the knife wasn't the murder weapon. But it's still on the 'odds-and-ends-yet-to-do' list."

"Talking about odds and ends, what about Trumpington's death … Anything new on that?"

"Sergeant Croft has completed collecting everyone's statements, sir," Ford said, and he picked up Croft's file. "We haven't had a chance to go through it yet."

Brownlee lumbered to his feet.

"Well, let me know how you're getting along. Is there any help you need? Perhaps I should requisition another dozen blackboards? The Home

Secretary is very supportive, incidentally, in the matter of Lady Canderblank's complaints. Evidently she is not well loved; he'd be delighted to slap an obstruction of justice charge on her. Do you have enough men, Ford?"

"Sir, with Sergeant Croft at my side, I have an army."

◆        ◆        ◆

Victoria Canderblank had chosen a small *ristorante* in Soho for their dinner engagement. Ford arrived early and stood on the pavement outside, waiting and smoking, searching his feelings with distrust.

She arrived in a taxicab and swept him into the restaurant. The place was crowded and noisy, but the proprietor welcomed her profusely and with a snap of his fingers and a burst of voluble Italian, summoned up a quiet table for two with a plate of antipasto and a bottle of Chianti to place upon it.

She smiled, and he felt as if he had been run over by the Flying Scotsman locomotive at full steam.

"Thomas, you have neglected to interview me about young Callaway's death," she said when they were seated and the Chianti had been poured. "I decided that it was long past time for you to take my statement, and so I thought I'd fit myself into your busy schedule as a matter of public duty. Cheers! Do you like the Chianti?"

She had a way of wrinkling her nose before she laughed, and her giggles and chuckles burst out of her like a stream of soap bubbles.

"Shall I begin?" she said.

Ford again felt the pleasant sensation of being bathed in her warm companionship and her endless cheerful conversation, and nodded in compliance. He wondered whether her monologues would grow irksome in time, or if she would always be a wellspring of exuberance, an emotional battery to which he could attach his own weaker soul and be recharged with her vitality.

"On the Saturday before last," she said, "I was forced, by filial duty, to attend a gruesome performance of Gilbert and Sullivan at Kings, followed by an even more gruesome soiree in the Master's Lodge. In my search for an escape from the successive layers of gruesomeness, I faced two choices: I could sneak from the house and murder the first person I saw, or I could go up to bed. We were, after all, condemned to spend the night at the Lodge."

She paused dramatically. "It was not an easy decision, but in the end, I elected to go to bed. The Bishop of Gloucester escorted me to my bedroom door but, you will be delighted to hear in the interest of the moral rectitude of the Church of England, no farther."

"I am relieved to hear it," Ford said with a smile.

He wondered if she were describing her activities in order to be beguiling, or to divert his attention from something she did not wish him to know.

"I awoke the following morning to the cheerful chirping of chaffinches. I assume there were also busy bees a-plenty, but the sounds of their bustling buzzing did not penetrate my casement. I was cheered by the thought that I would not have to accompany my mother on her daily ride."

She sat back.

"That's my statement. I shall permit you three questions, after which we will order our main course and pass on to other things. I recommend the *saltimbocca*. You may begin, Thomas."

Ford wished desperately that he could take her account at face value. He wished he could sit here and sip his wine while she twisted him delightfully around her little finger. He wished she were here because she wanted his companionship, although that could not possibly be true.

This evening she had chosen to wear her hair in long luxurious waves, and her face was shadowed and mysterious in the candlelight. He fought a brief and inconclusive battle with his emotions and forced himself to respond.

"What did all the others do at the end of the gruesome gathering?" he asked in a bantering tone that he forlornly hoped matched hers.

"That's a multiple question, provoking several answers, and therefore probably cheating. You're obviously a highly skilled interrogator, and I see that I shall have to be careful ... My mother and father went out for a walk, every one else went up to bed, except for Doctor Thornby who retreated to his study to review the schedule of the next day's events, and Mrs. Thornby, who was supervising the staff in clearing up. You have two questions left."

"Is it your parent's normal custom to take a stroll before retiring?"

"It is my father's custom to smoke a cigar before going to bed. He usually goes out on the veranda or for a walk at home, because my mother complains about the smell of stale smoke the following day. The choice of the veranda or a walk is determined by rain or lack thereof. It's a case of 'weather or not.'"

She grinned at her own joke.

"On the night in question, my mother was in a snit because the boiler was broken, and she couldn't take a bath. She often leaves the house when she's being particularly pissy. At home she often takes a pair of pruning shears and attacks some helpless shrub. You have one remaining question."

"What, if anything, did you hear after you retired—in the interval between the Bishop's nocturnal departure and the chaffinches' auroral arrival?"

She grinned, and Ford wished heartily that this was just a delightful game.

"Before surrendering to sleep, I heard my mother berating one of the servants—not an infrequent occurrence. She was insisting that she should have a bath, and the servant was refusing—I don't know why. The altercation took place outside my door. The clock struck three quarters, and I slipped into virtuous repose."

She held up her hand.

"Wait, there's more. I was awoken by another outburst of my mother's less than dulcet tones, although they were strangely muffled, as if far away. I arose and traced their source of origin to the basement, where I discovered that the household had reassembled to observe an antiquated and inoperative example of late Victorian domestic plumbing. I was subsequently re-escorted to my chamber by the faithful Bishop, bade him goodnight, and again surrendered myself to the arms of Morpheus. There,

Cassius—there are your answers, and I wish you joy of them. Now it's my turn."

The voluble proprietor arrived on cue and was ecstatic that the young lady had selected *saltimbocca*, for it was unquestionably his establishment's finest offering.

"To begin with, a word of explanation," she said with a toss of her head when they were alone again. "I've decided to call you Cassius. I recently had the misfortunate to suffer through *Julius Caesar*, but that particular evening was redeemed by the fact that I realized that you have a 'lean and hungry look.' Cassius is quiet but dangerous, like a smoldering volcano. Everything seems peaceful, and yet there's always a hint of danger, a whiff of brimstone, as it were, just as there is about you. Anyway, I asked myself what one should do if one is being snooped upon, particularly when one is being snooped on by a smoldering volcano."

"I am not *snooping* on you!" Ford protested, wishing his heart would not insist on turning summersaults every time she smiled.

"Indeed you are! I am a suspect, and you are Sherlock Holmes, albeit with a five iron instead of a violin, and Sergeant Croft is your faithful Watson. I'll bet you say 'Elementary, my dear Croft,' to him several times a day. I am under your magnifying glass, being dissected by your cold and ruthless logic. I must endure your minute and probing examination."

She took a sip of wine while Ford's mind raced hither and yon. If only this were real …

"Anyway," she said, "I decided to do a little snooping of my own. Through friends of friends and acquaintances of acquaintances, I have traced the hot flows of lava beneath your placid surface, my dear Cassius."

"You have?" he asked, wondering what on earth his expression must be like.

"Indeed so; much has been revealed. At Cambridge your virtuosity with a cricket ball was matched only by your brilliance as a student of Plantagenet history. Your record in the war is as distinguished as it is unblemished. Building upon these early triumphs, you are now a rising star in the Metropolitan Police Force."

"Your friends and acquaintances are given to great exaggeration."

"Perhaps, and perhaps not, my dear Cassius, for my investigations have far exceeded mere records of accomplishment."

"They have?"

"A portrait has emerged, as enigmatic as the Mona Lisa's smile. The brilliant young student who was destined to pen the definitive history of King Richard III, the last of the Plantagenets, unexpectedly shunned the ivied walls of academia and entered the constabulary. Why, one asks oneself? The fine left-handed bowler, the master of the *googly*, whatever that may be, distained the sun-drenched fields of Lords and Old Trafford, and now skulks in the shadows of Scotland Yard. 'Why so?' one asks again."

Ford began to speak, but she hushed him into silence.

"The plot, already thick, thickens again; my friend Veronica De Fitz-Roy, now the Countess of Steppingham, recalls you in your prewar days as a well-known poppet, much admired at May Balls and sought after in the boudoirs of Belgravia; and yet you have evaded the coils of matrimony, in spite of your universally acknowledged poppetude. Indeed, I am reliably informed that, had Cambridge University been organized as a pyramidal poppetocracy, you would have been found at its peak, on its highest, most poppetesque pinnacles."

She did not say if she would have joined the consensus, and he could not ask her.

"In sum, my dear Cassius, you are a riddle."

She leant back, smiled luxuriously, and took a sip of wine; Ford thought her the perfect picture of poppetudinosity. He searched in vain for an apt response, but was saved when their *saltiboccas* and a string quartet arrived simultaneously. Ford thought wildly, "If music be the food of love, play on."

"Now, Cassius," said Miss Canderblank, "I granted your three questions, and you must return the complement. My answers were open and forthright, and I expect no less from you. To begin, why did you decide to join the police force, rejecting a promising academic career and forsaking your potential as a cricketer?"

Ford felt he could either say nothing or speak for several hours. It had been a mistake to accept this invitation—he had advised himself against it, but he might just as well have advised a moth on the dangers of a candle flame.

"Cambridge was wonderful," he said slowly. "It was like a dream. But, like any dream, eventually one must wake up and return to reality. I needed a change."

"An interesting answer, my dear Cassius, but not an answer to my question, and in any case, your premise is open to question, for there is no reason one's life cannot be a perfect dream. I retain my right to three questions. Why the police force, and not some more conventional career?"

Ford's answer rang loudly in his head. "Because I crave order and discipline and predictability. Because I know that in 1930, I will have completed twenty-two years of service and be entitled to a Long Service Medal and a pension. Because the ladder of advancement is foretold; I shall, in another five or six years, become a Superintendent.

"Because I belong to a lesser breed of men who don't take risks or aspire to prizes they may not achieve. Because I loathe competition, and most careers, like cricket, are inherently competitive.

"Because I was scarred by the war and have crawled under a rock to hide. Because police work is solitary and expands to fill one's waking hours, leaving no time for thinking about all the things one doesn't have. Because if one does not try, one does not fail. Because—though you look utterly delicious, Miss Canderblank—I am terrified of rejection."

But Ford only thought these things and said none of it.

"Well," he said lamely, "society needs law and order, and someone's got to do it."

"That's completely pathetic, Cassius, and well you know it!" she snorted. "You're like an oyster!"

She leant forward across the table.

"But I shall crack you open—I promise you!"

Ford found himself wishing that he could be struck dead by a bolt of lightning at that very moment. In those circumstances he wouldn't have to pursue the ugliness at Kings; he wouldn't have to remind himself that the delightful Victoria Canderblank was almost certainly an agent for her repulsive mother, and therefore not to be trusted; and he could die in the happy belief that she was flirting with him because she wanted to.

"I shall retain my right to three questions, and pass on to other things," she said, breaking into his thoughts and attacking her saltimbocca with gusto. "Let me give you a brief synopsis of my life, starting with my first memory and concluding with this dinner engagement."

And then she was off and running—through the remainder of the saltimbocca, through a tart lemon sorbet to clear the palette, through crumbling pastries oozing fresh cream for desert—pouring out a droll and self-deprecating account of her childhood, her service as a volunteer nurse during the war, and her present vapid existence in society.

"All my friends are married. I'm the only spinster left. Jimmie Fanshaw-Bigsby is very keen to marry me and make me his Duchess, and I'm running out of excuses. My mother has declared herself in favor of it, as has the Dowager Duchess. Bigsby Hall has at least two hundred rooms, of which more than a hundred are afflicted with dry rot. Jimmie is Master of the Bigsby Hunt, and breeds foxhounds."

Ford's heart sank. His daydreams had not included the obvious possibility of a rival suitor.

"So, Cassius, if you need to find me a few years from now, I'll be in the South Downs, covered in flakes of mildewed ceiling plaster and surrounded by yapping dogs. My only hope for salvation is that an oyster in shining armor will come galloping up on a white charger and save me in the nick of time. But there isn't an *R* in the month—it's June and oysters are out of season. Let me see ... July, August, and then September. I shall wait until September before surrendering to a *Bigsby-ettic* fate."

She sat back and regarded him with her enormous eyes, creating a silence into which he would be compelled to step.

He needed to get away to think. Was there, he wondered, the slightest possibility that she was not saying these things in jest, and was actually inviting him to pursue her? Or, as was far more likely, was she throwing up a clever smokescreen to divert his attention from some aspect of the case? Which aspect? Surely she must be an agent of her mother's, trying the velvet touch where the iron fist had failed?

Coffee was served and Ford found himself talking about the case. It was a wholly stupid thing to do, but any other possible line of conversation led directly into emotional quicksand. He was desperate to see her again, and the case offered the only legitimate way of doing so short of a passionate declaration of his fascination. An irrational hatred of Jimmie Fanshaw-Bigsby surged in his veins.

"At the rate I'm going, I'll still be grinding up and down the hill to Kings in September," he said finally, again attempting to match her light tone but merely managing to be utterly prosaic. "Most cases of sudden death are never really explained; they just become dusty files in some archive. I'll probably just write a long and boring report and leave it at that."

He heard himself taking a risk.

"Nevertheless, I appreciate your account of that evening. I'll have to ask you to make it a formal statement that I can include with all the others. Perhaps it will give me an opportunity to return your invitation?"

"Oh my goodness, Cassius! Is that a crack I see in your shell?" she asked, mischievously batting her eyelids.

He noticed that she did not immediately accept his invitation, and he was left squirming in uncertainty—precisely the position he had been determined to avoid.

"But surely, Holmes, you cannot be baffled? Have you not discovered a rare South American poison in poor Callaway's body and traced it to a blowpipe hidden in the woodpile?"

"My dear Watson," Ford responded, finding at long last a safe basis for talking to her, "I wish I had. But I am being drawn, unfortunately, toward an inescapable conclusion, that young Trumpington caused his own death through a series of tragic errors—exposing himself to some form of black-mail, killing Callaway to silence him, and then killing himself in remorse."

He stopped himself in alarm.

"I hope you were not close to your cousin?" he said. "Whatever caused the blackmail is completely irrelevant. The only good thing about the entire affair is that the details need not become known. My report can be inconclusive, and no harm will be done."

She rewarded him with one of her superb smiles.

"Perhaps it's a good thing you did become a policeman. I've never associated sensitivity with the police force, but I see I have been wrong. Just to complete your already masterful grasp of the situation, I assure you there was no love lost between my cousin James Trumpington and me. He was a cad masquerading as a prig. When and where can I expect to be given my statement to sign?"

Ford said the first thing that came into his head.

"The Savoy Grill? For lunch on Friday?"

"I'm supposed to travel down to Bigsby Hall on Friday," she said, "but I shall take great pleasure in canceling, my dear Cassius. Great pleasure!"

Outside on the pavement, she did not offer him her hand, as if their relationship had advanced beyond such formality. Against her custom, she did not leave him with a cheerful monologue, but with a silent smile that, in his fevered imagination, spoke volumes.

He walked slowly south to Leicester Square and traveled by Underground to Scotland Yard, where he telephoned Croft and woke him from his righteous slumbers.

"That's all right, sir. Good Lord! Very well, sir. First thing in the morning, sir, as soon as it's light."

Ford fought an internal battle. He could return home and sink into a similarly righteous slumber, reflecting on his evening in Victoria Canderblank's company, or he could read Croft's file on Trumpington's death.

It was approaching midnight, and tomorrow would be a busy day. Surely he had had far too much to drink to concentrate? Surely it would be best to make a fresh start in the morning? The reasons for going home were compelling.

He groaned and opened the file.

> To: DCI Thos Ford, CID
> From: Sgt Rbt Croft, GC
>     Sgt Dthy Jackson, GWC
> In re: Accounting for whereabouts of persons at time of Trumpington's murder

Boys—all boys present and accounted for in their houses except as follows:

> Connelly: Trumpington told him approximately at 9 p.m. that he would be caned by T for "habitual tardiness at band practice." C decided to run away home, but changed his mind and returned. Caught climbing into Trafalgar at 11.30 p.m. by Mr. McIntire.

> (Note: White was in the sanitarium with an intestinal infection)

Masters and Staff—all accounted for in their places of residence except as follows:

> Mr. Robinson: Duty Master out on patrol from 10.30 p.m. until 11.30 p.m. when he discovered Trumpington. Saw all of the others as indicated below. States that all doors to the Gymnasium were locked at 10.30 p.m. Staff door found open upon discovery of the body.

> Mr. Bottomly: out for his evening run. States that he paused for a few minutes to catch his breath at rear of Gymnasium approximately 10.45 to 11.15 p.m. where he chatted with Miss Larue.

> Miss Larue: out for her evening walk, confirms encountering Mr. Bottomly as above.

> (Note: 30 minutes is a long time to chat, particularly on a rainy evening.)

> Mr. Jaspers: out walking his dog. Walked around the great lawn from 10.45 to 11.15 p.m. Saw (dog has nervous disposition and barks at all comers) those referenced above. Dog also barked at 11.00 p.m. at unseen person (clock was striking), possibly the killer.

Others—

> Miss L Green: out for a walk and unaccounted for; says she walked up to the School but did not go in.

> Miss V Canderblank: visited Lodge in the period 10.00 to 10.30 p.m. to return a library book. Said book wrapped in brown paper, per Master's wife.

Please find detailed reports attached. Please note that the Master's missing key has not been found."

"Good old Croft," Ford thought. He leafed through the attached details without curiosity or energy. Croft had noted that the gym master and the French teacher had spent an awfully long time together in the shadows, perhaps doing more than chatting. The note on White's whereabouts confirmed his claim that he had had other priorities on the night of Callaway's murder, and supported his alibi.

The notes on Lucy and Victoria were cause for concern, although for very different reasons. He remembered that when Croft had awakened him on the night of Trumpington's fall, Lucy was still dressed, and her bed had not been slept in. He, or the redoubtable Sergeant Jackson, would have to interview her again. As for Victoria, why had she not told him she had been at the School? If she had nothing to hide, it would be the natural thing to do.

Of all the people Ford least wanted to suspect of murder, these three—the wretched Connelly, the hapless Lucy, and Victoria—ranked the highest. But someone or something had attracted Mr. Jaspers' dog's attention, and it could well have been Lucy or Victoria, or Connelly sneaking back to Trafalgar. Now, as he closed the file and set off for his bed, he found his pleasant memories of the evening ruined by dark suspicions.

# Tuesday

The following morning, a bleary-eyed Ford presented himself to an elderly assistant librarian at the British Museum. Her iron-grey hair was drawn back tightly into a bun, and her faded blue eyes regarded him cautiously through pince-nez spectacles.

He handed her Callaway's copy of *Serving the Raj,* and she riffled through it, comparing it to the Museum's copy.

"They appear to be identical; I see nothing to make your copy special. We have dozens of similar reminiscences, regimental histories, and that sort of thing ... Sorry, Chief Inspector, I cannot help you. I believe you are also interested in the *Times of India* in 1903?"

"Yes, in the social pages—birth announcements, that sort of thing."

"Well, let me help you," she said and led him to a small private reading room. For the next hour they searched the papers together.

"Aha," she said finally. "Here is the person you're interested in, Chief Inspector. 'To Captain and Mrs. James Callaway, a son, Michael, born on December 12$^{th}$, 1903.' Is there anyone else you're interested in?"

She removed her glasses and rubbed her eyes.

"An occupational hazard," she told him.

"I'm sure it is," he replied, suppressing a yawn. "In my job it's lack of sleep ... I admit, Miss Parsons, I really don't know *what* I'm looking for. Any reference to a Doctor Roger Thornby, or a Lord and Lady Canderblank ... I know that a boy was fascinated by this book, and now he's dead under mysterious circumstances. I keep hoping for an explanation. I hope I'm not delaying you from your duties?"

"On the contrary, Chief Inspector; I love riddles, and this is a welcome relief from the tedium of cataloging, I assure you."

The next hour produced three references to Lord Canderblank in connection with his official duties and three to Lady Canderblank, who had evidently been a pillar of society. Miss Parsons was clearly better than Ford at this form of research—like a determined truffle hound in search of an elusive acorn—and he left her to it while he again stared at the pages of Callaway's hidden volume.

There was still nothing there; still nothing about his father or his father's regiment—no Canderblanks, no Thornbys, no Trumpingtons. There were no annotations written in Callaway's handwriting saying: *"In future I shall refer to the following person as* 'Oh, it's you,'" nor was there a glossary of terms identifying *Dearest Mummy.*

The end of the book contained photographic plates of British families at work and play under the benign imperium of British India. He thumbed through them idly. There were carefully grouped officers outside regimental headquarters, a Great White Hunter in a basket atop an elephant, languidly posed families reclining in wicker chairs, victorious polo teams accepting well-earned trophies with studied modesty, and …

"Holy *mackerel!*" yelled Ford, startling Miss Parsons to such as extent that her glasses flew off her nose. *"Eureka!"*

"Whatever is the matter, Chief Inspector?" she demanded, scrabbling shortsightedly for her pince-nez.

Ford almost danced a jig. He slammed the book down on the table in front of her, and stabbed his finger at a photographic plate. Miss Parson's adjusted her spectacles with agonizing deliberation before studying the page.

"Look! Look, Miss Parsons!" he demanded.

The photograph showed ladies wearing improbable hats being awarded prizes after an equestrian event, a gymkhana in Lahore, in November,1903. The caption below it listed their names—including *Mrs. James Callaway* for first prize in the Ladies Point-To-Point.

"That *is* your boy's mother, Chief Inspector, but what is its significance? Why are you so thrilled?"

"One moment, Miss Parsons," Ford crowed, scuffling among the copies of the *Times* to find the announcement of Callaway's birth, and laying them side-by-side.

"Now tell me, Miss Parsons, does that lady look expectant? Could she have given birth within thirty days?"

"Good Lord! Ah yes, now I see it, Chief Inspector! Where are the references to Lady Canderblank?—Aha, look at this social report. *'Lady Gloria Tendon's Charity Ball, blah, blah, blah ... and Lady Deborah Canderblank, newly returned from her long convalescence, blah, blah, blah.'* She was no more *convalescing* than I am!"

"Do you have military records in the library?"

"We have some, but only those that have been published. We are not a government repository."

"Then I must thank you for your efforts, Miss Parsons," Ford said as he hurriedly gathered up his papers and files, "and take myself off to the War Office."

"So, this Lady Canderblank was indiscreet, shall we say, to put it mildly," said Miss Parsons, evidently more pleased than shocked by the revelation. "It's typical of the arrogance of the aristocracy; this is precisely the sort of reason that led me to join the Labor Party."

Ford tucked his materials under his arm and shook her hand, grinning. "When this case is over, I may join it too!"

He thanked her profusely and then hurried to the War Office; thence to Highgate to interview Callaway's father's former commanding officer; and thence to Camden, where he left Mrs. Markham much distressed. Back at Scotland Yard, he spoke urgently to Superintendent Brownlee and left him telephoning Colonel Dagenham, while Ford himself raced in a police car—with its alarm bell ringing—to Paddington Station.

◆　　◆　　◆

Colonel Dagenham received Ford with his customary grace. Ford was pleased to see that Croft and Sergeant Jackson were there already, enjoying the tea and biscuits that Dagenham now pressed upon Ford.

"We searched the bushes they uprooted, sir, just like you said to when you telephoned me last night," said Croft, his face alive with excitement. "Actually they saved them, on account that they have very good root systems and will grow back nicely. They're just planted in mulch near the potting shed. Anyway, we found this, sir, wrapped around a rhododendron branch. It's the same color as the branches—that's why it was missed."

Croft held up a scrap of brown material.

"It's heavy oriental silk, sir," added Sergeant Jackson. "I'm not an expert, but it must be very expensive. My mother has a blouse like that, and it came from India. I checked with Ethel, the maid at the Lodge, and she says Lady Canderblank was wearing brown that evening."

"Why did you suddenly have the bushes searched, Ford? Why didn't you do so before?" asked Dagenham.

"An oversight, sir; in fact, a big mistake. Lady Canderblank had given orders that all the shrubs should be ripped out and burned, and I naturally assumed they were gone. Thank God, they weren't. Anyway, I was interviewing Miss Canderblank, and she made an allusion to physical evidence at the murder scene. It occurred to me it was worth a try, even if it was a long shot. May I bring you up to date on what I've discovered?"

Ford recounted the relevant portions of his meeting with Victoria Canderblank, his discoveries at the British Museum that morning, and his subsequent dashes through north London.

When he was done, Croft was reduced to saying, "Well, I never!" repetitively. Sergeant Jackson put the entire matter in social terms—a rich woman could simply buy her way out of trouble and get on with her life untarnished, while the likes of poor Lucy Green had to live with the consequences of her actions without support, and with her reputation indelibly blemished. Ford wondered if she, like the Librarian, were a member of the Labor Party.

"This is not good, Ford," said Dagenham grimly. "This isn't good at all."

"I agree, sir," Ford replied in the same tone. "We appear to be facing a first class scandal involving either the Canderblanks or Sir John Trumpington."

"Or both—we'd better get over to Canderblank Hall and have it out this evening," said the Colonel. "There's no point in delaying the unpleasant."

He consulted an elderly grandfather clock ticking solemnly in a corner of his study.

"It's dinner time. We'll preserve the social niceties as best we can and let them dine in peace. We'll go over afterwards. In the meantime, let me see what Mrs. Bond can rustle up for us."

"What about Lucy Green, Sergeant Jackson?" Ford asked. "I've been so involved with the Canderblank affair, I haven't had time to ask you."

"Well, sir, you were right," she replied. "We all made the same mistake and assumed that the boy she went to see—*'him that was killed,'* I think were her exact words—was Callaway. But in fact it was the Trumpington boy. He was the father of her baby."

"Oh my God," Dagenham groaned. "This case has more twists to it than I can keep up with!"

"It's another reason for blackmail, sir," she continued. "Provided Callaway knew, of course. It takes away the Greens' motive for killing Callaway, but adds a major motive for them killing *Trumpington*. I'll bet that five pound note in Trumpington's wallet was destined for Lucy."

"It's still possible that the two deaths are completely unrelated," said Ford. "The Canderblanks, or Connelly, for that matter, could have killed Callaway; and the Greens, for example, could have killed Trumpington for a completely different reason."

The Colonel's housekeeper entered the room.

"Supper's on the table in the dining room, sir."

They sat at an ancient refectory table watching the sun sinking splendidly in the west over the Severn valley. Colonel Dagenham telephoned to Canderblank Hall to warn them of their coming, and was then called to the telephone again. He returned with annoyance replacing his usual affability.

"That was Jim Trotter. He's fallen over and cut his hand on his bicycle chain. He can't play tomorrow. Damnation!"

"That leaves us shorthanded, then, sir," said Croft in alarm. "Assuming that I'm still free with all this Canderblank business, we'll still be one man short."

"Cricket match tomorrow, Ford," Dagenham explained. "Annual one day match against the School First Eleven. I put together a scratch lot, and we have a charity bazaar."

"P.O.D. Dagenham's Police Eleven," sir," added Croft. "Known informally as 'the Pods.' The Colonel draws on all the local police stations for miles around, all the way to Cheltenham. Inspector Trotter runs the Stroud station, and he's our demon left-hander."

The Colonel fixed Ford with a determined stare.

"Ford …" he began, but Ford cut him off.

"Oh no, sir, I couldn't possibly; I haven't played since before the war!"

"Nonsense, man! I had the pleasure of seeing you against Oxford in, let me see, '11, it must have been—8 for 32, if I recall correctly!"

"That was a long time ago, sir. I simply couldn't …"

"It would be a pleasure to keep for you, sir," said Croft.

"Just a few overs, I promise you," said the Colonel, and Ford knew that he had lost.

"Duty before pleasure," said Dagenham, before Ford could refuse. "Let's get to Canderblank Hall and get it over with."

◆     ◆     ◆

Colonel Dagenham had telephoned Canderblank Hall a second time, to advise the Canderblanks that he would be arriving shortly, accompanied by other police officers. When they arrived they were escorted to the Blue Sitting Room where they were greeted frostily.

His lordship let his displeasure be known.

"Dammit, Dagenham, this is the height of inconvenience. What the devil is it?"

Lord Canderblank's expressive range was limited to blandness and petulance; Ford discovered no middle ground, and he reflected that a politician does not require a broader array of emotions.

"The Chief Inspector has made certain discoveries which may have a bearing on the case, Canderblank. I think they need addressing."

"Who *are* these persons?" Lady Canderblank demanded, as if Dagenham had not spoken. "And *what* are they doing in my drawing room?" Her hand swept over Ford, Sergeant Jackson, and Croft.

"They are police officers going about their lawful duties under my command," Dagenham responded firmly.

"They belong in the servant's hall." Her tone was fierce and final.

"If you prefer it, Lady Deborah, we can transfer this meeting to any room you wish," Dagenham replied waspishly, clearly determined not to be browbeaten.

"That is not what I meant, and well you know it. Kindly tell them to wait below stairs while you speak to us. Do not presume to order me about in my own home, Percy."

Colonel Dagenham turned to appeal to Lord Canderblank.

"This doesn't need to be more unpleasant than it already is, Canderblank. I really don't want to be forced to take action."

His lordship held up a hand to restrain his wife's next barrage.

"Let's just get this over with, as quickly and inoffensively as possible, Dagenham," he growled.

Dagenham gestured Ford to begin.

"More impudence and innuendo, Austin?" Lady Canderblank demanded of Ford. "Will you not rest until you have ruined Sir John Trumpington's reputation, and Kings' along with it?"

"Lady Canderblank," said Ford, ignoring her habitual refusal to use his correct name, "I wish to advise you of certain facts that have come into my possession. I do not wish to form any firm conclusions without giving you the opportunity to comment upon them."

"Nothing could possibly be of less interest to me than your conclusions, Morris," said Lady Canderblank. "James, I insist that you speak to Edward Shortt!"

Lord Canderblank did not move immediately to telephone the Home Secretary, to whom all domestic police forces reported, and Ford continued.

"The first set of facts concerns Major Callaway. Seventeen years ago, in July of 1903, Major Callaway, then Lieutenant Callaway, was involved in an incident on the North West Frontier that resulted in the death of several men under his command. The court of enquiry issued a verdict that exonerated him of explicit misconduct, but indicated that he had exhibited extremely poor judgment. His commanding officer made it clear that his career had been ruined, and that he could expect no further promotion."

The Canderblanks had now formed a tableau of unmoving hostility. Lady Canderblank was sitting rigidly in an armchair in a bronze colored evening gown, with her head turned in such a manner that she did not have to look at Ford or the sergeants standing stolidly behind him. His lordship stood to her side and a little behind, in white tie and tails, all making it seem as if they were posing for a formal portrait. They absorbed Ford's words without blinking.

"A few months later, in November, Mrs. Callaway won the Ladies' Point-To-Point horse riding competition staged by her husband's regiment. Immediately thereafter, in December, Lieutenant Callaway was transferred to another regiment and received a promotion, over the strenuous objections of his commanding officer. The transfer and promotion were arranged by you, sir, in your position as a senior member of the Viceroy's staff."

The tableau remained in place.

"The Callaways arrived at their new post with a new baby, young Michael, who grew up and in due course came to England to live with the Markhams, Mrs. Callaway's relatives. At that time, you endowed the Canderblank Scholarship at Kings, and young Callaway became the first—and only—recipient. Prior to her marriage, Mrs. Callaway had been employed by you in the capacity of governess for your daughter, Victoria; a fact that explains your intervention in Lieutenant Callaway's career and your subsequent financial support."

His lordship stirred impatiently, and when he spoke, his voice was tight with annoyance.

"Inspector, the fact that we have assisted the Callaways in the past can have no bearing on the boy's death, and well you know it. I am reminded of the expression *'no good deed will go unpunished.'* Colonel, this is not the first time I have had to speak to you about this officer's conduct. I would, frankly, have expected you to assert more discipline. It is the height of impudence that he should continue to try to weave some bizarre fairytale that strains credulity beyond its breaking point."

Dagenham gathered himself to respond, but Ford cut him off.

"It is straining credulity beyond its breaking point, my lord," responded Ford, "to imagine that Mrs. Callaway would have engaged in vigorous equestrian competitions less than one month before the birth of her child."

Ford's previous words had had no visible impact upon the Canderblanks, but *this* time he could see the effects sinking in, like a rock tossed into some pool of viscous liquid, setting off great, slow ripples that expanded in ever-increasing circles.

Lady Canderblank prepared to speak.

"Shut up, Deb," growled Lord Canderblank, and the reaction was postponed.

"During the months preceding December, 1903, when young Callaway was born, Your Ladyship was suffering from an illness which required you to withdraw from the Viceregal Court. You returned to society at the same time that the Callaways received their new posting.

"As for my sources of information, Major Callaway's old commanding officer is now retired here in England, and I interviewed him this afternoon with regard to the circumstances of Callaway's promotion. He was flabbergasted—that word is contained in his written statement—to hear that Mrs. Callaway gave birth immediately before or during her husband's posting. His wife has also made a sworn statement to the effect that Mrs. Callaway was not visibly pregnant, and was, at the time of the posting, expressing concerns to the other ladies on post that she had been unable to conceive."

The Canderblanks stared back like sphinxes.

"I obtained reports of your illness and subsequent return from old contemporary copies of the *Times of India* in the British Museum. I became aware of Mrs. Callaway's equestrian success from a photograph in a book describing life in the Army in India, entitled *Serving the Raj*. I found the book among young Callaway's possessions. He had purchased it from a secondhand book shop."

The tableau remained in place, but seemed diminished, as if the Canderblanks had shrunk a little.

"I believe that Callaway realized, from that photograph, that Mrs. Callaway could not be his natural mother. He therefore cast about to someone else who could be, and he reached a conclusion, perhaps erroneously. He approached that person, but she denied it, and even at the time of his death, he remained an unacknowledged son."

"You cannot possibly know that!" Lord Canderblank burst out.

"Among Callaway's effects was an unfinished letter dated the day of his death, which began *'Dearest Mummy, Why do you deny me …'*"

"A tissue of falsehoods, suppositions, and lies!" his lordship spluttered.

"I have taken an affidavit from Mrs. Markham in which she states, under oath, that young Callaway was not Mrs. Callaway's natural child. And that Lady Canderblank gave the child to Mrs. Callaway, who accepted it as her own in return for favors to be granted."

*"Hearsay!"* Lord Canderblank barked.

"I have asked the authorities in India to obtain similar statements directly from Major and Mrs. Callaway."

"Circumstantial codswallop!"

"I have also asked the authorities to find the doctors who treated Your Ladyship, in order to determine the precise causes and nature of your ill health."

"Doctors are bound by patient confidentiality …" his lordship snapped.

"And by the laws governing obstruction of justice and contempt of court," Ford responded, interrupting him.

"You will put a stop to this, Percy, *immediately!*" Lord Canderblank demanded.

"You know I can't do that, James," Colonel Dagenham replied. "We are investigating a capital crime."

"I deny it! I deny it!" Lady Canderblank spluttered in fury, speaking for the first time since her opening salvos.

Ford gazed at her. Under what bizarre circumstances had she given way to an illicit passion whose fruit was the late, unlamented Callaway? Had her evident distain for her longsuffering husband led to repeated betrayals of her marriage vows? She had taken enormous risks of discovery and ostracism; did she secretly despise the very society in which she moved?

"I deny *everything!*" she hissed vehemently, as if reading his thoughts.

"Indeed, my lady," Ford said, "I believe you have already done so."

Lady Canderblank then began a tirade punctuated by her husband's ineffectual efforts to shut her up. Colonel Dagenham and Ford stood passively waiting for the eruption to run its course. When, at last, she had subsided sufficiently that others could make themselves heard, it was Colonel Dagenham who addressed Lord Canderblank.

"There is absolutely no reason for this information to be placed in the public domain, Canderblank, if it is not germane. Chief Inspector Ford has been acting exactly as his duties require, which are to determine the full circumstances of the boy's death. It is very much in your interests to hear him out."

Lady Canderblank's flow of invective ceased immediately. Clearly she had her anger under total control.

"The facts of this relationship may or may not have anything to do with the boy's death," Ford said. "Although it certainly suggests a motive, it is not the only motive that has come to light in this case, and a motive alone does not prove a crime. However, it is critically important that you answer certain additional questions, and I would urge you to do so in all candor."

Lord Canderblank, red of face and tight of lip, asked bleakly, "What is it you wish to know?"

"There have been certain matters about this case that have puzzled me. For example ..."

"You are *puzzled*, officer?" Lady Canderblank's diatribe switched back on in full force, now seasoned with a wicked sarcasm. "My house has been invaded because this incompetent officer is *puzzled*? Percy, you can protect this fool no longer!"

Ford looked at Lord Canderblank and continued to speak in a normal voice beneath her strident tones.

"For example, why Lady Canderblank went to such lengths to destroy potential evidence."

"What's that?" Lord Canderblank asked, straining to hear him. He turned abruptly to his wife. "For God's sake, shut *up*, Deborah!"

She stopped. Perhaps, Ford thought, the best way of countering her venom was simply to ignore her, and let her husband control her if he could.

"For example," he repeated, "why Lady Canderblank went to such lengths to destroy evidence. Immediately following the report of Callaway's death, she had the entire area in front of Trafalgar rooted up, with instructions that the rubbish be burned, against the objections of Sergeant Croft, telling him that Colonel Dagenham had given his permission. That was, of course, a false statement to a police officer. The Colonel not only did not give his permission, but would certainly have refused any such suggestion."

"An obvious misunderstanding," Lord Canderblank began, but Ford continued to speak.

"Lady Canderblank told the Sergeant about the Colonel's approval at ten o'clock. You did not telephone the Colonel until half past ten. Therefore there was no misunderstanding, sir. The statement was false."

Lord Canderblank opened his mouth and closed it again.

"Ten o'clock, or half past ten," Lady Canderblank sneered. "Such details are completely inconsequential. I have no doubt, Percy, that ..."

"Lady Deborah," interrupted Colonel Dagenham, "your actions were reprehensible, to say the very least. You deceived the Sergeant. You deliberately and falsely misrepresented ..."

"Come, come, Percy," she began to retort.

"I am the senior police officer of the county, madam," Dagenham roared. "I promise you the Home Secretary will be very, *very* displeased if this matter is brought to his attention. Indeed, your behavior throughout this incident has been completely unsatisfactory. Your statement to Sergeant was not just a lie, but a criminal offense for which the penalty is imprisonment."

"I am unimpressed by such officious fiddle-faddle, Percy," she snapped. "I remember when you were a small boy in knickerbockers—always ordering everyone about and spouting rules as if ..."

To Ford's delight, Dagenham gave way to his anger.

*"Canderblank,"* he bellowed. "If you cannot control your wife, I will have her taken into custody. Do I make myself clear?"

"Shut *up*, Deb," his lordship snarled, for the second time that evening.

Ford spoke into the ensuing silence as if he had not been interrupted.

"The groundskeepers, however, decided to salvage and replant the rhododendrons in another location. This morning a team of policemen led by Sergeant Croft searched the remnants of the bushes, and found a scrap of material torn from a lady's gown. There are credible witnesses who will testify that Lady Canderblank's dress was torn when she returned to the Master's Lodge. The material is an expensive silk, possibly of Indian origin, but we have not yet brought in the appropriate experts. We have instigated a search for the dressmakers who made the gown from which it was torn. Such searches take time but usually yield results."

"While walking, I encountered a stray cat," her ladyship shrugged. "The animal scratched me."

"Ah, that would explain it, Lady Canderblank," Ford said without inflection. "I fear so obvious an explanation had eluded me. Did you witness this assault, sir?"

His lordship spluttered indistinctly, and Ford continued.

"Another source of puzzlement has been the failure of Major and Mrs. Callaway to send any cables in response to the news of the boy's death. Such a shattering blow would surely have resulted in at least one, if not several communications. Doctor Thornby has not received a telegraph, and nor have the Markhams. One wonders whether they did in fact respond, *but to another party.*"

Ford paused. The still life portrait had reconstituted itself.

"As I said at the outset, my purpose this evening was to present this information to you, and to provide you with an opportunity to comment before I draw any conclusions. However, in the circumstances, I must warn you that anything you say will be taken down and may be used as evidence against you."

A long silence ensued.

"We wish to speak to you privately, Dagenham," said Lord Canderblank at last.

"If you wish to speak to me about the case, Canderblank, you must speak to the investigating officer."

"It was the Trumpington boy," Lady Canderblank hissed, as if Trumpington were a stranger and not her own nephew.

"Very possibly, Your Ladyship," said Ford, "But I have not reached that conclusion."

◆    ◆    ◆

The police driver had been inspired by his trip to Oxford, and was now becoming a devotee of high speed driving. He particularly liked the effects of rapid acceleration, and the forecourt of Canderblank Hall offered a perfect opportunity to demonstrate his newly acquired skills. The party therefore departed in a spray of gravel, as if propelled by Lady Canderblank's venom.

"Perhaps it really was the Trumpington boy," said Colonel Dagenham, half turned in the front seat as the Humber lurched forward. "God, what a mess that woman has got herself into!"

"It's nothing worse than she deserves, if you ask me, sir," said Sergeant Jackson, as she sat jammed between Ford and Croft on the narrow back seat. "It's him I feel sorry for—married to a cow like that all these years and now facing scandal and ruin because of her. Trumpington's her nephew, for God's sake—or was; did you hear her trying to blame the murder on him?"

Colonel Dagenham reflected.

"If, for the sake of argument, she did kill Callaway, does that mean that she also killed Trumpington?"

"That's a bit of a stretch, sir," Ford replied. "We know far less about Trumpington's last hours than we do about Callaway's. I must admit I've been a bit obsessive about Callaway. But now that I understand the significance of that damn book, I think I'll set all that aside and concentrate on the second death. Tomorrow morning we'll start focusing on that."

"Tomorrow morning is the cricket match," Croft said. "We'll have to find you some togs. He's about Inspector Farrell's size, Colonel, I should say. I wonder if Farrell's got any spares."

While Croft and Dagenham debated the most likely sources of sporting equipment for Ford, Ford's spirits, exhausted by the pressures of the day and drained by the encounter with the Canderblanks, sank even lower. The driver down-shifted dramatically as they climbed Birdslip Hill, and Ford envied him his simple pleasure.

# Wednesday

Wednesday dawned brightly. As the sun rose higher into the cloudless sky, Ford's spirits drooped in proportion. Rain could have saved him from the Colonel's cricket match, but now it looked as if he were trapped.

The match would be played on the Great Lawn at Kings. It seemed bizarre to Ford that he was committed to a sporting event to be played at the scene of two murders, on a lawn flanked by the Gymnasium on one side and Trafalgar on the other—the two buildings from which the young men had fallen—and with murder suspects scattered among the milling crowd.

He should have refused. He would make a spectacle of himself. After one over—six successive balls bowled by the bowler—his leg would start hurting. He would have to be polite to large numbers of people that he loathed. He would be wearing a borrowed pair of shoes, whose owner might or might not share his own views on personal hygiene. The entire event would be a disaster.

As Ford was waiting for breakfast at the Kings Arms, Croft appeared with borrowed cricket gear in hand. The boots looked brand new, thank God. Haltingly, Croft asked Ford if he would like to try a few practice deliveries in his backyard. Ford was working himself into a nervous panic and accepted the offer.

There was just room between the stone lockup and the chicken coops to measure out a twenty-two yard cricket pitch. Croft squatted down with his back to the coops and pulled on his big wicket keeping gloves, and Ford retreated down the vegetable garden path, pacing out his run-up.

"Ready when you are, sir," called Croft.

Ford took five quick paces and bowled in Croft's direction. In his youth he had bowled thousands of overs, and his body remembered the familiar rhythm. It seemed like putting on a pair of old and comfortable shoes. The ball bounced midway between him and Croft, and Croft caught it chest high.

"Very short," Ford said, and Croft tossed the ball back to him without comment. Ford retreated toward the vegetables. His second delivery was far too long, bouncing almost at Croft's feet. After ten tries he was able to bounce the ball consistently eight feet in front of Croft.

The art of spin bowling consists of tossing the ball with a flick of the wrist and fingers, so that the ball spins as it approaches the batsman. Unlike the American game of baseball, in cricket, the ball bounces before it reaches the batsman. An appropriate spin can cause it to veer or "break" to one side or the other when it strikes the ground. This sudden and unpredictable change of trajectory makes it difficult for the batsman to hit the ball correctly, and if the ball is bounced the correct distance or "length" from the batsman, he has very little time to react.

Ford's forte was making the ball break sharply to left or right, an "off break" or a "leg break" as they are termed, thereby confusing the batsman, who might therefore miss the ball. If the ball struck the wicket—the three vertical wooden stumps that represent the "strike zone" in baseball—the batsman would be out.

"Just like riding a bicycle; you never forget, sir," said Croft. "You'll be fine, if I may make so bold. You've got your length back already, sir."

The back door swung open.

"There's no time for a full breakfast," said Mrs. Croft, "so I've just done fried sausages and eggs and mushrooms, and baked some rolls. Oh, and there's bacon, of course, and I can fry some kidneys. It's not much, but it should keep you going."

◆    ◆    ◆

An hour later, the Colonel won the toss and elected to bat. This had the advantage of saving Ford from immediate humiliation, but condemned him to sit amongst the masters and their wives, waiting for his turn to bat while making polite conversation and pretending to enjoy himself. The

Canderblanks were there *en masse*, occupying the largest deck chairs in the center of the crowd, with Mrs. Thornby twittering around them serving tea and pastries, and the lesser luminaries spread out around them in strict order of precedence.

Lord Canderblank summoned up a minimal nod to Ford and Dagenham. Lady Canderblank ignored Ford completely and managed to have her back to him at all times. Victoria gave him an opaque smile. Obviously her mother had given her a vicious account of the previous evening, and he found that he very much cared whether or not she now saw him as her mother did.

The game settled into the snail-like progress of most cricket matches, and Ford found his attention wandering.

The Great Lawn was divided into two by the Kings Oak, a massive tree whose limbs were falsely rumored to have hidden Bonnie Prince Charlie in the rebellion of 1745. Every new boy was forced by the seniors to climb it by night, and scratch his initials high on its upper boughs. It was also a target for ambitious cricketers who would attempt to hit the ball over it, and invariably fail.

The First Eleven cricket pitch occupied the half of the lawn closest to the Gatehouse. From his deckchair, Ford could see both Callaway's window and the roof of the gym. Two very different murders had taken place, bound together by the closeness of their timing and the actual cause of death, but very different in all other respects …

Callaway was almost universally disliked, evidently with good reason, while Trumpington was much admired. In Callaway's case Ford had too many suspects, in Trumpington's, too few. He *had* to decide whether to consider this as one case or two. If one, for example, then Lady Canderblank must be a suspect in Trumpington's death; if two then she …

"Better get your pads on, Ford," the Colonel intruded into his thoughts. "You're next up after Jameson."

Ford jerked back to the present, and to the immediate prospect of making a fool of himself in front of Victoria. He was fifth or sixth in the batting order. He had been hoping that the openers would do well, and that he would never have to bat at all, but while he had been daydreaming, the Colonel's team had been going down like ninepins.

The Colonel was entertaining a guest from the New York Police Department, and was vainly trying to explain the rules. "Yes, the entire team bats in succession, and then the other team ... There are two 'home plates,' as it were, separated by twenty two yards. A bowler bowls six times from one end toward one batsman—that's called an 'over'—and then another bowler bowls to the other batsman from the other end ..."

Ford fervently wished that Jameson, whoever he was, would score a century. Croft was at the other end, batting defensively with a dogged determination. The School's bowlers were young giants who obviously believed that speed was far more important than accuracy, and their deliveries were flying around the batsmen's heads.

Jameson had evidently decided to fight fire with fire, and was flailing away with his bat as if he were an American baseball player. He connected with a ball at chest height, and sent it into the oak trees by the Chapel for six runs. "Yes, old chap," he heard the Colonel saying, "what you call a 'home run' earns six runs in cricket." Jameson missed the next ball completely; the next he hooked high over the square leg boundary for another six, scattering the spectators; the next sent the leg stump of his wicket spinning, and Jameson was out and Ford was in.

Ford swallowed and started out for the wickets, passing Jameson halfway, as the crowd clapped politely. Croft walked down the pitch to meet him.

"You'd better watch out, sir. They're both young hooligans. Only one ball left in this over."

Ford knew that negative thoughts, like "don't make a complete fool of yourself," are completely self-destructive, but no positive thoughts sprang to mind. He settled his cap firmly on his head, took his stance, and muttered, "don't make a complete fool of yourself."

The bowler took an extravagantly long run-up, and hurled the ball straight at Ford's left ear. Ford crouched and instinctively lifted his bat in self-defense. There was a loud rap as the ball struck his bat, and it flew past the wicketkeeper's outstretched glove and reached the fine leg boundary in three hops.

Ford found himself shaking with excitement and relief. The fielding team changed positions for the next over, and Ford nonchalantly leaned on his bat and crossed his ankles, as if a boundary earning four runs off his first ball was a matter of complete routine.

Croft batted with extreme caution, as if he were Horatio guarding the bridge. To Ford's delight, Croft pushed the last ball of the over through the gulley for a sharp single, Ford and he changed ends, and Croft was batting again. Ford was sufficiently relaxed to glance around, and saw that Victoria was regarding him through a large pair of binoculars.

For the next four overs, Croft got almost all of the batting, and Ford was glad to stay out of the limelight. When lunch was called, he felt that he had not been a complete disaster after all. Perhaps he would get a chance to speak with Victoria; her parting smile in Soho still burned in his memory.

◆        ◆        ◆

As soon as he joined the crowd around the buffet table, he found Victoria at his elbow. He had time to note how charmingly her broad rimmed straw hat framed her face, and how its ribbon perfectly complemented her eyes.

"May I speak to you, Chief Inspector?" she asked him, without discernable emotion.

Without waiting for a reply, she turned through the crowd and began to walk slowly in the direction of the Chapel. When they were out of earshot of the crowd, she turned on him and began abruptly in a steely voice.

"You have *really* upset my mother—and not for the first time, I may add!"

He was immediately on the defensive. He stomach had turned to water and he found he was almost stuttering.

"I regret any distress I may have caused her—or you, for that matter, Miss Canderblank." This was definitely not the occasion to address her as *V.* "It was certainly not my intention to upset her."

"Perhaps," she said icily. "But everybody is trying to put this unfortunate incident in the past. When all is said and done, while the boy Callaway's death is regrettable, it is not the end of the earth."

Ford was seized by a sense of grave injustice.

"It was for *him*, Miss Canderblank. Are you suggesting that his death should not be investigated? That the person or persons who murdered him should not be brought to justice?"

"I am simply saying that I see no particular sense in stirring up a hornet's nest. It's not even certain that he was murdered at all."

Ford's sense of injustice deepened.

"I agree it is possible that his neck was broken by accident, although it seems somewhat unlikely that someone stabbed him four times by mistake." Her eyes widened and he caught himself. Injustice or no injustice, an argument would do no good. He controlled his tone. "But even if he was not murdered, the sooner all the facts can be laid out clearly, the sooner this unfortunate incident can be *put in the past*, to use your words. I am simply trying to establish those facts, Miss Canderblank; that is all."

"Then I suggest you do that by ceasing this personal vendetta against my mother. It is absurd to think that a person in her position could possibly be involved in murdering a schoolboy. Frankly, I find your behavior unbecoming."

In contrast to her habitual vivacity, she spoke without emotion. Her coldness disturbed Ford far more than her mother's ranting ever could. Her manner in the restaurant had indeed been an act, he was forced to accept; he was now staring at the real Victoria Canderblank, to whom he was merely an inquisitive policeman.

A sort of savage anger began to burn in the ashes of his daydreams.

"Oh, I fear there is indeed a case to be made against your mother," he said, hoping he sounded as brutal as he felt. "First, she went to great lengths to conceal or destroy evidence. Second, she lied about her whereabouts on the night of Callaway's murder. Third, she lied about her relationship with Callaway, which, had it been revealed, would have ruined her. Callaway was threatening to expose the relationship; thus, I fear your mother had nothing to lose and everything to gain, from his death. Further, it was very much in her interest that he be silenced as soon as possible—before the story could come out."

"Even if those things were true," she retorted "which they *cannot* be—she could not possibly have killed him!"

"I beg to differ, Miss Canderblank, he said inexorably. "Your mother could have disguised herself and gone to Callaway's door, unremarked amongst the other costumed actors, and pushed him through the window. It was perhaps the one night of the school year when a woman could enter the dormitories and not be recognized as such. Then she could have gone downstairs, still unremarked, taken a knife from the kitchen, and stabbed the body several times to ensure that the boy was dead."

Victoria's face wrinkled in distaste and disbelief, but Ford was not finished.

"When she returned to the Master's Lodge, she insisted on bathing, even though a few hours before, she had complained bitterly about the lack of hot water. Her clothing was torn and her hand was scratched; both are consistent with her having crept through the bushes at night, and for both, her explanation is, to be blunt, ludicrous."

Victoria dismissed his words with a wave of her hand.

"You simply cannot expect me to believe my mother capable of such a thing! She may be a bit overbearing at times, I admit, and she may insist upon having her own way, but *murder* …"

Perhaps s she was appealing to him for help in dealing with the inconceivable notion that her mother was capable of cold-blooded killing, but Ford was in no mood to offer comfort.

"Would you have thought your mother capable of an illicit love affair, and the concealment of the fruit of the alliance?"

"It's all so—so *squalid!* It makes me sick!"

His anger was abating, but he said with priggish formality: "I regret having distressed you, Miss Canderblank."

She turned to face him directly, and it was hard for Ford to accept she was the same person who had bewitched him on the golf course and at the dinner table.

"Is there some special pleasure you derive from finding the worst in people?" she demanded viciously. "Is that why you chose to be a policeman? Do you enjoy ferreting out a person's petty vices and foolish indiscretions, real or imagined, and ruining their reputations?"

He groped for a reply. "Miss Canderblank, two boys have been murdered, and ..."

"This interview is at an *end!* I see I have misjudged you completely. I suggest you return to the gutter, Chief Inspector; it seems to be your natural milieu."

Miss Canderblank swept back toward the pavilion, leaving Ford to watch her retreating back helplessly. His leg began to ache.

◆     ◆     ◆

The remainder of the cricket match flew by in a whirl. Ford was seething with righteous indignation that his character had been impugned, furious with himself that she had pierced his armor so easily and so deeply, and full of self-doubt as to whether he would be able to conduct the remainder of the investigation with anything remotely resembling objectivity.

It was so *unfair!*

He had swallowed Lady Canderblank's insults, endured her attempts to derail his investigations, and pressed on until he had uncovered her secret. It was not *his* fault she had had a fling in India. It was not *his* fault that the boy had been murdered, thereby setting in motion the train of investigation through which her peccadillo had come to light.

Yet Victoria Canderblank was blaming him for the whole squalid mess.

Turning his inner furies against the School's cricketers, he abandoned caution and attacked the bowling. His eyesight seemed unnaturally good, and the ball seemed to approach him at a preternaturally slow pace, so that he was able to hit it anywhere he wanted. He felt no pain in his leg.

He was determined not simply to defeat the bowlers' efforts—he would *humiliate* them. He was particularly anxious to hit the ball extremely hard in the Canderblanks' direction, and he felt a fierce shaft of triumph when Lady Canderblank leapt out of her chair in a most undignified manner for fear of being struck.

Croft, meanwhile, continued his dour defensive play. After an hour, he and Ford had added a hundred runs, and Colonel Dagenham declared the inning over.

The School came in to bat, and in due course it was Ford's turn to bowl. His senses remained supernaturally sharp and his mood, if possible, was even blacker than before. The sharp stabs of pain in his leg had returned, but they acted as a spur rather than a deterrent.

From time to time in his earlier cricketing career he had been able to get leg breaks to break so sharply and at such a perfect length that they were unplayable, and this afternoon was another such occasion. A parade of batsmen faced him, and he overwhelmed them; by teatime the match was turning into a rout, and half an hour later, the School was all out.

The players straggled in from the field to polite applause.

Now that the tensions of the match were over, Ford's leg ached fiercely, and he was limping badly. When he saw the Canderblanks' Rolls Royce sweeping away toward the Gatehouse, he felt a cruel sense of loss. There was a steady trickle of people congratulating him on his performance, but it was an effort to summon up any vestige of civility. He refused, as politely as his mood permitted, an invitation to take tea in the Lodge, and hobbled back to the police car.

Croft judged his mood correctly and was silent as they rumbled back down the hill to the village. At the Kings Arms, Ford left the car with a curt nod to Croft and painfully climbed the stairs to his room. It was in his mind to take a bath, but instead he slumped down in the uncomfortable armchair and let his thoughts race unhindered.

◆     ◆     ◆

An hour later, Ford finally roused himself and soaked in a hot tub, but neither his leg nor his outlook had improved. He went downstairs and ate an unappetizing meal of cold, fatty ham and overcooked baked beans, served by a sulking Lucy, thinking all the while of the feast he might have had if he had had the civility to walk across the green and be sociable with the Crofts—an easy and indeed pleasant course of action, but one of which he was incapable tonight.

He knew that Croft was very pleased to have kept wicket for him, and delighted that he had stumped two batsmen and caught three more off Ford's bowling. He had no right to deny Croft his moment of celebration, but he simply could not rise to the occasion.

He dragged his protesting leg back up the stairs, propped it up on a pile of pillows, opened a fresh page in his note book, and wrote, very carefully: *"Who killed Callaway?"*

He stared at the page, which stared back at him. Inspiration eluded him. He turned to a fresh page and wrote: *"Who killed Trumpington?"* Inspiration still eluded him.

He rearranged his leg. His alarm clock ticked loudly. He tried a final page: *"Did the same person commit both murders?"* He closed his eyes but he was not sleepy. He tried swearing, but that did not clear his mind.

He returned to the first page and almost *wrote "Lady Canderblank"* beneath *"Who killed Callaway?"* but his pen hovered above the white surface. He had no question that she was sufficiently malicious, merciless, and ambitious, to kill her natural son, and then to kill her nephew Trumpington to protect herself and her reputation.

Doctor Thornby had telephoned her after meeting with Trumpington on the evening of his death. He would certainly have told her that Trumpington had been at the scene of Callaway's death, that while there, he had observed a female figure—or figure appearing to be feminine—entering the bushes, and that Ford was going to continue the interview with Trumpington in the morning. Therefore she would *have* to kill Trumpington for fear that Ford would extract the information from him. It was a risk she could not run.

His mind veered to the cricket match and that exquisitely delicious moment when she had fled his cricket ball. She had jumped out of her deckchair, spilling her tea on her dress, tripped over her husband's chair, and ended in an ungainly heap on the grass. Her impenetrable hauteur had been shattered. People had tittered behind their hands. It had been *delightful!*

He paused. In order to kill Trumpington she would have had to climb in and out of the Gymnasium attic window, and navigate the slippery tiles of the roof. The woman was in her fifties and heavily corseted. Would she have removed her corsets in order to kill Trumpington? No. The whole idea was bizarre.

The clock ticked and ticked, and Ford thought and thought, and his mood grew steadily blacker.

If Lady Canderblank had *not* killed Trumpington, then someone else had, which meant that there were two murderers and two unrelated murders. Kings would then be housing two people capable of murder, and with two separate and overpowering reasons to kill. Did that really seem likely? Would Lucy Green actually murder Trumpington over a few pounds for a backstreet abortion? Did she have the force of character or bodily strength to do so?

Or would Green have killed Trumpington in fury for deflowering his daughter, even in the midst of an ongoing police investigation in which Green was already a suspect? Would the arrogant Trumpington have actually gone to the roof to meet Green, of all people? Again, it was simply not credible.

He turned to a fresh page and wrote out the list of suspects. The three Canderblanks headed the list. He considered the Greens, but he did not write them down. Similarly, he could not find it in himself to keep young Connelly on the list. He stared at the page; he had only three credible suspects for either murder, and they were all Canderblanks.

His mouth tasted sour from too many cigarettes and the bitterness of Victoria Canderblank's condemnation.

"Right," he said out loud. "So be it. Tomorrow I'll solve the crime and then go up to London in the evening. On Friday I'll review the case with Brownlee, and then we'll come back down and make the arrest on Saturday. Nothing to it!"

The case would be over, apart from the tedious processes of writing long reports and briefing the lawyers. He would take some time off to play golf, and he would never, ever, have to think about Victoria Canderblank again.

He undressed and settled into bed, but his mind was racing and his leg was merciless. The clock ticked on.

Even if it *was* a Canderblank, which one? Was his lordship a man of action? It didn't seem very likely; murder demands more than petulance.

Surely Lady Canderblank would never stoop to such a menial task as actually murdering someone—she'd have instructed her secretary or a trusted servant to see that it was done ...

*"Caruthers—I wish you to dispatch a schoolboy immediately!"*

*"Of course, Your Ladyship, at once; and the afternoon mail has arrived—do you wish to see it?"*

The whole thing was absurd! And Victoria had gone to bed before Callaway was murdered, unless ...

"Oh no, please, no," he groaned aloud, as a whole new avenue of ugliness opened up before him. Her words came back to him: *"I suggest you return to the gutter, Chief Inspector; it seems to be your natural milieu."*

Exhaustion overcame him, and he fell into a fitful sleep.

# Thursday

"**G**ood morning, Mrs. Croft," said Ford when she opened to his knock. He was feeling remarkably cheerful despite his wretched night. "I'm sorry to disturb you so early. Is your husband about, by any chance?"

"That's all right, sir. He's out the back attending to his roses."

"I'm afraid I owe him an apology."

"Oh no, sir. You have a great deal on your mind."

Obviously Croft had told his wife about Ford's black mood.

"A murder must play on the nerves, I should think. How's your leg, sir, after all that running about, if you don't mind my asking?"

"Much better this morning, thank you; it's my own damned fault for doing too much. Well, I'll just have a word with him."

"Spot of breakfast, sir?"

"That's awfully good of you; I'd love some."

"Well, I'll just see what I've got."

Ford walked around the house and found Croft at the end of his back garden, loading evil-smelling glutinous muck into a wheelbarrow.

"Nonsense, sir," said Croft, when Ford apologized for his black mood on the previous day. He straightened and eased his back.

"I didn't even notice," he lied cheerfully. "What's on the calendar for today?"

"Well, Croft," Ford said, "we've probably got all the facts that we're ever going to get until the murderer or murderers confess. So we'll spend the day reviewing the information and seeing if we have a real case against anyone."

Sergeant Jackson arrived while they were having breakfast.

"No thanks, Mrs. Ford," she said, "I've already had something to eat."

"Well, Dorothy, there's some deviled eggs left over—I hate to see them go to waste—and the last piece of ham. Here, have some tea and toast to keep you going while I get a plate."

"I hear you two did rather well, yesterday," Sergeant Jackson said, sitting down and bowing to the inevitable forthcoming meal.

Croft grinned, and between bites of ham and egg, said, "The Chief Inspector scored 78 not out in an hour and a half, and his bowling was 6 for 18. It was a pleasure to watch."

"They were only schoolboys," Ford protested. "Besides, you did rather well yourself."

"I hear you dropped a six into Lady Canderblank's lap," Dorothy Jackson said. "I wish I'd been there to see it."

"She made a right fool of herself," said Mrs. Croft succinctly as she reentered carrying a fresh plate. "Tripped over her own feet and went ass over teakettle, if you'll excuse me, and wouldn't stop complaining for the rest of the match. Now we all know the color of her bloomers," she said, grinning at the memory. "Who'd have expected it?"

Ford hadn't caught sight of Lady Canderblank's nether garments, but refrained from asking the obvious intriguing question. "Speaking of the Canderblanks," he said instead, "I fear we have some work to do. I sat up half the night reviewing where we stand."

"Stay at the table, if you're comfortable, sir, and I'll clear away to give you some room."

"Are you sure we won't be in your way?"

"Not at all."

Ford closed his eyes to summarize the jumble of information in his head. He must be learning that habit from Brownlee, he reflected.

"Let's begin by summarizing incontrovertible facts. As far as Callaway's death is concerned, Lady Canderblank was in the bushes; Connelly was in the bushes and in Callaway's room, by his own admission; and Trumpington was all over Trafalgar. All of them had motives. Agreed?"

"Agreed, sir," said Croft, writing copiously.

"Lady Canderblank was back in the Lodge by ten forty-five, raising holy hell, so it's unlikely that she could have killed Callaway, messed around with the knife, and returned in time. We don't know what Connelly did after he went to Callaway's room, and we know that Trumpington met Lucy Green at five minutes before eleven. Therefore we should focus our attention on Trumpington and Connelly."

"If it's one of them, I hope it wasn't Connelly," said Sergeant Jackson.

"I agree. Now, as far as Trumpington's death is concerned, we have no direct evidence, so we must rely on two things—motive and opportunity. In terms of motive, we also have the two Greens, George and Lucy. Lucy was out for a walk on Thursday night, so in that sense she had opportunity. Connelly had argued with Trumpington earlier in the evening and was attempting to run away from Kings; he, too, had motive and opportunity."

He steeled his voice to remain neutral.

"Miss Canderblank was at Kings. She might have had motive if she was aware of her mother's situation, and she also had opportunity. So, we have Lucy, Connelly, and Miss Canderblank."

"With Connelly on both lists, unfortunately," said Sergeant Jackson sadly.

"I fear so."

Fifteen minutes had elapsed since breakfast, and Mrs. Croft was sure they would all be dying of thirst. A large teapot appeared under a handsome tea cozy crocheted in the shape of a plump hen.

"I like your tea cozy," commented Sergeant Jackson. "My mother has one a bit like it, but not as well made. This is very handsome—a work of art."

"Oh, it's not *my* work—Bob's the crochet and knitting expert in this household."

"Now, why did you have to tell them that?" Croft growled, turning red with embarrassment while Ford struggled to control a grin.

"It's the long winter evenings, sir," Croft appealed to Ford. "You have to keep yourself occupied."

"Quite so; I can't even darn a pair of socks, I'm afraid. I wish I had your skills."

"I'd be grateful if you didn't repeat it, if you don't mind."

"I won't tell a soul."

"Nor will I," Sergeant Jackson said. "Although if it slips out by accident in the Kings Arms one evening ..."

"You wouldn't, would you?" Croft asked her in alarm.

"I might ... I've a dress that needs altering—how's your hemming?"

"Let's move on," said Ford hurriedly. "Let's address the case concerning Trumpington. Let's consider our suspects one by one. As far as Lucy is concerned, why on earth would Trumpington want to meet her in the Gymnasium attics, of all places?"

"Well, sir," said Mrs. Croft, "I hope you don't mind me interrupting, but it would be private, like, if they were going to, well ..."

"By Jove you're right, as always," Ford responded. "Sergeant Jackson, would you mind going across to the Kings Arms and fetching her? We'll settle it once and for all."

"Right, sir," she said, immediately departed, and fifteen minutes later returned with Lucy.

They moved into the comparative formality of Croft's parlor. By unspoken consent, Ford and Croft left it to Sergeant Jackson to do the questioning.

"Now then, Lucy," she began in her inimitable way, "Where did the Trumpington boy take advantage of you? In his room? In the fields? In the attics of the gym?"

Lucy had lost her former truculence and already seemed on the verge of tears.

"You went there on that Thursday, didn't you; went there to meet him just like you had before? You thought if you gave him what he wanted again, he'd give you some money, didn't you? One good turn deserves another?"

"Yes I did, but I never did it with him that night ..." She faltered. "I saw him in the village in the afternoon, and he told me to be in the attic at eleven o'clock sharp. I asked him for money, and he said that depended on whether I was nice to him, like. I didn't have a choice, did I?"

She shuddered with an impending bout of weeping.

"Anyway, I got to the School on time, but there was a car parked where I usually climb in, so I had to go the long way, and when I was coming up, I saw them teachers gathered round a body, and Mr. Jaspers' dog was barking its head off. I got frightened and ran home, thinking how I'd never get a penny from him if he was dead … Then Sergeant Croft came upstairs in the pub to get the Inspector, and I thought 'Oh my God, he's going to arrest me!' Then you came out of your room, sir, and …"

"Whose car was it?" asked Ford, interrupting the flow.

"Who's what, sir?"

"You say you saw a car parked outside the grounds," Sergeant Jackson said. "Who was in it?"

"I couldn't see: it was pitch black raining."

"What kind of car?"

"A big fancy one, with one of them statues on the front. You've got to believe me—it's the truth."

Ford intervened.

"Lucy, Sergeant Jackson is doing her best to help you. She's the best hope you have. Lying to us won't help."

"I know that, sir, I do! It's the truth, I swear to God!"

"Is there anything else to tell us? Anyone you saw, or anything that didn't strike you as right?"

She screwed up her eyes in concentration, and finally shook her head.

"All right, Lucy, thank you," Ford told her. "I think you're being honest. If you think of anything more, tell the Sergeant."

"I will, sir."

Sergeant Jackson patted Lucy on the shoulder and escorted her as far as the front door. They returned to the kitchen. Mrs. Croft had taken the opportunity to bake the fresh scones that now sat, still hot and steaming, on a platter in the center of the table.

"The strawberry preserves are from the garden. I'll just finish whipping the cream, and it'll ready in a moment. Was I right about Lucy, if I may ask, sir?"

"Right, as always, Mrs. Croft," Ford said.

He squared his shoulders to face the unpleasant as directly as possible.

"Now, let's take the case of Victoria Canderblank. A big car with a stat-uette sounds like the Canderblank Rolls, although Lucy might have been mistaken in the darkness. She—Miss Canderblank—delivered her library book, left the grounds, and then parked. Can anyone suggest a legitimate reason for doing so?"

Croft seemed embarrassed. He must have guessed at Ford's internal predicament and remained silent.

"The case against her would be based on her desire to silence a potential rumor against her mother," Ford prompted them, as if she were a com-plete stranger. "If Callaway had boasted to Trumpington that they were, in fact, cousins, then Trumpington could have been a threat."

"Would she kill her own cousin?" Croft asked.

"Lady Canderblank had no reluctance in trying to pin Callaway's mur-der on him, so why wouldn't her daughter share her animosity? No, I think Miss Canderblank is very much on our suspect list—if we're inclined to believe that Lucy has finally told the truth."

Was he being completely objective, he wondered, or was he being vin-dictive following her cruel words at the cricket match? He hurried on.

"Which brings us to the wretched Connelly, threatened with a thor-oughly undeserved caning, and God knows what else, in dire trouble with the Captain of the School."

"It's just not fair, sir, the way he was treated," said Croft.

"I agree, and I must say I simply can't imagine he would kill either Cal-laway or Trumpington—I'll bet he was too afraid of Callaway, and he probably regarded Trumpington as a god. It's extremely unusual for chil-dren to commit murder, even in the most extreme circumstances. Cer-tainly children commit deliberate acts of cruelty, but not to the point of homicide. Nonetheless, he must remain on both lists ... Incidentally, these scones are superb, Mrs. Croft." He held up his third scone and smiled.

"Well, thank you, sir! I'll pop another batch in the oven."

"God, no! I'll scarcely be able to stand as it is! Let's clean up a few loose ends; we'll see Connelly and see if the Master can tell us what he did with that knife. Then I'll run up to London. I must see my boss in the morning."

The telephone rang—by coincidence, it was Brownlee.

"Ford, I've a snippet for you ... in fact, two snippets. They found a dressmaker who has identified that bit of torn dress as belonging to Lady Canderblank ... Thank God my wife doesn't care very much about clothes—the price of that material is *staggering!*"

Ford could hear him smiling.

"Then there's the other snippet, Ford. There's one thing you can say about me, and that's that I harbor grudges ... It probably makes me a bad cop, but I'm too old to change. If someone rubs me the wrong way, it brings out the worst. The snippet concerns this chap Shipman, the Canderblank's secretary. I thought I'd check to see if he has a record, and it seems he's been a bit of a bad lad; let me give you the details."

Brownlee spoke for five minutes while Ford said little but "Good Lord!" several times.

"Bit of advice, Ford: you're sometimes too nice for your own good. Harden your heart and use this, old chap—see what you can stir up!"

◆       ◆       ◆

Ford did not feel any better entering the grounds of Kings regardless of how many times he had done so before. In his youth, the place had been a source of great misery, but now it also had the added quality of housing sinister secrets. He wished desperately for this case to be over, to put all its wretched twists and turns into the past, to wake up in the morning and not to have to ponder, ever again, the wellsprings of Lady Canderblank's malevolence or Trumpington's arrogance, or the enigma of Victoria Canderblank.

Brownlee had said that he was sometimes too nice for his own good. He would take his cue from that; the sooner he was done, the sooner he would be free. Today he would let his distaste for the School and everything it represented get the better of his politeness.

He and Croft presented themselves to Miss Grantly.

"Good morning, Miss Grantly. Is the Master in, if you please?"

"He's in, but he's busy. I wouldn't want to disturb him."

"Would you please tell him I'm here?"

"That would require disturbing him."

"How true. I'll return in half an hour."

"He may still be busy, or he may have left for another appointment."

"True again, Miss Grantly. I'll ask Sergeant Croft to remain here so that he understands it is important that I see him before he goes to that appointment—if appointment there be."

"That will offer no guarantee of his availability."

"Indeed it will not, Miss Grantly, but it will afford him the opportunity to reflect upon the results of declining to be interviewed in a criminal investigation, and the consequent necessity of being escorted to a police station. In the meantime you may wish to telephone his solicitor, so the Master can be fully informed as to his exact legal options, and as to my authorities as investigating officer."

Miss Grantly's complexion, which normally resembled parchment, now took on the tone of *mildewed* parchment. Ford gave her one last withering glance, and left abruptly before his patience deserted him completely. As Ford went out, Croft placidly assumed a waiting posture by the door.

Ford trod the too-familiar corridors to the Masters' Common Room. It was empty, but he discovered from the overflowing notice board that Connelly would be studying Shakespeare under Mr. McIntire's direction.

As he walked through the School to Mr. McIntire's classroom, he heard the sounds of lessons oozing under the classroom doors—the droning of Latin declensions being recited by rote, the scarcely controlled hubbub of Miss Larue's fifth form French class, laughter from some joke by Mr. Feely—and he smelled the noxious vapors from Doctor Howard's chemistry laboratory.

He knocked on Mr. McIntire's door and entered.

McIntire looked squarely at him. *"What bloody man is this?"* he demanded. The class tittered but none replied.

*"What bloody man is this?"* demanded Mr. McIntire a second time, glaring round the classroom, whose occupants were convinced this time Old Mack really had gone ga-ga.

*"I can report, as seemest by my plight, of the revolt the newest state,"* replied Ford, coming to everyone's rescue.

"You idiots, this is the Sergeant," said McIntire, *"who like a good and hardy soldier fought 'gainst my captivity: hail brave friend, say to the king the knowledge of the broil as thou didst leave it."*

*"Doubtful it stood, as two spent swimmers that do cling together and choke their art,"* Ford replied.

"*Macbeth*, you collection of *morons*! Act 1, scene 1. We read it last term, and since Shakespeare has been dead for three hundred years, I doubt he's changed the words in the last three months. What can I do for you, *brave friend*?"

"You can lend me Connelly for ten minutes, sir, if you would."

The boy blanched at the sound of his name, and as he rose from his seat, Ford thought he saw his hands trembling.

He led Connelly out onto the lawn where they would not be disturbed, and came abruptly to the point.

"Connelly, what did you talk about to Trumpington the night he died?" The boy's eyes were rimmed red.

"He said he was going to cane me—twelve strokes. He said it was a warning in case I ever mentioned anything Callaway had ever told me."

Connelly's face was rumpled, as if it had been cast and extracted from the mold before his features were quite set. Every emotion telegraphed itself. Ford realized Connelly's inability to dissemble must have made him an easy prey for Callaway's cruelty and Trumpington's manipulation.

"He couldn't have just caned you without real grounds; he'd have to have a reason to give to Mr. McIntire."

"He said I'd been late for band practice twice. Normally that calls for a hundred written lines times the number of minutes each time. But he said more than once made it habitual, and you can be caned for habitual offenses."

"I remember. Did he offer you a way of getting off?"

"He said that Callaway had stolen money from him, and if I got it back before the end of the evening he'd let me off."

Ford was taken aback, and paused to digest this; it was something he hadn't considered before.

"Did he, by Jove? What did you say?"

"I said I didn't know anything about the money, which is true, and I said the twelve strokes wasn't fair, sir. But he said that was questioning his authority, which is another twelve strokes in and of itself. In the end, he told me to get the money, which he assumed was hidden in Callaway's room, and bring it to him that evening—or else, sir."

The boy's propensity for tears was beginning to reappear.

"So either I had to break into Callaway's room, which Mr. McIntire has said is completely out of bounds, or get caned."

His face disappeared behind a large and dirty handkerchief.

"So I—I just couldn't face it anymore. I decided to do a bunk—to get away from here. I got as far as Twenty Acre Field when it began to rain like hell, and it was pitch black, and somewhere over there, there's a dangerous bull, and so I sat under a tree in the rain, and in the end I just came back, except Old Mack—Mr. McIntire, I mean—caught me climbing in, sir."

"What did he say? Did you tell him what Trumpington had said?"

"I only told him Trumpington had said he'd cane me. So Mr. McIntire said people could do a lot of mean things to me, but they couldn't stop me growing up. One day I'd get out of Kings, and I just had to lump it in the meantime and try to make the best of a bad job. He said the trick was to find something I liked and ignore everything else—like he likes Shakespeare."

"That's very good advice."

"Is it, sir? A lot of people say he's not good enough for Kings."

"Why? Because he got to university on his own merits instead of his father's money? Is it intrinsically superior to be born of wealthy parents, or to have brains? Is it morally superior to buy things rather than to earn them?"

"Well ..."

"Let me give you some advice, Connelly. If you're ever in trouble, or you don't know what to do, go and ask Mr. McIntire or Mr. Jaspers. Callaway and Trumpington were both more than you could handle, in their different ways, and it's no disgrace to ask for help."

The boy's transparent misery reminded Ford vividly of his own hatred for his schooldays.

"And permit me to add one thing more. When I was at Kings, I worked out how many days I had to be here before I could get out. It was a frightening number—over a thousand. But each day I subtracted one, and gradually the number came down. Each day I was able to say to myself that I'd survived another day. I felt proud of myself, like a runner in a long distance race. You may want to do the same."

"What did you do the day you left, sir?"

"We came out through the Gatehouse and started down the hill. The sun was shining. I didn't look back—that was my revenge. I just didn't spare Kings a second glance. Kings had controlled my life, and now it was powerless; not worth even a fleeting look."

Connelly stared at him.

"Is that irony, sir?"

"Exactly so. Now, I'm not necessarily the best person to be giving you advice—Mr. McIntire and Mr. Jaspers and your parents are much better bets ... Let me ask you, on your honor, are you telling the complete truth about Trumpington?"

The boy lifted his chin.

"Yes, sir, I swear it."

"Did you see him later and give him five pounds?"

"No, sir, of course not," he grinned. "I promise I've never had a fiver in my life! Honest!"

"Good! Let's get you back to class before Mr. McIntire calls me a bloody man and means it and sends me to see the Master!"

Though not sent by McIntire, Ford returned to Doctor Thornby's office. The Master was pacing his study while Croft stood impassively at the doorway. Thornby was furious.

"Listen, Ford, this is highly inconvenient. Do you realize you've kept me waiting almost four minutes? You'd better have a damned good reason!"

"Yes, sir, good morning. Sergeant, please make a note of the Master's dissatisfaction and bring it to Colonel Dagenham's attention."

"Right, sir," Croft stalwartly replied behind him.

"Now, sir, the reason I asked to see you is this: where is the knife that Tobias Jones, the undertaker, gave you?"

"The knife that ... I have no idea. Of what relevance is it now that young Trumpington's role is tragically clear? Is this going to be another of your obsessions, like that book of Callaway's?"

Ford tried not to gasp—Lady Canderblank must have told him about the book, following Ford's interview at Canderblank Hall. Why would she reveal so painful an intimate secret to the Master? He dragged himself back to the present.

"Where did you put the knife, sir?"

"Put it?"

"The knife is material evidence in a murder investigation. Where did you put it, sir?"

Thornby stared about vaguely, as if expecting to find the knife somewhere amidst the clutter of his desk.

"I must have put it down somewhere ... It's of no consequence, surely; it was cleaned ... I suppose I may have lost it."

"You *lost* it, sir?"

"Yes, Ford, I must have lost it. Just like that!"

Ford could have sworn he heard a barely audible snort of disbelief behind him.

"I would like to see the library book that Miss Canderblank returned to the Lodge on the evening that Trumpington died, sir, and any other contents in the package."

"The library book that—oh, I vaguely remember something of the sort ... I expect it was returned to the Library."

"What book was it, sir?"

"I have no idea."

"Did you return it yourself?"

"I really can't remember ... Really, Ford, I would have thought you would realize that there are hundreds of books in a school. I can scarcely be expected to remember one specific volume!"

"It was of sufficient significance that it was wrapped up and delivered to you by Miss Canderblank late in the evening, sir, after you had spoken to Lady Canderblank on the telephone."

"Is that all, Ford? I have duties to attend to."

"Have you found your key to the Gymnasium, sir?"

"No, I haven't. And now I must insist you stop pestering me."

"Yes, sir. Sergeant Croft, please make a note that the Master is unable to account for the whereabouts of the knife, the library book, and the Gymnasium key, all of which were last seen in his possession and all of which are material evidence."

"Right, sir," Croft repeated.

The Master sat down at his desk and observed Ford calmly.

"Ford, for your own good, I must say that your investigation—if it is worthy of that name—is becoming tedious as well as disruptive, and your relentless pursuit of these irrelevancies, this minutia, this mountain of trivia, is becoming somewhat embarrassing."

He leaned forward. He had spent many years giving advice to recalcitrant boys, and his manner demonstrated it.

"Tenacity is admirable, but stubbornness is not," the Master continued. "I suggest you complete your efforts by concluding that both boys died by accident, rather than embarrassing yourself further in a fruitless attempt to discover foul play, and somehow punish Kings for the fact that your career here was undistinguished. To be completely frank, people are beginning to make jokes about you!"

Ford returned his stare. He sensed that Croft, still standing behind him, was turning pink with fury.

"I shall take note of your advice, sir."

"I hope so, Ford. I really hope so. Class jealousy is really so very ugly. When someone from a humble background such as yours acquires a little power and attempts to take revenge by attacking his betters, such as the Trumpingtons and the Canderblanks, the effort is always futile."

He spread his hands in appeal.

"You are jeopardizing your career, such as it is. I urge you, for your own good, to accept the inevitable before you become a public spectacle and suffer the consequences."

"Thank you for your advice, sir. I shall take it into consideration."

Ford and Croft left Old School.

"Christ, sir, I don't know how you didn't punch him in the nose," Croft growled as they emerged onto the lawns. "I'd have kicked him from here to Timbuktu!"

"Well, he simply isn't worth it ... but on to more important matters. I'll run up to London now and write up our conclusions and then see my boss in the morning. I think we're finally getting close to the end of this investigation. I'll telephone you after I see Brownlee."

◆　　◆　　◆

Back in London, Ford sat down at his kitchen table. The room was bleak and depressing; the window was high and small and looked out at a neighboring brick wall. The gas stove was old and used for little except boiling water. The cabinets were a particularly vile color of green that clashed with the pinkish linoleum floor. The table itself was of the utilitarian, enameled sort, with chipped corners.

A loaf of bread—stale but not yet rock hard—and a rolled-open tin of sardines constituted his dinner. The contrast with Mrs. Croft's kitchen, or even the cheerful disorder of the Brownlees' kitchen, could not have been more vivid. He imagined the room being inspected by Doctor Thornby with approval: "Well, Ford, at least this room reflects your fundamental mediocrity."

The one redeeming feature was Mrs. Croft's geranium cuttings, which now stood in an old jam pot filled with water. He peered closely at the stalks, but no roots were appearing; perhaps the ambience had robbed them of their will to grow.

He cleared away the dishes and washed them, and made himself a pot of tea. The milk was two days old but still marginally usable.

Reluctant to begin his report, he foraged through the bookshelf to find a pamphlet on careers in the Metropolitan Police to send to White. He dallied over the inscription and then wrapped the book and addressed the package with excessive care.

Bereft of other delaying tactics, he sighed, pulled out a pad of lined notepaper, and filled his fountain pen.

He wrote: *"Circumstances surrounding and leading to the deaths at Kings School."*

He paused, lit a cigarette, and his pen hovered above the paper for a moment.

*"All the known facts in this case support a conclusion that one person committed both murders, and that this person is one of two possible suspects."*

He poured some tea and continued.

# Friday

"Sir, I've encountered a problem I haven't faced before," Ford told Brownlee on the following morning. "You may want to replace me on the Kings School cases. Not to beat about the bush, the evidence is tangled enough as it is, and I'm concerned that I may be losing objectivity."

Peering over his teacup, Brownlee's eyes searched Ford's face.

"If you're concerned about disliking this wretched Canderblank woman," he said, "I wouldn't worry about it. Even the Archangel Gabriel would find it hard to tolerate her. Just because she deserves to hang doesn't mean you're going to cook the evidence to charge her with murder, simply out of spite. Knowing you, you'll be twice as cautious."

Ford hung his head in embarrassment but drove himself on.

"It's not that, sir, I'm afraid. The fact is I'm obliged to tell you it's her daughter, Miss Canderblank, and the problem is the reverse."

"*Is* it, by Jove! *Is it*?" Brownlee chuckled. "Between you and me, my dear wife was telling me the other day that you needed to get married and settle down. She simply can't abide the idea of bachelors evading the clutches of unrequited spinsters."

He lowered his teacup and placed it carefully in the center of its saucer.

"Still, that's none of my damned business. To tell you the truth, I had a very similar problem a number of years back, but unlike you, I didn't have the common sense to recognize it. Put myself in a real pickle ... But that's another story ... Sufficient unto the day is the pickle thereof." He paused to chuckle, then solemnly asked, "Has Miss Canderblank become a more likely suspect?"

"I'm down to two," Ford said, "her and one other. You remember the chart we drew on the chalkboard? I believe the answer is right there, at least as far as she's concerned."

"Really? How did you come to that conclusion?"

"Do you have a minute, sir?"

"Of course."

They walked down the corridor to Ford's wreckage of an office. Some kindly soul had opened the windows to let the dust escape, but there must have been something in the atmosphere that made the room immensely attractive to bluebottle flies.

"Er, are you going to take me off the case, sir?"

Brownlee chuckled.

"Don't be a damned fool, Ford!"

"Very well," said Ford, squaring his shoulders. "Now, sir, if you consider the timing, there can only be two possible explanations."

They discussed Ford's conclusions until the flies drove them from the room.

"Cartwright!" boomed Brownlee down the corridor, and the constable appeared.

"Ah, Cartwright, catch those flies immediately."

"Yes, sir," responded Cartwright. "What's the charge?"

"Breaking and entering."

"If I may, sir, there's no evidence they opened the window themselves, so technically it's probably trespass, sir.

"Well, that's true, but kindly remove them anyway, Cartwright, and bring me some more tea."

He referred to his watch.

"Ford, it's time you went to meet Miss Canderblank."

◆     ◆     ◆

Ford waited in the ornate foyer of the Savoy Hotel feeling like a complete fool. There was absolutely no possibility that Victoria Canderblank would keep their luncheon appointment after their encounter at the cricket match, and yet here he was, standing in his best suit outside the oak doors of the Grill. He took up his position well before noon, in case she came early, and watched the steady flow of diners entering the restaurant.

By twelve fifteen, he was wondering how much longer he should wait; the maitre d' had glanced at him curiously more than once, and his leg had still not recovered from the cricket match. He looked at the clock for the thousandth time and wondered if he was a sufficient fool to wait until two when the restaurant closed.

"I'm not remotely hungry," a voice said. "Let's just sit down over there and talk for a minute."

Victoria Canderblank had appeared before him miraculously, as she always seemed to do. She was calm and collected, although Ford thought he detected tiny lines of strain about her eyes. They sat down side by side on a huge leather sofa. Ford had planned to be distant and formal, but the seating arrangement made that impossible.

"I hate my mother," she began without preamble, "but she didn't kill that boy—I know she didn't."

She removed her hat and tossed it onto the coffee table before them. Today she was dressed in a conservative suit. Ford would have observed how its severity seemed to complement her figure, had he permitted himself to do so.

"It's Daddy I worry about," she continued. "A scandal will destroy him. He's put up with her for all these years, absorbing her domineering temperament and swallowing his pride over her peccadilloes, just to keep up appearances ..."

She seemed to be compelling herself to continue.

"Anyway, I understand that you cannot be dissuaded from your investigation just because innocent bystanders may get hurt. The point is that I *know* she didn't do it. Callaway was alive at a quarter to eleven. And by then she was already back in the Lodge, making everybody's life miserable—as usual."

Ford regarded her face intently for a moment, then said softly, "No, I don't believe she did it."

She turned her gaze upon him, and he felt like a rabbit staring into the headlights of an onrushing motorcar.

"I'm here to offer you a deal, if that's the right expression," she said. "I'm offering it for Daddy's sake, although I'm scarcely in a position to do so. If I tell you what I know, you have to promise that you'll try to protect him. He's worked long and hard to get into the government, and I think he will, if this wretched scandal doesn't come out."

Her stare did not falter.

"I expect you think I'm just a spy, trying to worm my way into your good graces. I expect you think I've had an ulterior motive for my flirting. But these are chances I have to take. You see, I think you'd rather be honest and unhappy than dishonest and happy."

Ford felt he had been pierced to the soul.

"I can't make any promises," he managed to say. "I have to discover the facts, and then let them lead me to the logical conclusion, regardless of what it may be. That's my job."

"You know, you're a very hard man to trust," she said. "One can usually trust people, because one knows ultimately they'll do things that are in their own best interests—but you won't."

Ford attempted to make his voice harsh, but with little success.

"If you have information that exonerates your mother, you should tell me. In fact, if you wish to tell me something, you should come to Scotland Yard and tell my superior officer and me. In addition, you must make a complete and candid statement about your movements—not only on the night Callaway died, but also on the night of young Trumpington's death."

She searched his face as if she were trying to see into his soul, and indeed she was.

"Let's get it over with," she said stoically.

They took a taxi down the Strand and along Whitehall until they turned and came to Scotland Yard. On the way, she sat in uncharacteristic silence, and he did not feel he could break the strain between them. The blood had drained from her face so that she resembled an alabaster statue. Once in the building, he led her through the maze of corridors and staircases until they came to Brownlee's office.

The Superintendent made a show of seating her comfortably and sending for tea. Then he returned to his desk and clasped his hands in front of him as if he intended to say grace. Ford perched himself awkwardly on the windowsill behind him, shifting his weight to his sound leg.

Victoria appeared to be collecting her thoughts and then began her statement as if reciting lines she had committed to memory.

"I became aware of Callaway's relationship to my mother only two weeks ago, three or four days before the school play," she said. "Astonishing, isn't it, that I had lived this long and not known. Yet, it's true.

"I had been aware for some time that the atmosphere between my parents had become particularly poisonous. So I confronted them, and it was then that they told me the truth—because they assumed I'd eventually find out anyway."

She spoke in a completely expressionless voice, her eyes upon Brownlee's folded hands.

"Apparently, Callaway was threatening to make the news public. He was insisting that my mother acknowledge the relationship, and that my father should somehow make him his heir. He wanted to inherit the title. It wasn't possible, of course, practically or legally, but that was what he was demanding."

Brownlee made a neutral clucking sound and shook his head. It might have signified sympathy or understanding for the Canderblanks' plight, or perhaps it might not.

"If there was to be a scandal, my mother's position in society would be ruined, and Daddy would never get a job in the government. My mother ..."

She paused, gathered herself, and began again.

"My mother decided that the only possible course of action was to silence the boy permanently. She announced that we should murder him after the school play."

She made it sound as if her mother had announced a family outing. Perhaps living with Lady Canderblank inoculated one against even the most outrageous displays of behavior. Ford managed to limit his react to shifting his weight on the windowsill.

Brownlee made no movement at all.

She continued, "There would be a lot of people about and general confusion, and the houses would be open late. It was all a question of arranging impenetrable alibis."

This admission was so startling that even she was reduced to silence. She continued to study Brownlee's hands.

"I knew she was in earnest," she began again eventually. "Daddy argued, of course, but in that mood she is unstoppable. In the end, he agreed, and I agreed in support of him, although I had no intention of permitting it to happen."

Brownlee repeated the indeterminate sound.

"There's something else you should know. Mummy's tastes are somewhat extravagant. She got used to having lots of servants in India, and she insists on a large household, which costs a fortune here. She also does a lot of entertaining; she likes to play the hostess, and, to be fair, it helps Daddy's career. Anyway, they've just about run out of money."

She sounded as if she were talking about some other family with whom she was vaguely acquainted.

"If Daddy gets into the government, they'll have an excuse to put the Hall into mothballs and cut back and live in a modest flat in London. And they'd be able to borrow, because Daddy could do favors in return for high paying directorships when he leaves, so they'd be able to repay the debts."

Brownlee used the sound once more. It was impossible to tell if he was condemning official corruption or simply recognizing its inevitability.

"Anyway, when the play ended and we were all milling about, Callaway came over and called her *Mummy*, loud enough that other people might have heard. He was in that bizarre outfit and ghastly greasepaint. He was shaking with excitement, barely under control. My mother told him she'd meet him, just to shut him up, and he said he'd wait in those wretched rhododendrons. It was absurd and undignified, but she had no choice." She paused, took a deep breath, and continued. "And I realized that she was determined to go through with it."

Having admitted to conspiracy to commit murder, a crime for which she could spend the rest of her life in prison, Victoria Canderblank at last fell silent.

Ford realized he must have stopped breathing some time ago. Even Brownlee was too stunned to use his sound. The silence lengthened as she prepared for her next admission. Ford couldn't stand to watch her trying to summon up her courage. He drew a deep breath, and spoke, filling the void.

"Let me see if I understand your plan correctly," he said, as gently as he could. "After the refreshments at the Lodge, your parents went out for a walk, and you retired to bed. The Bishop, a witness of unquestioned rectitude, saw you to your door. Your mother met Callaway in the bushes while your father kept guard, loitering as he smoked his cigar. In the darkness, she stumbled and tore her dress. Presumably she told Callaway to return to his room where they could speak privately, without fear of interruption. She would wear a floppy hat and pretend to be one of the Major General's daughters. Perhaps she intimated that she would acknowledge him as her son."

Victoria nodded slightly.

"Your parents returned to the Lodge. When you saw them approaching, you climbed down from your bedroom window using the trellis, and they told you where Callaway would be. Your father re-entered the Lodge; your mother tried unsuccessfully to hide her dishevelment, and then she went in also, in order to make a loud fuss outside your bedroom door at the correct time, using words and phrases you had agreed upon in advance. Thus you would be able to recount the argument, proving that you were in the Lodge while, in fact, you had gone to Trafalgar and were ascending to Callaway's room. It is, indeed, the very alibi you gave me on Monday evening."

Victoria nodded again and had the decency to blush.

"There were boys dressed up as women all over the place," he continued, "and that meant a woman could go up to his room undetected. You wore a large floppy hat, as your mother had planned, which covered your face, and the boy or boys you encountered on the stairs assumed you were one of the Major General's daughters. Subsequently you returned to the Lodge and entered by the French doors in the rear. In the meantime your mother had ensured that everyone had been drawn down to the basement, so that you could go down and appear there, as if you had just been awoken. Thus you could be both unquestionably in your room and at the scene of the crime."

This time she nodded with an air of submission.

"Therefore, Miss Canderblank, the only remaining question is, what happened when you entered Callaway's room?"

"Quite so," she said calmly. "Contrary to my mother's wishes, I intended to buy him off. I planned to explain that there was no point in ruining the Canderblank name in order to join the family—that would be self-defeating. It would be better to keep quiet and accept our money."

She shook her head.

"However, I was not sure how long blackmail might keep him quiet, so I'd prepared an alternative. I understood he had literary aspirations, and I had therefore arranged for people I know in the business to publish a book of his. In that manner, I could offer him a chance to achieve a worthwhile life in his own right."

That was an astute plan, Ford thought. She would be offering him a way to earn the private and public esteem he craved.

"Unfortunately, when I got there, I found the room empty. But the window was open, and I looked down and thought I saw something in the darkness. I ran downstairs and peered into the bushes. Callaway was dead. I couldn't really see, but I felt him, and there was a knife sticking out of his chest. There was nothing to do but return to the Lodge and enter through the veranda doors, so that I wouldn't be seen. I must admit that I was utterly confused; I thought my mother must have murdered him, but if she had, then why had she sent me on what amounted to a fool's errand?"

She sat back while the policemen absorbed her statement. Ford's head was awhirl.

"Do you possibly have a cigarette?" she said. "I seldom smoke, but on the other hand, I seldom confess to a crime. What's the penalty for conspiracy, by the way?"

"That depends," Brownlee answered phlegmatically, as Ford offered her his cigarette case. "Conspiracy is tricky. The most important thing for you to consider is that the Chief Inspector and I have to decide whether or not to charge you. Conspiracy is hard to prove, and it's often used as a threat to frighten witnesses who do not cooperate fully. The police have a great deal of discretion … Personally I would be very reluctant to charge an entire family with conspiracy … What did you conclude when your mother claimed she had not killed him either?"

"At first I thought she'd done it anyway. If she were capable of killing her own son, she was capable of deliberately pinning it on me, her daughter. It didn't make much sense, but there was no alternative, and she was frantically trying to cover up the evidence and obstruct the investigation, as you know. Then, when my cousin James Trumpington died, it seemed pretty obvious that *he'd* done it, although I didn't really know why."

"Yes," said Ford, "let us now consider the night young Trumpington died, if we may." Ford's leg was hurting and he changed positions on his perch again. "What were your movements on that night?"

"Oh, that's easy. I drove to the Lodge and dropped off a library book my mother had borrowed—Doctor Thornby wasn't there—and then I came home again."

Ford nodded. "Doctor Thornby spoke to Trumpington about eight in the evening and then telephoned your mother. Your mother subsequently appears to have felt it essential to return a school library book that very evening, and sent you off with it. Shortly thereafter Trumpington died in highly unusual circumstances, and your mother and Doctor Thornby spoke again. What made the return of the library book so important?"

"I … I don't know."

"Did it contain a note, perhaps, or was it simply a pretext in case you were observed in or near the School after visiting the Lodge?"

"I thought it was ridiculous myself, but one learns that sometimes one simply bows to my mother's demands."

"What book was it, may I ask?"

"I have no idea; it was wrapped in a brown paper package and tied with string. She had even sealed and stamped it with her signet ring. Anyway, when I got to the Lodge, the maid let me in. Mrs. Thornby told me he wasn't in, so I left the package on his desk in his study."

"Did you see any keys on his desk?" Ford asked, watching her closely.

"What? Keys? I don't think so … I didn't pay much attention, to tell you the truth; I was preoccupied. Anyway, I left the School, parked beside the road, and had a smoke. Then I drove home."

Ford could see nothing in her face to suggest that she was lying, but—as he thought bitterly—she had lied effortlessly on previous occasions.

"In what manner were you preoccupied?" Superintendent Brownlee asked. "Were you concerned with your mother's actions on the night Callaway died, or perhaps on *this* night?"

"With a totally unrelated matter, I assure you, Superintendent."

"I fear you will have to tell us."

Victoria stared at him.

"I must confess my feelings as well as my actions?"

"It is often very important for the police to understand motivations, Miss Canderblank."

Her eyes returned to the Superintendent's hands.

"Very well, Superintendent. I have been contemplating marriage with an eminently suitable man for whom I feel no strong affection. His wealth offers a ready solution to my parent's financial difficulties, and his social position could greatly buttress my father's political ambitions. However, I have recently met another man many would judge entirely unsuitable, but for whom I believe I could feel a very strong affection. This is probably not an unusual occurrence in the general scheme of things, but it is new to me, and I find it extremely disconcerting as well as powerfully beguiling."

A long and awkward silence ensued. Ford again found himself struggling with wild thoughts.

"Miss Canderblank, let me summarize," Ford said finally. "You entered into a plot with your mother to murder Callaway, your unacknowledged half brother. And you actually went to the intended scene of the murder. However, you say it was your intention to dissuade him from his course, not to murder him as your mother had instructed. When you arrived for this confrontation, he was already dead, presumably at your mother's hand."

"Exactly."

"Four days later you brought a library book to the Master late in the evening, a mission you have described as ridiculous. You then remained near the School grounds, lost in thought, while your cousin was killed in a manner almost identical to your half brother's death. Thus you were present at the murders of two close relatives, but uninvolved with either."

"Precisely." She gave him a sharp, questioning look. "Do you believe me?"

There was another long and awkward silence.

"What we believe is irrelevant, Miss Canderblank," said Brownlee. "It's what the jury will believe that counts."

# Saturday

Now that the moment had come, Ford hesitated on the steps of Canderblank Hall, wondering for the thousandth time if he had made a mistake. He'd agonized all night and all day in search of a flaw in his argument and had found none, and yet he wished he felt more confident. Brownlee patted his arm in encouragement while Dagenham pulled the ornate bell handle. Croft, Sergeant Jackson and the police driver brought up the rear.

Now it was too late to turn back, for the supercilious footman was opening the door, and the next moment, they were marching down the gilded hallway. Croft and Sergeant Jackson discretely detached themselves and headed for the servant's quarters, while the others continued toward the now-familiar drawing room.

Lady Canderblank was sitting in her customary armchair. She appeared calm, even bored, yet Ford was certain she was simply conserving her strength before giving rein to her invective. Lord Canderblank and Victoria stood behind her. His lordship had his habitual expression of petulance, while Victoria's face was in shadow.

On the opposite side of the fire, Doctor and Mrs. Thornby were similarly posed. Mrs. Thornby sat with her shoulders hunched as if to ward off an impending disaster. The Master stood behind her, and Ford guessed he was rehearsing a variety of deprecating remarks. Sir John Trumpington stood rigidly with his back to the fireplace.

The police arranged themselves as if occupying the fourth corner of a square. Colonel Dagenham and Superintendent Brownlee stood together facing the fireplace and Ford placed himself a little behind them. The police driver softly closed the door and stood in front of it.

The Colonel cleared his throat and began the proceedings.

"Thank you all for coming here this evening," he said. "Let us hope that we can draw these tragic events to a close. It is now almost exactly two weeks since Michael Callaway, a pupil at Kings, fell to his death. I requested Superintendent Brownlee of Scotland Yard to assist us in our investigations."

He nodded slightly in Brownlee's direction.

"Four days later, there was a second tragedy, when Sir John's son also fell to his death. I have already extended my sympathies to you, Sir John, and I extend them to you again now."

Sir John squared his shoulders but did not reply.

"Chief Inspector Ford, who has been conducting the investigation, has now reached his conclusions and reported them to the Superintendent and me. We are satisfied with his report, and we will be instituting legal proceedings accordingly. The purpose of this gathering is to share his conclusions with you."

"Percy," Lady Canderblank broke in, "I have told you on several occasions that this—this *person* is neither fit nor qualified for his position. Regardless of what he may insinuate this evening, I have already instructed my solicitor to take whatever actions may be necessary to have him censured."

Colonel Dagenham acknowledged her comment with a solemn nod. "The gentleman has already telephoned me, Lady Canderblank. However, Superintendent Brownlee and I are completely satisfied that Chief Inspector Ford's conduct has been entirely appropriate. On the other hand, I have a very compelling case of obstruction of justice which could be brought against you. If you continue to attempt to interfere in this officer's conduct of his duties, I shall also be forced to take action. Do I make myself clear?"

"Perfectly clear," answered Lord Canderblank for his wife. "For God's sake, Deborah, let's just hear the man out and be done with it without a lot of fuss and nonsense."

But Lady Canderblank was no more easily deterred than a pit bull terrier. "I have no intention of listening to malicious gossip in my own drawing room. Nor do I intend to sit here while Percy threatens me. I fully intend ..." She began to rise from her chair, but Lord Canderblank laid a firm hand on her shoulder.

Superintendent Brownlee took a step toward her. "Lady Canderblank," he boomed, "I'm not sure you quite recognize the jeopardy in which you have placed yourself."

Brownlee seemed to Ford to have grown larger than his normal stature, and he projected an authority before which even Lady Canderblank quailed.

"In the next thirty seconds you can be arrested," Brownlee continued. "You would spend the next thirty-six hours in His Majesty's Prison in Gloucester, in the company of others charged with criminal offenses, until a judge hears the charges against you on Monday morning. In view of the present and continuing nature of your obstruction, we would request that you be remanded without bail, and returned to prison until your trial, a period of several weeks. Judges invariably support the police in such situations. Alternatively, you may now remain silent unless and until you are spoken to. Having visited Gloucester Women's Prison, I strongly suggest you take your husband's excellent advice."

A long pause ensued in which Lady Canderblank's face registered a variety of emotions until it settled into sullen hostility.

"Good," Brownlee said. "Now I suggest you will all give your full attention to Chief Inspector Ford."

Brownlee's gaze swept over the Thornbys and Sir John, none of whom seemed prepared to argue with him. He stepped back, and Ford stepped forward into his place.

"Good evening," he said politely into the silence. "My purpose here is to summarize for you what has taken place, and the conclusions that my colleagues and I have reached."

He swept the group with his eyes, pausing for only a painful instant on Victoria's face. Then he continued.

"The initial problem with this case was finding a motive for young Callaway's murder. He was disliked, even hated, but there was no evidence of an overwhelming reason for ending his life, or ending it on the particular moment when it was. While we were still attempting to find a motive, regretfully, young Trumpington also died."

He glanced at Sir John to acknowledge his bereavement.

"It became immediately apparent that Callaway had been blackmailing young Trumpington, and that Trumpington's future career was severely threatened. Thus we had an explanation for Callaway's death and, unfortunately, a reason why Sir John's son might, tragically, have chosen to end his own life while his mental balance was disturbed."

Ford was determined not to look directly at either Lady Canderblank or her daughter, for very different reasons. In the end, he divided his attention between Lord Canderblank, Sir John, and Mrs. Thornby.

"Shortly thereafter, the circumstances of Callaway's background became apparent. Since they have a direct bearing on his death, I have to review them."

He willed himself to continue. The hatred glistening in Lady Canderblank's eyes was palpable.

"During the Easter holidays, Callaway—we'll continue to call him that, for the sake of simplicity—came across a book which contained a photograph of *Mrs.* Callaway engaged in strenuous sports one month before he was born, and he realized that Mrs. Callaway could not possibly be his natural mother. He jumped to the conclusion that Lady Canderblank was, in fact, his true mother."

Mrs. Thornby was visibly shaken. She stared at Lady Canderblank, who stared back coldly, and then twisted in her seat to stare up at her husband, who ignored her.

Ford paused, moved slightly to minimize the throbbing in his leg, and continued.

"He jumped to that conclusion because Lady Canderblank was in India at the time of his birth, was also Mrs. Callaway's former employer, and was additionally paying for his schooling. He began to write to her, demanding that she acknowledge him, but she denied that demand. Perhaps his purpose was blackmail, or perhaps his purpose was simply to be recognized; we will never know for sure."

"On the night of the performance of *Pirates of Penzance*, Callaway insisted that Lady Canderblank meet him, presumably so he could make further demands. Following that meeting, Lady Canderblank returned to the Master's Lodge, where she had an altercation with the maid. Some of those present described Lady Canderblank as being in a disheveled state. The following morning, she had the entire rhododendron patch chopped down and replaced with new bushes. However, we recovered a torn patch of material that has now been identified by a dressmaker as coming from a gown made for Lady Canderblank."

Sir John glanced at the Canderblanks in surprise, but no one else moved.

"Following this meeting in the rhododendrons, Callaway went up to his room, and shortly thereafter fell to his death from the window. A witness, a young boy named Connelly, has sworn he saw a female figure descending the staircase in Trafalgar that leads to Callaway's room. It is not unreasonable to suppose that this was Lady Canderblank, having followed Callaway up to his room and having pushed him out to silence him."

Lady Canderblank stirred, but her husband laid a restraining hand on her shoulder. By now, Mrs. Thornby was softly sobbing.

"However," Ford continued, "the female figure on the stairs was observed at the same time that Lady Canderblank was having her altercation with the maid in the Master's Lodge. I am therefore completely satisfied that Lady Canderblank did *not* murder the boy who claimed to be her son."

Ford felt a wave of relief emanating from the Canderblank corner.

"Approximately ten minutes later, Mr. Green, the publican of the Kings Arms, observed a female figure returning to the Master's Lodge. Every lady in the Lodge was in someone else's physical presence, save one. Lady Canderblank, Lady Wimbleton, Mrs. Thornby, and the maid Ethel were in the basement, inspecting the boiler. The only remaining lady was Miss Victoria Canderblank, who was, on her own account, not alone in her room in bed, but in Callaway's room."

Utter silence.

"Based on the evidence I have presented so far, it therefore follows that, if the female figure on the stairs was the murderess, it was Miss Canderblank who killed her reputed half-brother."

Ford experienced an almost overwhelming temptation to look at Victoria, but somehow he avoided doing so. Sir John and Mrs. Thornby were staring from Ford to Victoria and back again in complete confusion, while the Master gazed at Ford as if waiting for him to make some foolish error of logic.

"The other possibility is that the female figure on the stair was a youth or man dressed in female costume. Young Trumpington was in Trafalgar at the relevant time and had charge of the *Pirates of Penzance* wardrobe. He could well have put on a Major General's daughter's costume and a floppy hat to hide his face. Following his own death it became clear that Callaway had been blackmailing him, which constitutes a powerful motive. Thus, in summary, I was drawn to the conclusion that one of two people committed the murder—Miss Canderblank or James Trumpington."

Sir John shifted uneasily, but Ford ignored him.

"As for motive, the revelation of Callaway's ancestry would constitute a social scandal of the greatest proportions. Lord Canderblank's political ambitions would undoubtedly be dashed. Miss Canderblank's marriage to the Duke of Bigsby would not be possible, and as a consequence, that avenue of financial rescue would be closed. Thus Miss Canderblank had powerful motives."

Lord Canderblank opened his mouth to protest, looked at Brownlee and Dagenham, and closed it again.

"As for young Trumpington's motives, if Callaway had revealed the circumstances of the Oxford scholarship examination, not only would Trumpington's own career be ruined before it had even started, but his father's reputation would be destroyed as well."

Ford wished that he could sit down, or that Brownlee or Dagenham would take over, but the only sound apart from his own voice was the ponderous ticketing of the grandfather clock. He wondered when Croft and Sergeant Jackson would return. There was nothing to do but continue.

"We must also consider the death of James Trumpington. As we now know, young Trumpington conspired with his father to cheat in his scholarship Oxford examinations, thereby achieving one last triumph to cap his school career."

Sir John stared at the wall above Ford's head, while everyone else turned to stare at him. Ford was certain that neither the Canderblanks nor the Thornbys had been aware of the Trumpingtons' conduct. Lady Canderblank's expression became even more malevolent, if such a thing were possible—now, Ford realized, she'd have a powerful weapon to use against her brother-in-law.

"Callaway, it seems, made a habit of snooping through other people's belongings, and discovered incriminating evidence in the form of a letter from Sir John to his son. Armed with this evidence, he proceeded to blackmail Trumpington. When Callaway was killed, young Trumpington should have felt an overwhelming sense of relief, but, alas, he was already embroiled in another disaster, for young Lucy Green had yielded to his advances and informed him that she was expecting his child."

Now everyone was shocked—except, Ford noted, the Master.

"Young Trumpington must have felt that he had escaped the frying pan only to discover that he was in the fire. Lucy demanded money to pay for an abortion, but Trumpington had already been bled dry by Callaway. He was desperate. He attempted to extort money from the boy Connelly, and intended to meet Lucy Green in the Gymnasium attics to pay her off. But Connelly took fright and tried to run away from the School, leaving Trumpington without the financial means to silence her. Trumpington also met the Master, perhaps to tell Doctor Thornby that he feared I was forming a case against him in Callaway's death."

The General's eyes glittered as his son's reputation, already in tatters, was shredded further.

"However, when Trumpington ascended to the roof for his assignation, he encountered not Lucy Green, but his killer, who flung him from the roof to his death. When Lucy arrived at the School a few minutes later, he was already dead."

Ford paused to catch his breath and gather himself for the last assault.

"When Callaway was killed in Trafalgar House, it surroundings were a hive of activity. In contrast, the night of Trumpington's death, the Gymnasium was deserted. The front door was guarded inadvertently by Mr. Jaspers and his dog, and the rear door, also inadvertently, by Mr. Bottomly and Miss Larue. The only *un*guarded entrance was the staff door. At ten forty-five when Mr. Robinson checked it, it was locked, and it was not unlocked until we arrived. Trumpington had a key on his person when I examined him. Therefore, we conclude that Trumpington had gone to the Gymnasium and unlocked the door with his own key."

His audience maintained a funereal silence.

"When he went up, his killer was awaiting him, but Lucy could not have entered the Gymnasium before him since she had no key; therefore Lucy was not on the roof. If he had been planning to commit suicide, he would not have taken a five pound banknote to give to Lucy—a five pound note he had acquired under circumstances we will review shortly. Therefore he did not end his own life; someone else did, and that someone had a key."

Now Ford gazed steadily around at every face but Victoria Canderblank's.

"There are four keys," he said. "Mr. Bottomly has one, but we know that he was otherwise engaged. Trumpington had one, which I found in his pocket. The duty master has one, but we know that he was making his rounds. The remaining key belongs to the Master, and it is missing. We can therefore reasonably conclude that Trumpington's murderer used that key to enter the Gymnasium."

Ford wished mightily that he did not have to continue. He was reaching the crux of his argument, however, and there was no turning back.

"We know that the key was not missing earlier in the evening, because the Master used it to attend an evening fencing session, and we know it was missing on the following morning when Sergeant Croft conducted an inventory. Therefore the key was removed from the Master's key ring between those two times. The only person in the Master's study, other than the Master himself, was Miss Canderblank. It therefore follows logically that Miss Canderblank removed the key and subsequently pushed the young man to his death."

The room had been still before, but it now became stiller. Ford wondered if some bizarre metaphysical force had petrified every person present except himself. The General's eyes had shifted away from him and were now staring at Victoria.

"But why would she do such a thing?" Ford asked rhetorically. "Her relationship with Trumpington was distant but not hostile. In what manner could he have represented a threat to her or her immediate family?"

The room waited for his answer.

"In my interview with him a few hours before his death, young Trumpington repeatedly referred to Callaway as a 'bastard.' At the time, naturally I assumed it was a pejorative figure of speech, especially since Callaway had so many reprehensible characteristics; but, of course, we now know that it was the literal truth.

"In addition, the note from Callaway that was recovered from Trumpington's study contained the phrase, *You know you're no better that I am.*' I assumed at the time that Callaway was comparing his blackmail and other sins to Trumpington's cheating, but we also know that Callaway's parentage was of uppermost concern in his mind. Therefore, upon reflection, it is equally likely that Callaway's note meant he had boasted of what he believed to be his true relationship to Trumpington; Callaway had told him they were first cousins, the sons of two sisters."

Inwardly, Ford groaned.

"This meant that Trumpington also knew the secret, and was as dangerous to the Canderblanks as Callaway had been himself. Thus Miss Canderblank had as compelling a motive for taking Trumpington's life as she had for taking Callaway's."

He shifted his weight, as much to give himself a moment as to relieve his leg.

"There remains the question of how she knew what Trumpington knew. The Master had met with Trumpington a few hours before his death. Trumpington was frightened that I might accuse him of murdering Callaway. It is inconceivable that he did not inform the Master of what he knew about Callaway's putative parentage."

He stole a look in the direction of the Master, whose eyes were two black coals afire with hatred set in his bloodless face.

"The Master telephoned to Lady Canderblank after that meeting, and shortly thereafter Miss Canderblank visited him to drop off a library book. Thus, the Canderblanks were informed and, we might guess, decided to strike immediately. The Master was not in his study when Miss Canderblank returned the book. Therefore, we may surmise that she was alerted to the danger by her mother following her mother's telephone conversation with the Master."

He was almost done.

"It would have been the work of seconds to remove the Gymnasium key. She would then have visited Trumpington in his room and instructed him to meet her later. She left the School so that the gatekeeper would note her departure, parked her car beyond immediate notice on a dark night, returned on foot, and entered the Gymnasium to wait for him."

Ford risked glancing round the room. Mrs. Thornby looked acutely uncomfortable, and would not meet his eye. Instead she seemed absorbed by the pattern in the carpeting, while her hands kneaded themselves in her lap.

Doctor Thornby was staring at the Canderblanks. The skin of his face was drawn back as if he were in profound shock. General Trumpington was glaring at Victoria, a vein pulsing at his temple, and his cheeks were red. He seemed about to leap upon her in fury.

When Ford permitted his eyes to glance at the Canderblanks, he saw three petrified statues with unblinking eyes boring into his.

"Thus, every fact at our disposal points to Miss Canderblank as the killer, egged on by her mother."

At that moment, Croft and Sergeant Jackson opened the door quietly and slipped into the room, unnoticed by all except Ford. Croft nodded to him, and Ford continued.

"The difficulty in solving this case has consisted of three elements: piercing the web of lies and obstruction which was thrown up, eliminating the red herrings and their consequences, and resolving several incongruous facts that stuck out like sore thumbs. I admit that I've been driven by the incongruous—the seemingly innocuous—facts that didn't fit the pattern.

"In Callaway's case, it was the book about military life in India. I simply could not fathom why he would go to the trouble of hiding such an innocent volume. Similarly I could not understand why Major and Mrs. Callaway did not respond to the news of Callaway's death. I take it you still have not received a telegram from them since we met on Thursday, Master?

"No." He managed to pour his loathing of Ford into that single syllable.

"Nor have the Markhams," Ford said. "We checked immediately before this interview.

"In Trumpington's death, it was a question of the five pound note he had with him when he died. Who might have given him so large a sum of money?"

Ford told himself he had to finish this, regardless of the anguish he was inflicting.

"But the most extraordinary fact, to me, concerned the leaking boiler in the Master's Lodge."

At the mention of the boiler, Lady Canderblank's self-imposed calm finally cracked.

"You were concerned about a *leaking boiler?*"

Ford continued before she could gain momentum.

"Let me ask you a question, Mrs. Thornby. On the night of Callaway's murder, Lady Canderblank created a fuss over the lack of hot water. It was sufficiently severe for you, the maid, the Wimbletons, and the Bishop and Lord Canderblank all to go down to the cellar to examine the boiler. Why did you not summon your husband?"

"I ... I didn't want to disturb him. He had to prepare for the morning."

"Lady Canderblank," Ford countered, "was sufficiently irate that her voice reached the Bishop in his bedroom. It roused the Wimbletons, who are hard of hearing. Green, the innkeeper, was fifty feet away from the house, and *he* heard Lady Canderblank. It is not possible that your husband was not disturbed."

"I—"

"I put it to you, Mrs. Thornby, that you did indeed go to your husband's study to fetch him, but he was not there."

"I … I have nothing to say."

"Are you prepared to swear under oath that you did not go the study?"

"I—"

"Mrs. Thornby, when did you become aware of the full circumstances of young Callaway's birth and parentage?"

"That's *enough,* Ford!" Doctor Thornby intervened angrily. "Leave my wife alone!"

"*Shut up,*" hissed Lady Canderblank. "He has no proof. He's just guessing."

"Get this over with immediately, Ford," Thornby demanded.

"*Shut UP!*" Lady Canderblank hissed again.

"Finish it, for God's sake, Ford!" the Master shouted.

"Roger …" began Mrs. Thornby to her husband.

"Silence!" he cut her off. "Ford, damn it—*do* it!"

"Very well, sir. Doctor Roger Thornby, I arrest you for the murders of Michael Callaway and James Trumpington."

It seemed to Ford that a minor earth tremor must have struck the house, for all the people in the room seemed to quiver and rearrange themselves in slightly different positions.

"*What?*" roared the General: "I demand an explanation! *He* killed my son?"

"Yes, sir," Ford said, "on the night of the play, Doctor Thornby disguised himself as a Major General's daughter. All the costumes had been stored in his office, and thus such a costume was immediately available to the Master."

Sir John stared at the Master in disbelief.

"The Master donned his disguise and left his study through the window," Ford continued. "He went to Trafalgar, ascended to Callaway's room, and pushed the boy to his death. Bizarrely, Miss Canderblank, dispatched by her mother on the same mission, followed him. The boy Connelly passed them both on the stairs, but was not able to discern the height of the Major General's daughter, and no wonder—as Connelly was going up he saw the tall Master coming down, and a few minutes later Connelly saw the shorter Miss Canderblank going up, and assumed they were the same person."

Ford continued to direct his explanation to the General.

"Your son was *also* at Trafalgar and saw Doctor Thornby entering the bushes to stab Callaway's body to make sure it was dead. Your son was certain he saw the rear view of a man *disguised* as a woman, rather than an actual woman. When I interviewed him several days later, your son was terrified that I might bring a case against *him.* That he might be accused of a murder he had seen Doctor Thornby commit."

"Good God!" burst from Sir John's lips.

"Following my interview, your son went to Doctor Thornby to confront him. In return for his silence, he demanded the money that Connelly had not given him to pay off Lucy, whom he was meeting later that evening. Doctor Thornby borrowed five pounds and gave it to him later. When we examined your son, we found a five pound note, which we have subsequently tested, and it bears Doctor Thornby's fingerprints. Thus Doctor Thornby knew where Trumpington would be later that evening, and went to wait for him. When your son went up to the Gymnasium attics for his assignation with Lucy, the Master was waiting and pushed your son to his death."

"*What?*" General Trumpington turned to the Master. "Thornby, is this true? God *damn* it, is it true?"

The Master was sputtering. "I had his reputation to consider, as well as the School's, and yours, and the Canderblanks' ... It was all bound to come out eventually, unless I did the decent thing ..."

"The *decent thing?* You *killed* my son to protect *reputations?* That's *absurd!*"

The General started toward the Master, and Croft and the driver rushed forward to restrain him.

"*Why?*" General Trumpington demanded. "*Why? Why?*" Croft had seized him from behind and lifted him bodily, so that the General's legs flailed in the air.

Disregarding the struggle with the General, Doctor Thornby spoke urgently to Ford. "What will happen if I plead guilty and provide no further statement? Is that possible? Will anything of this have to come out?"

"That's not my decision to make, sir," replied Ford, aching with relief. "I can only say that a plea of guilty to both charges relieves me of the responsibility of making a case in open court and proving it by demonstrating motives."

Colonel Dagenham intervened. "I see no legitimate cause that would be served by revealing the details," he said. "We will have to explain it to the judge *in camera*, but if it's satisfactory to him, no further public information need be supplied." He turned toward Brownlee. "Unless the Superintendent has another view?"

"No, I concur with you. That will be my recommendation to the Solicitor General."

"I still do not understand ..." Sir John began desperately.

"You do not need to," Lady Canderblank spat. "The case is closed. This incompetent officer has *finally* done his duty and *exonerated* the House of Canderblank."

◆    ◆    ◆

Croft and the driver led Doctor Thornby from the room. Sergeant Jackson took charge of Mrs. Thornby, who seemed to have entered a trance-like state. General Trumpington stared at Lady Canderblank and left abruptly, marching like a soldier, followed rapidly by Superintendent Brownlee and Colonel Dagenham, both of whom thought he might try to do violence to Doctor Thornby.

Ford was left to face the Canderblanks alone.

"Well, Austin," Lady Canderblank said, "you've managed to disrupt Kings thoroughly, for absolutely no purpose. The two boys are just as dead, and Kings has lost a fine Master." She turned to her husband.

"I think it might be best if we dismiss the Master for incompetence before the news gets out. In that way we can demonstrate that we had our suspicions and acted to prevent more boys from being endangered while the police were still fumbling. Just in case the facts leak out, we can say that, faced with our dismissal, he broke down and admitted his guilt."

Her hauteur and vindictiveness had returned in full. Her focus was on sweeping away the consequences of the past two weeks.

"If we appoint another Master quickly, perhaps the whole thing can be glossed over. As Chairman of the Governors you can appoint an interim acting Master, and we should do so as soon as possible. Anyone would do—perhaps that old fool Jaspers can fill in until we find someone more suitable ... We'd better contact the Prince's representative immediately ... In fact, it might be best if you were to go and see him personally first thing tomorrow. I'll go up to the School in the morning and make the announcements. I think we should get the Master's wife out of the Lodge by lunchtime—the last thing we want is for her to be moping around gossiping to everyone through her tears."

She looked back at Ford.

"Why are you still here? You entered my house against my wishes, and now there is no reason for you to remain. Oh, and there is one more thing, Morris, just so we understand each other. You have not one shred of evidence against me—not one. Now you may go."

"If that is what you wish to believe, Lady Canderblank, I will not disabuse you," Ford said.

"What the devil does *that* mean?" she demanded.

"Good evening, ma'am, my lord, Miss Canderblank."

"Wait," she demanded. "What evidence? *What* evidence?"

He left without looking back, wishing that he could march out as smartly as the General had done, but the polished wooden floors exaggerated the uneven sound of his footsteps.

◆    ◆    ◆

In the forecourt, Brownlee and Colonel Dagenham were squeezed into the back seat of the police car with Doctor Thornby crammed between them. Sergeant Jackson and the driver were in the front seats. The Colonel beckoned Ford over.

"Come and see me before you leave, if you would?"

"I'll see you at the Yard," said the Superintendent, and the driver, sobered by the seniority of the occupants he was conveying, for once set off at a funereal pace.

Croft waited beside the remaining car.

"You got the telegrams, Croft?" Ford asked. "It worked? Thank God I didn't have to use them."

"It went like a dream, sir. Shipman came on very strong and sarcastic like, until I mentioned what the Superintendent had found out—indecent exposure in a girl's school, of all things! After that, he was like a lamb. Took us straight to the study and found the telegrams."

He handed over a thin sheaf of papers and Ford glanced through them in the gloom. General Trumpington approached him, still in search of explanations, still trying to grasp the fact that the Master had killed his son.

"That man killed my son, Chief Inspector. I simply cannot comprehend it. I still don't understand why."

"Your son saw him commit a murder," Ford said quietly.

"But why did he kill this wretched Callaway boy in the first place?"

Ford handed General Trumpington one of the telegrams that Croft had obtained from the odious Shipman, the Canderblank's secretary. It was from the Callaways in India and addressed to Lady Canderblank.

OUR CONDOLENCES TO YOU AND ROGER THORNBY STOP NATURALLY WE WILL SAY NOTHING STOP ASSUME OUR ARRANGEMENTS WILL CONTINUE STOP

The General's eyes opened wide. "*Thornby* was Callaway's father? Good *God!*"

He shook his head in disbelief, trying to absorb this latest shock. He groaned, and looked blankly around the forecourt.

"You know, Ford, the irony is that the rest of us—myself included, over that wretched scholarship—will get away with whatever we did. Sometimes life feels completely futile. I've lived for my son since my wife died … What am I going to do now?"

"Sir, it's none of my business," Ford said, "but you are about to become a grandfather. The girl Lucy needs help. Perhaps you could supply it. As for your grandchild, with your support, who knows to what heights he or she might ascend? Of course, it's none of my business, sir, as I said, but I just thought I'd mention it."

Sir John did not reply directly; evidently Lucy Green's condition was one shock too many.

"I'm still very confused," he said. "You gave the impression that Victoria was the killer—right up until the last moment."

"That, I fear, was an impression that Lady Canderblank and the Master wished me to have. The library book—if there was one—was simply a ruse to put her in the vicinity. The Master pretended to lose his key to create the impression that she could have stolen it. They had not hesitated to kill their own son to protect their reputations; they were, I fear, equally capable of incriminating Lady Canderblank's daughter."

The General pondered, and veered away to a different topic.

"You know, I went back over my records after I met you the other day … I sent you off on that idiotic raid in '17. I didn't expect it to succeed; I just needed to show Division that I was being aggressive. As soon as you'd gone, I regretted it, but by then it was too late. Afterward, I recommended you for the Distinguished Service Order, but that somehow felt inadequate."

"I survived, sir, more or less. Now, let me just write down the young lady's name and address, in case you decide to help your grandchild."

◆    ◆    ◆

Ford was now consumed by a desire to get away as soon as possible. As he turned for the car, he saw Victoria emerge from the house and start toward him. He readied himself for her final assault. The pain he had suffered while recuperating from his wound would be trivial in comparison to the pain he anticipated in recovering from Victoria Canderblank.

If he had thought of his past life as dreary, his future was going to be desolate.

"Holy *mackerel*!" she burst out. "Even *I* thought I was guilty back in there! I've never been so scared in my life!" Her expression became serious. "Are you going to bring charges of conspiracy against us?"

"No, of course not! What possible benefit could it bring?"

"It would send my mother to jail—God knows she deserves it."

"That would simply hurt you and your father."

"Do you really have evidence against her?"

"I have her fingerprints on the five pound note, along with the Master's. That's what you carried in the library book."

Her lips parted in astonishment.

"She sent that money by *me?* Holy Moses! You're right. Don't send her to jail—it wouldn't be fair to inflict her on the other inmates!"

"Perhaps you're right."

An awkward pause ensued.

He said reluctantly, "I don't suppose you'll ever be able to look at me again without being reminded of this whole horrible mess, Miss Canderblank, if our paths were ever to cross …"

"No, I don't suppose I would," she replied somberly. "And you'll never be able to trust me, after all those awful lies."

"You lied to protect your father, not yourself; that's not the worst thing in the world."

"Yes, but I lied to *you*, and that *is* the worst thing in the world … If I swear never to lie to you ever again, would you believe me?"

"I would," he said solemnly.

"Then I swear it."

He stared down at his feet, not knowing what to say. Finally he looked up at her face, and discovered that her dazzling smile had returned. She started toward the car.

"God, I'm hungry, Cassius—I haven't eaten all day! It's far too late for the inn, and I'm certainly not going to stay here a moment longer. There's one café sort of place I know that stays open all night in Oxford, but that's miles away."

Croft emerged from the gloom and she turned to him.

"Is there an all-night teashop in Gloucester, Sergeant, or Cheltenham, perhaps? I'm starving!"

"Well, Miss Canderblank, I'm afraid there isn't, at least not one that's good enough for the likes of you. But Mrs. Croft usually lays out a little bite of supper when I'm out late, if that's acceptable? And you, of course, sir?"

"It that acceptable?" she asked anxiously, turning to Ford. "I need to know your opinion."

"It is," he replied.

"Then that settles everything," she said.

978-0-595-43777-1
0-595-43777-X

Made in the USA
Lexington, KY
07 April 2014